HEALING MAGIC

& Playboys

CASUAL MAGIC
BOOK THREE

LAUREN CONNOLLY

HEALING MAGIC & PLAYBOYS

LAUREN CONNOLLY

CITY OWL
PRESS

HEALING MAGIC & PLAYBOYS
Casual Magic, Book 3

CITY OWL PRESS
www.cityowlpress.com

Cover Design by MiblArt. All stock photos licensed appropriately.

Edited by Yelena Casale.

For information on subsidiary rights, please contact the publisher at info@cityowlpress.com.

Print Edition ISBN: 978-1-64898-458-7

Digital Edition ISBN: 978-1-64898-457-0

Printed in the United States of America

Also by Lauren Connolly

Casual Magic:

Fire Magic & Ice Cream

Earth Magic & Hot Water

Healing Magic & Playboys

***

Forget the Past:

Rescue Me

Read Me

Resist Me

Praise for Lauren Connolly

"Cleverly crafted, sweet and spicy, *Fire Magic & Ice Cream* is wittily written and explores all the emotions! With very imaginative world building, the elementals' that live alongside humans all have certain 'gifts'. Ms. Connolly has crafted a plethora of characters that are unusual, endearing, and full of loyalty." — *InD'tale Magazine*

"If you are looking for a fun, delightful, and super steamy romance that's a quick read, look no further! *Fire Magic & Ice Cream* brings it all in one charming package." — *Kat Turner, author of the Coven Daughters series*

"The relationship between Dash and Paige, in *Rescue Me*, will bring the warm-fuzzies, as both step out of their comfort zones to give it a chance, and boy is their chemistry sizzling. A page turner from start to finish, the reader will be reluctant to put it down!" — *InD'tale Magazine*

"If you're looking for a fun, low stakes, lighthearted, magical, and steamy read for the summer you HAVE to read *Fire Magic & Ice Cream*! This book was so much fun and I breezed right through it. I loved Quinn and how she had to learn to control her magic and the cinnamon roll ice Viking man August who balanced her out. Their chemistry was on point, and the way they navigated their relationship was so adorable." — *E.E. Hornburg, author of the Cursed Queens series*

"*Read Me* is a perfect sunshine-and-grump tale that is an absolutely delightful addition to the Forget the Past series! Readers will feel the gamut of emotions throughout this tale, from laughing out loud to reaching for tissues, and it will be worth every second. If one loves a second-chance-at-doing-life-right tale, this book is definitely one to add to the must-read pile! Unputdownable from start to finish!" — *InD'tale Magazine*

To the librarians that keep smiling even when they want to scream.

Chapter One

AVA

The evenings after I teach, I refuse to wear the proper stripper uniform. I'll still put on the lacy, bedazzled bra that adds enough push-up to make it appear as though my D-cups are about to spill out. And I'll tug on my matching panties that seem sheer but have crystals clustered over all the important parts. I'll even coat my skin in the glitter-infused lotion that makes my normally beige complexion look like I'm covered in glittering gems.

But I will not wear the heels.

The soles of my feet ache from hours standing in front of college students, trying to explain how Wikipedia may be a good starting point when learning about a new topic, but it is not a viable source to cite in a research paper. When I first applied to library school, I didn't expect there to be an instructional component. I imagined I would be tucked away in some archive, examining old books, or I'd be cataloging collections in a public library. But I settled into higher education, and academic librarians wear many hats.

Though, I'm not sure how many of my colleagues across the country have a stripper hat in their skillset closet.

I technically don't have a hat either. But I do have a mask. I tie the lacy disguise over the top half of my face and secure the material to my hair with a few strategically placed bobby pins.

But—due to my five-class-in-a-row-day—I do *not* put on the six-inch-tall pleaser heels.

Barefoot, trying not to wince at how even flatfooted my soles are still tender, I push through the door that leads from the dressing room to the area behind the main stage.

Without the soundproofing, I can hear the last bit of "Champagne Shit" by Janelle Monae. As the final cords trail off there's the sound of cheering, the crowd showing their appreciation for the performance.

"Club is busy for a Tuesday," Blue says. They pause beside me with a janitor broom. The cleaning implement looks badass with its chrome handle and pitch-black brush head. The Air Elemental is in charge of cash collection tonight, sweeping up all the loose bills after each dance. They make a big show of moving the broom around, but us magic types know Blue is actually manipulating the air currents to direct the money off stage. Making sure they don't miss any. On slow nights we collect the bills ourselves, since it's only a handful.

Not that I keep the cash.

"Oh," I say. "Good."

Blue snorts, hearing the lack of conviction in my voice. Most dancers would love a building full of eager customers. A part of me is glad to hear there's a decent showing.

The problem is, I only need a few audience members to earn the payment I'm looking for. The more people there are, the more likely there's someone in the crowd who voices dissatisfaction over my not-so-classic stripping style.

Also increases the chances someone might recognize me.

Stop it, I silently scold myself. *No one from your job would come here. And even if they did, they wouldn't recognize you on stage.*

The curtains part, and Jade saunters in, her light green G-string stuffed full of bills. Normally we're the same height, roughly five foot six, but since she didn't forgo her pleasers, the woman towers over me. Jade swings a curtain of braids over her onyx shoulder to show her top is equally adorned with cash.

"A birthday party," she announces by way of explanation, gesturing at her haul. Blue sneaks around the dancer, ducking through the velvet curtains and heading out to sweep up any earnings Jade received that didn't end up in her panties. "Though, this one"—Jade tugs out a bill that sat snug under the bikini strap running across her collarbone—"was from your man."

She waves the hundred dollars in front of my face and my heart rate trips. But not because of the amount.

He's here. Of course, he's here.

"I don't know what you did to that man." Jade grabs my face in a gentle but firm hold and plants a loud kiss somewhere in the mass of my white-blonde waves. "But gods, I love you for it. He tips me like he thinks I'll put in a good word for him." She tilts my chin up to grin directly into my face. "So here's my word. Keep making him into a needy puddle of goo for at least a few more weeks. I'm almost done saving for my trip to Brazil."

Jade—who's working under a nom de plume like we all are—shared with me that she started stripping to pay off the student loans from her computer science degree. But she decided to keep going because The Jewelry Box is a decent place to work, and the combined salaries means she can fill her condo with luxuries and jet off to locations all around the world whenever she wants. Also, sitting at a computer all day is a demon on the body. Pole dancing is her workout.

I roll my eyes. "I didn't do anything to him. I do the opposite of *do*. I ignore him just like I ignore everyone else."

Jade lets out a husky chuckle. "I know! It's delicious. I'm going to see if I can find a lap near him to dance on so I can watch his face when you give him nothing." She kisses my cheek then lets me go. "You make Tuesday nights my favorite of the week."

The beginning strains of "In Too Deep" by WDW drift to us just as Blue reappears, pushing a stack of crumbled bills in front of them.

"You're up, Pearl." All of us dancers choose what songs we perform to —after running them by our boss Yasmin for approval—and we can change them up as often as we like. But this is one of my favorites and everyone knows it. I'm a sucker for a good boy band.

Jade smoothly squats so she can scoop up handfuls of the cash and deposit her earnings into a nearby bin with her name embossed on it.

There's a container for each dancer. Ruby's is also partially full from her earlier performance.

It might seem odd to leave cash basically lying around back here. But the workers at The Jewelry Box respect one another. Plus, a protection witch spelled the boxes to only allow the dancer whose box it is to reach inside.

The pros of working at a strip club run by and staffed with magical beings.

Speaking of magic, time for me to go get some.

I breathe through the tingle of nerves that always sends goosebumps racing across my skin the moment before I step in front of a crowd. I had the same reaction this morning before I walked into the intro level history course where I was set to teach a group of thirty about research databases. Now I'm preparing to tease a crowd of half-drunk club-goers with my body.

An interesting life I live. But I'm used to it.

Mostly.

As my fingers clutch the heavy velvet, I pull on my emotionless mask, wearing it underneath my masquerade one, then I step onto the stage.

Eyes turn toward me. Another jewel on display.

I saunter down the thin stretch of elevated walkway that leads to the round main stage, my bare feet making no sound on the cool wood. The bulbs along the edge of the platform fade from green to a soft white glow. Jade to Pearl, the shift silently announces. Though the lights highlight me, there's no spotlight. No strobe lights or disco balls. Yasmin, the owner of The Jewelry Box, wanted her club to stand out and stand apart from the seedier joints in Phoenix.

The moment a patron makes it past the bouncer, they know this isn't an average strip joint. The floors and walls are different shades of dark wood, the surfaces polished to the point they reflect a muted glow of the candles flickering on high shelves around the perimeter of the spacious room. All the club's lighting is warm and low, providing a sensual ambiance. All the seating is simple and comfortable, and the couches in the VIP section are soft supple leather. Strips of silk dangle from the ceiling, appearing gauzy and delicate as the material shifts in subtle air currents, but each one is plenty strong enough to support the acrobatic dancers that dangle from them as part of their routine. Elegant chandeliers hang from the ceiling where the silks don't, the only items that sparkle in this room other than me.

The first time I toured the place, the word that came to mind was *speakeasy*.

The Jewelry Box provides a sense of elegance along with erotic tantalization.

There is still a pole, and that's where I head, knowing once I reach it my tender feet can leave the ground. Still, this short walk already has my body relaxing. Partly because I'm comfortable up here, completely in charge of this space.

But more than that, my tranquility arrives on a cloud of lust.

The men, and some women and thems, stare at me with hungry expressions, dragging their eyes over every bare inch of my body. In their gazes, I can see them imagining what it would be like to touch me. To fuck me.

Go ahead and wonder, I silently encourage them. *Get creative.*

I want them to fantasize about me. To play out personal pornos with me as the star.

Because every ounce of lust directed my way fills my internal magic cauldron. The often empty well in my chest that holds mystical fuel so I can cast spells.

The problems of a half-witch, half-succubus.

Well, more like a quarter, since it was my grandmother who decided to summon an incubus demon and sleep with him without using birth control. Two generations later, and I'm a healing witch who needs other peoples' arousal to power my spell work. My mystical fuel is all external. Without these dancing shifts, I wouldn't be able to access my magic.

And without my magic, I'm fucked.

A few more steps to the pole, and I'm already juiced up. So much that I'm tempted to direct some of the power toward my feet to ease the ache.

Don't do it. You need that power. You'll regret using it.

Since I've got my stoic stage mask on, I don't sigh in annoyance. But the aggravated noise wants to get out. After working with Elementals like Jade and Blue, and most of the other Jewelry Box employees for the past two years, I've grown envious of how they seem to have an endless supply of magic. Jade, a Fire Elemental, can bring flames to her fingertips with only a touch of concentration. The heat lives in her always. And if she wants to supercharge it, she merely needs to strongly feel a particular emotion. For her, it's annoyance, but each Elemental is different. Fire, water, earth, air, and metal. More often we use the silly nicknames, Pyro, Squid, Petal Pusher, Airhead, and Stoner.

Descendants of the Elemental gods, they carry magic in themselves and don't have to syphon power from the surrounding world like I and many other witches have to.

To distract myself from my pity thoughts, I turn the last few steps into light skips then grab the pole and swing myself around, adjusting my grip and eventually bringing my legs to the smooth surface. With a burning flex of my biceps and a strategic squeeze of my legs, I climb, knowing by the end of the night I'll have light bruises on my inner thighs from the moves I plan to do, all to keep my feet off the floor. As I let the set of songs I picked out guide my body, the pain eases to the back of my mind, and I enjoy the strength and sensuality of my movements.

And I keep my focus away from the VIP section.

Away from him.

I know he's here. I would've realized even if Jade hadn't said anything, though I don't like how she labeled him as my man.

But I guess it's better than calling me *his*.

That's what he wants. I can tell from the way he continues to show up. Continues trying to get me to the edge of the stage by holding up larger and larger bills. Bills that I ignore, just like I ignore him.

But I ignore everyone, so he's not special.

Only, he is. Slightly special.

Not that I'd ever tell him.

His lust tastes different. When the power converges on me, I breathe the force in, the magic passing over my tongue on the way to my chest where the force settles and heats my skin from the inside out. Lust magic tends to taste like cocoa, and it's like everyone hands me a generic milk chocolate bar. But he slips a decadent peanut butter cup between my lips.

A little different.

A little more delicious.

And not something I plan to thoroughly examine. I'm here for magic. Not for some rich playboy interested in a stripper only because she's the first person to ever ignore him.

Still, I should get a medal for effort because the guy is hard to disregard.

Even now, as I hang upside-down on the pole, my attention tries to latch on to him. I spy a perfectly tailored suit covering a tall, lithe body. A flicker of golden-brown hair, the color richer in the club's warm lighting.

But I force my gaze away before I'm caught in his dark eyes.

I right myself and slide the rest of the way down the pole in a sensual glide that belies how strong my grip is. My toes touch the ground, and I let my body drop lower into a crouch, then arch my back and try not to shiver at the onslaught of lust that tastes largely of chocolate but leaves a lingering aftertaste of peanut butter.

My last song in this set is almost done, and I stand, considering if I want to climb once more. I like being high above everyone.

Then a movement at the edge of the stage teases the corner of my eye.

It's him. My body knows it's him.

My tastebuds tell me how much he craves my attention.

How high will his offer go this time? He went up to a thousand two weeks ago. But even if I want the money—which I don't—he still eventually lets it fall. Those ten hundred-dollar bills scattered at my feet when I wouldn't look his way.

I didn't keep it. I don't keep any of the money. One more wall of safety, like my mask.

Still, I find myself curious.

Instead of climbing, I hook my leg waist-height on the pole and take some lazy spins that match the beat. Meanwhile, I allow my peripheral vision to focus on his hands.

No bills appear in them. Not this time.

His fingers cradle a velvet box.

Different. Intriguing.

I expect him to open it. To show me whatever treasure he brought to draw me in. Instead, he sets the box down on the edge of the stage and waits. The hand that didn't deposit the mystery gift in my territory clutches a glass with amber liquid. He brings the drink to his mouth, but I don't watch him sip the rich alcohol. Don't risk a glimpse of his lips.

Leave it. Walk off the stage at the end of the song like normal.

The problem is...it's a box.

Money is money. I know what that is. But a box...

It's a mystery.

Damn the gods, I love a good mystery. My favorite part of my day job is when a student brings me a fun research puzzle to solve. When we search through databases to discover an answer together.

The box is a puzzle.

Don't do it, I tell myself even as I slow my spinning. *This dancing is for you. Not for him. He doesn't get anything from you.*

But...looking inside the box isn't giving him anything, I reason as I step toward the gift.

A gift I swear I won't keep. Still, I need to see what it is.

What does he think will win me? What price has he placed on my attention?

In a graceful move, I glide across the stage and drop to my knees, thighs spread so the velvet box sits between them.

A wave of lust rushes down my throat, and if I didn't have my mask of disinterest in place, I'd let out a dry chuckle. Or a groan of relief. My internal magical caldron is filling to the brim, and I'm set for at least another week if not more.

He likes seeing me on my knees.

But who cares what he likes? I'm not here for him. I'm here for the box. Impatient for the mystery to be solved, I open the lid with a snap, the velvet soft and teasing against my fingertips.

Inside, nestled on a silk cushion, is a string of pearls.

Pearls almost the exact same shade as my milk-pale skin and the white outfits I wear and the mask I don. Pearls like my stage name.

Pearls like the person I pretend to be.

And nothing like the woman I truly am.

Disappointment creeps up my spine and through the nerves in my body, shoving out the brief respite of dancing and leaving behind all the new and old aches of the day. I extend a single finger, hooking the necklace and lifting it from the box until the jewelry dangles in the low light of the club. There's a gasp from nearby that sounds like Jade. She must've found a lap with a good view to occupy.

I lift my eyes to the unbuttoned collar of his dress shirt, up the strong, tan column of his neck, past his defined chin, and stop at the easy grin on his face. No need to meet his eyes when I can spy plenty of self-satisfaction in the pleased curve of his mouth.

He thinks he found my price. A string of gems in exchange for one.

Pompous playboy.

When will he learn that I can't be bought?

Before he realizes my intention, I extend my arm, the pearls swinging in my grasp. But they settle with a satisfying thunk when I drop the entire necklace into his glass of whiskey.

The song ends, and I rise to my feet in a smooth move I perfected by the age of eight. There's money strewn across the stage, tossed there while I spent my entire set on the pole.

But I'm not here for the cash. Blue will sweep it up, and Yasmin will donate it to the local animal shelter.

I leave every bill behind as I stride off the stage.

And I leave Sammy Reyes behind, too, not feeling even a pinch of guilt over the shocked expression on his handsome face.

The Squid can keep his meaningless gifts.

All I need is the decadence of his peanut butter lust.

Chapter Two

SAMMY

"I'm in love with her."

"You don't even know her real name."

"Who cares? Names don't mean anything. There're thousands of other Sammys in the world but not one of them is entirely like me."

"That's true. There is no one like you. Let's hope the gods keep it that way."

I recline on a poolside lounge chair in the backyard of Damien Cortez's house, the same man who has no sympathy for my romantic plight.

"I'm telling you. I love this woman. Can't you help me? Don't you want to see me all happy and gooey like them?" I wave toward the people in the pool.

Aspen Baumann, a mountain of a man, an Earth Elemental, and one of my best friends, stands chest-deep in the salt water. In his massive arms, he cradles my other best friend, Rafael Aguado, a Water Elemental who doesn't seem to mind that his boyfriend is periodically dunking him under the surface. Their girlfriend, Cat Byrne, a Fire Elemental with a temper almost as short as her stature, clings to Aspen's back and laughs as Rafael pretends to protest the manhandling.

They're so adorable it borders on disgusting. I love that for them.

But I want it for myself, too.

"That is more than enough of that," Damien says as he tips his chin toward the three.

"You are *no* help." I roll off my chair and settle on the lip of the pool, my legs in the water, hoping the liquid will sooth my tormented emotions. Small waves rise and fall around my legs in response to my proximity and the pull of my magic. When I'm wretched, water answers easily to my slightest movement, swirling and dancing for me as if the liquid wants to gain my notice. I feel a strong kinship with my element.

For a brief shining moment, I thought I'd finally gotten Pearl's attention. And I did.

Only badly, it turns out.

She *hated* the necklace.

What other reason would she have for not only rejecting it but doing so by tossing it into my drink?

I used to be better at this. Wooing women. In college, I barely went a night without a bed partner.

But were you really wooing them? Or was your money?

The harsh, internal voice has me rubbing a sore spot on my sternum.

The truth is, I don't know. I never seem to know when someone truly likes me.

"Cat," I call out to the redhead, and she turns her flushed face my way, her grin staying firmly in place. I love that she smiles at me now. For the longest time, I thought Cat and I had a teasing, torture-each-other-because-it's-funny relationship. Turns out she *actually* wanted to torture me because she hated my guts.

One more example of my apparently shitty ability to form a genuine relationship with a person.

But I apologized, sincerely, and I've worked on being someone the Pyro might like to spend time around. From the way she's softened toward me, I think I'm making the right steps.

If I can win Cat over, then maybe I can figure out a way to get Pearl to give me a chance.

"What's up?" she asks, detaching herself from Aspen's back to drift my way.

"You're letting her get away!" Rafael wails dramatically reaching for

Cat as if they're shipwrecked in the middle of an ocean instead of playing in a luxurious pool in the backyard of a house in Phoenix, Arizona.

Aspen heaves Rafael into the air, and the Squid lets out a bird-like squawk before landing in the middle of the deep end. Meanwhile, the Petal Pusher appears behind Cat, grabs her by the waist, and lifts the woman onto his shoulders, where she sits, giggling and digging her fingers into her boyfriend's shaggy brown hair for balance.

Now I'm staring up at her deceptively sweet face as she asks, "What's up, Sammy?"

"What's up is that I will give you anything if you tell Pearl that I'm not an asshole." I clasp my hands in front of me and try to appear as pitiful as possible. Cat is a waitress at The Jewelry Box, which means she has access to Pearl in a way I don't. "What do you want? A boat? I'll buy you a big boat. A yacht."

She rolls her eyes. "We live in the middle of a desert. What am I going to do with a boat?"

"We'll put the boat in the water...somewhere. Then you take these two lucky bastards for a sex-cation on the water. You and Rafael can geek out on all the fish"—they work at the local aquarium—"and Aspen can make sure you don't get lost at sea. Then when you return, all three of you can stand at the altar beside me as I marry Pearl, the woman of my dreams."

Cat stares at me, a sardonic expression on her face, not seeming even slightly tempted by my willingness to arrange a sex-cation for her on a luxury yacht.

"Her name isn't even Pearl," she says.

"I know," I groan, digging my fingers into my hair and only restraining myself from pulling it out by the roots because Carlos, my barber, is very proud of my hair and will Sweeny Todd me if I come in with stress bald spots.

"Hey, man." Rafael appears at my side, heaving himself out of the pool and throwing a wet arm around my shoulders. "I know what it's like to pine." He waves a hand toward Cat and Aspen, the two people he loved since high school but didn't get with until a few months ago. "But it seems like you're tying yourself up over a woman you don't know. Did you consider you might be in love with the idea of her, but not actually her?" He gives me a reassuring squeeze. "For all you know, she could be super annoying and self-centered."

"She's not, though," Cat says offhandedly, proving that she knows Pearl. Knows her real name. Has spoken to her. Hell, they're probably friends.

"Cat." Rafael sighs. "I love you, but you're not helping me get Sammy over this woman."

The Pyro shrugs, her lips tilting into an evil smile.

"Why do you like her?" The question comes from Aspen, the most levelheaded of the bunch.

He's also a lawyer, and probably best able to talk me out of my infatuation.

But if he could turn me off of Pearl in a single conversation then I don't deserve to know her, do I?

I know my friends think I'm only interested in Pearl for her appearance. When I've been a self-described one-and-done guy for most of my life, I can't blame them.

In their minds, I'm a playboy.

But I haven't had a one-night stand in two years. Haven't slept with anyone at all in that time. Sure, I still flirt like it's my job. I can't help it. I like flirting. And teasing. And joking. Plus, I've never been great at taking life seriously.

Which is why, even when I talk about something or someone I'm serious about, I still sound like I'm playing up the dramatics. But I *do* care about getting to know Pearl. The real woman off the pole and behind the mask.

"I freely admit, my initial attraction was all about the physical. She's gorgeous. And that ass..." Thoughts of Pearl's round behind, all peachy and plump and asking for a bite, threaten to distract me. I push the image to the back of my mind and continue. "But then there is the fact that she wouldn't take my money. What's up with that?" I glance at Cat, but the Pyro shrugs again, though I get the sense that she knows, or at least has an idea. "Then there's how she dances. Sexy, true. But skillful. When she's on the stage, it's like the dance is all she cares about. And if she makes a mistake, even a small one, her lips pucker in this adorable frown. Like she cares about perfectly executing her performance more than provoking a reaction from the randy crowd. And her laugh..." I sigh at the memory of the breathy, reluctant chuckle.

"You heard her laugh?" Aspen asks.

I nod eagerly. "About a month back, I spilled my drink on my lap. When I stood up it looked like I pissed myself. Pearl was on stage, and I heard it. The most beautiful fucking sound."

She still hadn't met my eyes that night, but her gaze landed on my crotch for long enough that I knew why she was giggling. Long enough that my dick didn't care it was covered in ice and tequila.

"You're in love with her because she doesn't want your money and she laughs at you?" Damien asks, disbelief coloring his voice while he roasts peppers on the grill for whatever dinner he's making. The Squid is a grill master in addition to always being the host.

And he doesn't get it. I can tell none of them do.

Damn it to a hell dimension, maybe they're right. Maybe I'm piling all my longing onto the idea of a woman. But I can't help thinking that despite wearing a mask, Pearl reveals more of herself on stage than any other stripper at The Jewelry Box.

That she's independent and driven. Talented and strong. She doesn't take shit and has a sense of humor.

Plus, she's curious.

When I placed that jewelry box on the stage, it was the first time I truly earned her attention. Not because I'd found the expensive item that would finally buy her affection. But because I set a mystery at her feet, and she wanted to learn the answer. As unimpressive as that answer ended up being in her eyes.

Gods, and the way she rejected my gift. Not simply walking away, offering her normal cold shoulder.

No, she went for brutal. Showed me exactly how much the three-thousand-dollar necklace was worth to her.

She's honest.

Pearl—with her stage name and mask—has more secrets than most people I've come across, but I don't think the woman takes naturally to deception. And brutally honest is one of the hottest things a woman can be as far as I'm concerned. I've had too many false friends in my life.

"She might think you're creepy," Rafael offers.

Present company obviously not included.

My gut churns at the thought that has crossed my mind more than once.

"Cat?" I hold the Pyro's gaze, knowing she'll give me the harsh truth. "Does she think I'm a creep?"

The redhead's expression turns thoughtful as she idly traces her finger along the shell of Aspen's ear. The Petal Pusher's face goes hazy with happy contentment from the affectionate petting.

Lucky bastard. That's what I want.

A partner to stroke and love and bicker with. A person that will call me an asshole when I'm being an asshole but then kiss me and tell me it's okay because they still love me.

But then also tell me they're going to peg me later because that's the treatment assholes deserve.

My whole body clenches in wanting at the thought.

"If she does, it's only a little bit. Not enough to truly bother her."

"How do you know?" I press.

"We have a monthly meeting," she explains. "Yasmin always asks the dancers to give her names or descriptions of customers that make them uncomfortable. Those people either get banned from the VIP section or from the club entirely. Neither has happened to you, so you're not creepy enough to concern her."

Not creepy enough to concern her.

"I was hoping for a slightly more enthusiastic, 'No, Sammy! Of course not! Pearl doesn't think you're a creep at all. In fact, she has a crush on you and is too shy to figure out how to tell you.'"

The redhead smirks. "You want me to lie to you?"

"No," I grumble. "I want you to tell Pearl I'm a cool guy that will worship the ground she walks on if she gives me the time of day."

Cat flicks water at me, and I let the droplets land on my bare chest, my skin warm from the late spring sun. If I'd wanted to flick my fingers and send the droplets back at her, I could have. My water magic currently rocks through my body, a pulsing force wanting free. Doesn't help that my powers are fueled by sadness, and I'm feeling quite melancholy at the moment. The pool, normally a still surface, rises and dips in agitated waves because I can't seem to completely tamp down the magical force inside me.

That's the thing about being an Elemental. We have these super cool abilities to manipulate an element, but the magic also randomly chooses one of our emotions to draw fuel from. Cat's fire magic goes wild when she's angry, Aspen tends to make nearby plants sprout and flower when he's happy, and Rafael once set off the sprinklers in The Jewelry Box when he got jealous.

Meanwhile, I get mopey and the beer in my can starts sloshing around.

What kind of magic does Pearl have?

With the thought in my mind, I lean forward, bracing my elbows on my knees, sharing a glance between Cat and Aspen. Aspen works security at The Jewelry Box and likely knows as much as Cat about my mystery woman, but the guy isn't chatty like I need my informant to be.

"What kind of Elemental is Pearl?" I ask. "Tell me that at least."

Cat quirks her head. "Who said she was an Elemental?"

"She's..." My mouth bobs open as I search for words. "W-what? She's not one of us? B-but she works for Yasmin!"

"So?" Cat flicks more water at me. "Most of the staff are magical, but not all of them. And I'm not sharing that info about her either. Get it through your head, Sammy. I'm not about to crack on this. And throwing your wallet at Pearl isn't going to win you any favors. Like you said—she doesn't care."

Cat is right. I know she is because Pearl's lack of interest in my money is one of the things that got me stuck on her in the first place.

She might be human.

That's not a deal breaker, but it's also not ideal. My mom is a human and accepted my dad's magical heritage. But she's not exactly normal when it comes to interacting with the world. Humans don't know about the magical people living among them, and if they panic when they learn, then a memory witch has to wipe all trace from their mind.

I don't want to earn Pearl's affection only for her to freak out when she finds out I'm a Squid. I *really* don't want to have every trace of me erased from her memory.

But that's a future worry for a relationship I can't even figure out how to get started.

"Food is ready," Damien announces, the guy never leaving off his grilling through all my romantic woes.

Aspen lets himself sink backwards into the pool, Cat squealing as she goes with him. Rafael gives my shoulder another commiserating grasp as he pushes to stand.

I don't rush to join them for food, mind still stuck on how I can get Pearl to take notice of me.

She opened the box. Maybe she just needs another mystery.

An idea forms in my mind, and a spark of hope clears out my pity party and subdues my sadness magic.

Next time, I'll have something new for my mystery woman.

Chapter Three

AVA

"I told you. Only send me PDFs. I don't want to open random internet links. That's how you get computer viruses."

Somehow, I manage to keep a pleasant smile on my face even as Professor Fellows lectures me. The guy is in his late forties with a decent-looking academic vibe going on, but his arrogant personality ruins his salt-and-pepper hottie potential.

"I appreciate your diligence when it comes to cyber security," I say, proud of my ability to fake a sincere tone, "And I'm sure the IT department does, too. But I thought since you were the one to initiate our email exchange—and because the links were to library databases—that there wouldn't be a problem." I explain this with my pleasant customer service voice.

"I'm not taking the risk." He leans across the reference desk, close enough that I can smell his cologne. The scent is pleasant, a subtle sandalwood. It does not match his condescending tone at all.

I can't decide if I want Abraham Fellows to be smelly so every part of him reflects his bad attitude, or if I should be grateful that I'm not under assault on multiple fronts.

"And this source," he continues. "Why did you send me this when I *told* you I'm not researching the Colorado River?"

Glancing down at the printout of the email I sent him, I see where it does in fact list a book titled *The Winding History of the Colorado River*.

I bite back a sigh.

"Yes. I recall that from your original message. But this book," I point at the citation and my extra note beneath it, "has a chapter that mentions the river you're interested in. Because it feeds into the Colorado River. I thought you might want to read that chapter specifically and take a look at the pictures."

Goddess save me. I swear Fellows just skimmed my email, printed the thing out in a huff, then stormed across campus five minutes before the end of my workday because he wanted a boost of superiority before heading home.

Meanwhile, I have a shift at the club tonight. A shift I'm very much looking forward to after this conversation.

Normally, I'm overjoyed to help faculty and students with their research. Emphasis on *help*. Because during a collaborative effort, I know they're learning how to discover sources themselves in the future.

But then there are the academics who think they're above looking for their own resources.

"Well. Fine." He straightens and taps a finger on the reference desk, the gesture scolding. "But I'll still need the PDF."

"The PDF of the book is attached to the original email I sent." *And I am not your personal research bitch*, I want to hiss at him.

But I don't, because he's a tenured professor, head of the history department, and has the power to decide if the instructional librarian will be invited to teach information literacy lessons in the intro level courses. An instruction I enjoy doing, is part of my job, and is necessary for the students at this college to succeed.

That last fact should make the decision about having librarians visit classrooms simple. But there's this ridiculous layer of politics in academia. Apparently, my predecessor was not a team player, and therefore never got invites to be a guest speaker. The past two years of working here, I've tried my hardest to change that mentality among the faculty, but it's been slow going.

And pissing off Fellows won't help.

"Good. Glad we straightened that all out." The man offers me a smile that I might have found charming if he hadn't spent the last ten minutes berating me.

"Happy to help." I already have all my things packed, so I can't even shuffle papers around to look busy and encourage him to leave. "And I'm looking forward to talking to your students next week."

"Yes. That's right. That'll be nice for them. To have you at the front of the room for a bit. I'm sure they get tired of staring at me." The comment sounds innocent. A casual joke.

But there's a sudden sweetness on my tongue and tingling flush under my skin. An influx of magic. Which can only mean one thing.

Abraham Fellows is aroused. And he's turned on because of me.

Over the years, I've had to figure out the parameters of my powers. I'm not simply a witch. I'm a *succubus* witch. A suck-witch.

No, I do not call myself that out loud.

But it seems accurate because my magic sucks energy from the arousal of people near me. The problem is the arousal also has to be directed at me. I've tried to simply be in the proximity of someone who is turned on, but I get nothing from them. The attraction must be elicited by me or pointed at me in some way.

Which means when I taste a power boost, I know someone has the hots for me.

I welcome the sensation at The Jewelry Box. Not so much at my day job, where I want to be seen as something other than a sexual fantasy.

"Okay then." I keep on a placid expression. "Have a good day." *Jerk*.

He nods, satisfied the librarian has been thoroughly chastised, and strolls out the door.

The moment he's gone I let my face relax out of the inauthentic smile. I move my jaw around and massage my cheeks. This is another reason I'm glad all I need to do at The Jewelry Box is dance. The other strippers put on an entire performance, simpering and coy smiles and sultry laughs. Everything to create a sensual reality for the customers that earns them large tips. Money they deserve by the end of the night because that acting is no easy feat. Just a few minutes of the falsity exhausts me.

Luckily, on the pole all I need to do is move my body and that earns enough lust to last me until the next week. Still tiring, but in a way I like.

The day after a shift, my muscles ache in a well-used way. The way that makes me feel as though I moved and tested myself.

Not that I forced myself into a personality that doesn't fit.

"Is he gone?" The squeaky question comes from my student worker Kathleen, who peers out from the doorway that leads to the staff-only space.

"You're not a Professor Fellows fan?"

She wrinkles her nose, then pushes her glasses back into place when they slide down. "He can be really critical. I'd rather not run into him outside of class if I don't have to."

I completely understand, but since Kathleen is a student first, I can't shit-talk a faculty member with her. The best I can do is offer a commiserating nod as I vacate my seat.

"Well, he's gone. And the desk is yours. Make sure to let Rodrigo know when you're leaving." I gesture toward the circulation library associate who's currently troubleshooting a computer issue at one of the public units.

"Will do." She settles at the reference desk, straightening in the chair with an eager grin. Kathleen may be a history major, but she told me she wants to get a master's in library science when she graduates. I'm fond of her and will be bummed at the end of the semester when she's gone.

"I restocked my cards." I point to the business card holder as I scoop up my bag and travel mug. "If someone brings you a question you can't answer, don't feel bad about sending them my way tomorrow."

"Yes, Ms. Bellarose," Kathleen intones with a teasing smile.

I wave at her, then call out a farewell to Rodrigo as I pass. He grunts in acknowledgment, but I don't take it personally. He always gets surly when the tech goes down because it's a stark reminder of how the college still hasn't gotten us the new computers we were promised a year ago.

The library always seems to land at the bottom of the list when funding is brought up. And then we get chewed out when we cancel database subscriptions to keep to our miniscule budget. I sigh and roll my head on my shoulders, trying to ease the tight muscles of my neck. Goddess, I'm looking forward to dancing tonight. I started at The Jewelry Box for the magical boost, but now I find it's my best stress relief.

Better than sex.

At least, better than any sex I've ever had.

As I walk across campus, a natural snarky smile comes to my face as I think about how horrified the administration would be if they knew what was going through my mind. If they knew what I do every Tuesday night—and sometimes weekends if Yasmin is short-staffed or if I've had a particularly stressful work week.

College of Freedom & Faith is not exactly progressive. They have a beautiful set of buildings and a gorgeous, old library I fell in love with the moment I took a tour. But they also have a strict morality clause in the hiring contract. One that I break on a weekly basis.

I refuse to feel bad about it. For one, I think morality clauses are ridiculous and archaic. Two, stripping is necessary for my continued physical health, aka my ability to perform my job.

Most healing witches have the freedom to use their magic to benefit others. But ever since I was fifteen, I've suffered from chronic migraines. The only solution: dosing myself with healing potions in an effort to stave them off.

I'm not about to risk that pain because my administration is full of prudes. Besides, as a magical being surrounded by humans, I'm used to hiding parts of myself from the world.

What's one more?

What I know is that I'm good at my job, and I'm passionate about helping students succeed. That should be what's important, so that's what I focus on.

My shift at The Jewelry Box doesn't start until nine, so I head home for a quick dinner, sighing in relief when I change into soft shorts and a loose T-shirt. If only I could strip in this outfit. But Yasmin does have an image of sensual elegance she seeks to maintain at the club, and I respect her reasoning far more than the strict dress code enforced on me at my day job.

Long pants or skirts that fall past the knee. All shoes must be closed-toed, and heels can't be taller than one inch—not that I *want* to wear taller ones, but I chafe at the fact that I've been restricted. Are my male colleagues afraid I'm going to tower over them? Plus, we live in the fucking desert, and I'm not allowed to wear sleeveless tops or necklines that fall below my collarbones to the library.

It's a cruel form of torture.

After double-checking I have everything I need in my duffle bag, I climb back into my car and head over to the club, parking in the gated lot for performers. A recent safety measure to keep over-enthusiastic customers from following us to our cars.

The backstage area is full of laughter and half-naked women. Well, *full* is an overstatement. There are only four other women because Tuesday nights are never as packed as later in the week. But the ladies are big personalities and seem to take up every inch of space.

Diamond waves at me from her makeup station, her acrylics glittering as brightly as her crystal-covered outfit. She leans toward the mirror and carefully presses adhesive gems to the corners of her eyes, decorating her sienna skin. All of us make an effort to match our outfits and makeup with our stage names. Amber has on a bikini that somehow shimmers both orange and gold, bringing out the natural golden notes in her complexion.

"Shit!" Ruby hisses as I pull out the cushioned seat in front of my station. "My strap snapped. I knew this top couldn't handle my tits." The woman holds up a scrap of crimson that's edged with gold discs. The red shade is warm against her beach-girl tan.

"Let me see." I extend my hand, and she passes it my way. "Give me a few minutes. I'll sew it."

"Really? Oh, my goddess, Pearl. You are perfection." She claps and gives a little happy jump that makes her brown curls bounce, then settles back at her mirror to apply a set of false lashes.

I sit three down from her and fish out my emergency sewing kit, smiling all the while. This brings me back to the days when I'd earn some extra cash sewing costumes for Mom's coworkers at the burlesque club. Not that I'd make things from scratch, but I was great at letting out or taking costumes in, fixing torn seams, and adding intentional tear-away pieces for those show-stopping moments.

Some people would probably find my childhood horrifying, but I had plenty of love and support from those ladies.

The Jewelry Box has the same vibe. Not competitive and cold like other clubs I've worked in over the years. The unique feel can be attributed to the owner.

Yasmin wants to own a strip club unlike any other, and happy dancers are a key part of that plan. Most clubs have their dancers working like independent contractors, coming and going with little control over their schedules and owing the house money to strip even if they don't earn tips. Yasmin, meanwhile, established a full-time option and offers it whenever interviewing a new performer. Get a salary, benefits, and keep all your tips as long as you work a certain number of hours a week.

My bet is this works so well because Yasmin is a marketing genius and is a master at bringing in high-end clientele. The club makes plenty of money from cover charges, VIP memberships, and drink sales. No need to shortchange the dancers who help bring in even more customers.

"Here you go. All good." I snip off the loose end of the thread and hand Ruby her top.

"You're a goddess." She hooks the clasp, slips the straps over her shoulders, and gives her tits a shimmy. Everything stays in place. "Thank you!" she sings while sauntering toward the door that leads to the floor of the club. Diamond already left that way, and Amber arrows toward the stage entrance, giving her arms a last stretch before she starts her silks routine.

Meanwhile, I slip into my outfit for the night then fish a book out of my bag and settle in a cushy chair in the corner. Amber usually goes for twenty minutes, then I'm on. Other women would work the floor right now, get some extra cash for lap dances.

But I only need some stage time. I get enough lust up there without having strangers up close and personal. I doubt anyone from College of Faith & Freedom frequents The Jewelry Box, but it's possible. Hence the mask and my distance.

Amber times her set perfectly, strolling off the stage with her handfuls of cash just as I finish my chapter.

"Good crowd tonight." She smiles wide and holds up her fistfuls. "They're in a giving mood. I'm gonna grind some laps so hard."

"Get after it." I salute her then take a moment in front of my mirror to settle my mask in place. Once I know it's pinned tight, I rub my trademark glittery lotion over every inch of exposed skin.

Time to shine.

As I push aside the velvet curtain, step onto the stage, and stroll toward the pole, my eyes make an automatic sweep of the club. Once again, sitting in the VIP section is a familiar form.

Samuel Reyes is back.

A slight jolt and tingle flow through my body. I tell myself it's a magical lust wave and not something naturally occurring within me. Because there's *no* reason for me to have any type of reaction to the Squid.

Yes, I know he's a Water Elemental. When I saw Cat chatting with him a few months back like she knew the guy, I questioned her at the end of my shift. Mostly to find out if he's potentially dangerous. I've had customers fixate on me before—more than simply deciding I'm their favorite dancer at the club. She told me he's a Squid, rich, and a cocky, charming playboy. Overall, her opinion was that he's harmless as an overeager golden retriever, but she wouldn't hold it against me if I asked Yasmin to slap him with a ban.

The Pyro wore a smirk when she said that last bit, and I got the sense she'd take a bit of evil pleasure in seeing Sammy barred from The Jewelry Box.

But he's a big spender, and none of the other performers have a problem with him. I don't have an issue with him either. Not really.

But I don't get why he finds me so interesting.

Maybe, like me, he enjoys a bit of mystery.

He wasn't here last Tuesday. I try not to ponder on why he comes to some of my shifts and not all of them. In the beginning, I didn't have a regular schedule. When I presented Yasmin my proposal of dancing without taking funds, only taking lust, she agreed and told me all I needed to do was text her at least twenty-four hours in advance when I planned to come in.

For the first year, that worked perfectly well for me. There were some weeks that I didn't come at all. But then the stress of my day job amped up my migraines, and I needed to be sure that I would have a regular fuel source. Hence my request to have a scheduled slot on Tuesday nights supplemented with other shifts when needed. Yasmin welcomed me. At some point, Sammy seemed to catch on that Tuesdays were my regular days.

At least I think he's caught on. For all I know, the Squid is coming multiple days a week, and he's drooling over more dancers than only me. Maybe it's just that when I am here, I'm his favorite. But other nights he could prefer Jade. Or Ruby. There are some dancers that I never cross paths with anymore because they don't dance on Tuesdays. Maybe Opal is his favorite. Or Emerald.

It doesn't matter, I tell myself. He can pant after every single woman who comes up here. If he wants to rub one of those big hands over the crotch of his pants while Amber twists herself up in the silk scarves hanging from the ceiling, then that's his prerogative. I'm not looking for anything else from him.

Just a touch of lust. Enough to keep my pain at bay.

Tonight, though, as I'm used to, Samuel's entire focus is on me. I don't let my eyes catch his. But I can still taste his attraction. The weight of his stare drags over the glitter I've massaged into my skin.

I tease the pole tonight, not in the mood to climb when my heels already have me towering. Instead, I pretend the pole is my lover. That it is a frozen, stoic being I need to seduce and make mine. There are moments when my lips are less than an inch from the metal, as if to kiss it. But no one sanitizes the prop between uses, so I keep my mouth to myself.

Halfway through my final song, I take note of movement in the VIP section.

It's him, of course. The Squid strolls up to the stage, clutching an item against his chest.

More jewelry?

Maybe tonight I'll see what emeralds look like in whiskey.

But when Samuel Reyes sets down his armful, the wooden box doesn't look like a jewelry case. Not unless the container houses a crown.

If it's a crown, I might keep it.

Only because wearing the regal adornment while I'm reading a fantasy romance novel would be fun.

No, I chide myself. *Ignore it. Ignore him. Walk off this stage without touching that super cool-looking wooden box!*

Only, I don't think I can...

Chapter Four

SAMMY

Once again, the box lures her in.

I knew it. Pearl is fond of a mystery.

This time I didn't go for something so obvious as jewelry. As my friends pointed out, the dancer seems uninterested in big-ticket items. Not that the box I set at her feet is cheap. There's a Petal Pusher in Washington that creates beautiful carvings, and I had this commissioned special.

Different shades of wood create a wave pattern on the lid of the box, the pieces fitting together seamlessly. When you run your fingers over the surface, you'll find delicate engravings of sea creatures and ocean birds. This is a one-of-a-kind piece.

If Pearl is intrigued by boxes, then I'll give her one hell of a box.

Hopefully, she doesn't chuck it at my head.

I watch her stroll toward me, trying not to let on exactly how eager I am. But she can probably still tell. Coyness is not one of my strong suits.

Like every night she's on the stage, Pearl is gorgeous. She's opted for a silky white outfit tonight that looks like something a woman might wear to bed. Which leads me to imagining her in my bed, only a thin sheet draped over her, a husky laugh tempting me to join her.

These are the thoughts she probably wanted to bring to mind when picking out the outfit. A strategic move.

Or at least it would be if she wanted to earn more money from besotted men like me.

Why does she dance if not for the payment?

I can't figure the puzzle out, and I don't have the mental capacity at the moment when Pearl stops in front of me. The entrancing woman doesn't kneel this time. She does something far more mind-melting.

Balancing in her towering heels, Pearl bends her knees and settles in a seemingly effortless squat. The thick muscles in her thighs flex under her glitter-covered skin, and her calves look carved from marble.

Does she ache at the end of the night? Does she need someone to massage her tight muscles until they're loose and pliant?

I could be that helper.

The exceptionally talented woman threatens to turn me into a puddle on the floor when I finally acknowledge that this position leaves her legs spread wide enough for me to stare directly at her silk-covered pussy. The fabric is scant enough to tease me with the curves of her ass cheeks.

When I raise my drink to my mouth, there's a shake in my hand. Pearl's fingers are steady as she unlatches the lid and lifts it open. I know what she'll see inside and wait with held breath to see how she'll react.

Her lips purse, maybe in the start of a frown, or maybe in the attempt to push away a smile.

I hope for the latter.

Pearl reaches into the box and pulls out the contents.

Another—slightly smaller—box. This one was also a commission, crafted with equal care and expertise.

She lifts the lid...and pulls out another box. This one is just as carefully wrought as the first, though slightly smaller.

Over the music, I could swear I hear the huff of her breath.

A frustrated sigh?

A disbelieving laugh?

My Russian doll-style gift continues, and I maintain hope as she opens the fourth box in a row. Her curiosity hasn't waned.

In the last container, which is small enough to sit snuggly in her palm, Pearl finally discovers something different. She plucks the card stock from its home and tilts the note, so the dim lighting illuminates the words. She doesn't have to read them aloud for me to recall what I wrote.

The message was simple:

Hi! My name is Sammy. Would you like to get dinner with me?

With nervous fingers, I clutch my glass tight while silently reminding myself to breathe and try to look attractive rather than desperate and creepy.

This could change everything. If she gives me a chance.

Then something amazing happens. Finally, after months of visiting The Jewelry Box and watching Pearl dance, she meets my eyes.

I suck in a gasp, her attention heavy like a hit. I feel like a ghost who's been haunting the VIP section, and now, finally, I'm acknowledged as existing.

But just as I come to terms with the fact that Pearl is looking at me, holding my gaze with hers, the dancer lets out a sigh so loud no background music can dampen the noise.

Then she rolls her eyes.

And finally, the dancer extends her hand, reaching toward me, the note pinched between her fingers. She drops the paper in my drink, the same as she did with the pearls. The amber liquid soaks into the cardstock, but I don't bother trying to snatch it out. My magic rocks through me, tugging on the alcohol until it swirls and wets the note completely. Demoralized, I watch as Pearl smoothly straightens, towering over me and this entire club on her raised platform and in her deadly heels.

My heart sinks out of my ribcage to land heavy in my gut as she steps away.

But then she pauses.

And turns back to me.

And I choke on air as she leans over, face getting closer to mine ...

Only to watch her scoop up the boxes into her arms and carry them with her when she struts off stage.

"Need another drink?"

I glance down to realize Cat hovers at my elbow, her crimson brows raised in question as she eyes my contaminated glass.

"Hey, Red," I greet my friend using her club name. For the same reason dancers use pseudonyms, the waitstaff can choose to be labeled as a color if they don't want their real names tossed around. "Sure. Did you see?" I wave at the stage.

"See you get rejected? Again?" She snorts with zero sympathy. "Yeah."

"That's not all that happened." I smirk at my friend, earning a scowl from her.

"What else happened then?"

My face warms with triumph. "She accepted my gift."

"You mean the boxes?"

"Exactly. The boxes."

Her crimson brows dip. "You didn't put a tracking device in them, did you?"

"Gods, no! Seriously?" I huff. "They're normal, beautiful, one-of-a-kind boxes that Pearl liked enough to keep."

Cat's suspicious expression fades, but she still appears skeptical. "And you find this promising?" From the Pyro's tone, she doesn't. But I hang on to my optimism.

"I do."

Chapter Five

AVA

Another Tuesday night and I'm at the club again. After multiple classes today, I decided to forgo the heels once more, and I find relief stretching my feet in the dance moves. The music flows through my body, and I relish the stretch and pull up my muscles. There's a good crowd tonight that is fueling me up nicely for the coming week. I let the magic of their longing fill the shallow well my magic became over the past few stressful days.

I'm grateful for the boost but wistful for the days when I rarely needed a refill.

Something shifts in the air. Not the mood of the entire club. That stays the same. But I notice something different about the atmosphere. There is a thrum of excitement. An awareness that another presence has entered the space. Without being obvious about it, I let my eyes scan the room.

There he is.

Sammy.

He's looking my way as he usually is, but I don't let my gaze settle on him. I continue to move and sway and tell myself that I'm dancing for no one but me. Even if I do try a new move that I've been working on that has my body upside down, hands gripping the bar as my shoulder presses against the metal and my legs spread wide.

That's for me. Not for him.

Still, I look forward to the taste of peanut butter, and from the corner of my eye, I track his approach to the VIP section. There's an odd slouch to the way the man moves. Normally he stands upright, striding along with a hint of swagger. A small corner of my brain wonders if he's injured.

Doesn't matter. It's not my problem.

If Sammy knew what I could do, he would probably make it his problem. He'd be at the edge of the stage begging not for my attention, but for my aid in healing whatever ails him.

I don't share my magical skills with other people in my community. They know I'm a witch and that's enough. There's already too much expectation in what witches can do. As if our magic can solve every problem. As if we just need to find the right words and the right combination of herbs and speak them with the right connotation, and we can change the world.

But we have limitations like everyone else. Me more than most.

I climb the pole and relish the height. Gazing down upon the gathering, knowing that they can see the ample curves of my ass cheeks in the bedazzled boy shorts I opted for today. The material under the crystals is stretchy, comfortable, and stays in place no matter what gymnastic move I make.

As I slide down the pole in a twirling glide, I realize that Sammy has approached the edge of the stage. I pretend not to notice, though I still wait for him to possibly offer up another pretty box.

I don't need another message of introduction. Or a silly quip.

But I did like the boxes.

I brought them back to my apartment and now I use them to store things. They're well-made with intricate designs on them. They don't make me like him any more than I did before, but I'll take a beautiful box if someone's handing it to me. Better than a string of pearls.

My toes settle on the stage, and just as I am about to sink to my knees for a little floor work, my eyes sneak over to Sammy once again. As if realizing I am aware of his presence, he pulls back the expensive lapel of his peacoat and retracts his hand from where it once hid inside the fabric. Kind of like a flasher, but the guy doesn't pull out his dick.

Cradled in Sammy's large hand is a furry ball with wide eyes. It blinks in the dim glow of the club and stares at me. Directly into my heart.

He brought a kitten to a strip club!

All thoughts of my dance fall out of my brain, and I dive across the stage to come to a kneeling position in front of him, my arms outstretched. It's a *kitten*. I can't keep away.

Sammy grins wide as he offers the little cat to me. Our fingers brush as I scoop the animal from his grip, but I'm too focused on the fluffy perfection to pay heed to the tingling spark of our contact.

The cat doesn't seem scared, only curious as I hold her against my chest. Her fur is luxuriously soft, and she lets out a little mewling sound that is sweeter than any lust I've ever tasted.

"She's yours." Sammy says the words clear enough to be heard over the music. "If you want her."

I'm just figuring out a way to respond to this wild turn of events when there's a commotion behind the man's back. My boss Yasmin appears, followed closely by one of our security guards, Aspen. Yasmin is a tall, slim woman who can don an imposing appearance when she needs to.

Right now, she looks menacing.

"Samuel Reyes," she snaps.

His happy expression falters, and he flicks his gaze over his shoulder. I watch those same shoulders droop when he realizes who is behind him.

"Yasmin. Hey—"

"You brought a *cat* into my *club*."

"Technically, yes. But—"

"You are banned," she declares, and the other people in the VIP section wince in sympathy. "For three months. Get out of here. Now." Yasmin shifts her body and gestures for Aspen to step forward. "You make sure he leaves."

"Three months?" Sammy's voice cracks with panic as he states the length of time.

While this exchange happens, I continue to hold the kitten against my chest, scratching underneath its chin with a gentle finger. I love animals, cats especially. I had one when I was growing up. When Mr. Wiggles died, the pain was so intense I swore I'd never adopt another animal again. But now I am officially in love with this fur baby. If Sammy tries to take it away from me, I will throw down against him. Same goes for Yasmin. She can be mad at the guy and ban him all she wants, but this kitten is an innocent victim in this situation.

"Sorry, Sammy." Aspen rumbles the words, even as he places a beefy hand on my customer's shoulder and pulls him towards the door.

Sammy doesn't put up a fight, but he does half turn, staring over his shoulder, eyes connecting with mine. His expression is so forlorn and baffled that I'm tempted to laugh.

He did this to himself.

And I don't know what he's looking for from me. Does he expect me to call out and say *I'll wait for you!*

Not gonna happen.

Thanks for the cat, I silently think to him.

Because that's the thing: I've never spoken to him before. Not a single word. And I don't see a reason to start now.

He should be grateful. Yasmin is being lenient with him. She must like the guy. Someone else who pulled the same stunt would've been banned permanently from The Jewelry Box.

"I don't know what we're gonna do with that," Yasmin says as she stares at the animal in my arms. "If you give it here, I'll take it back out to him so it's his problem."

"No," I say, cradling her close to my cleavage. "She's mine now."

Only when I get off stage and have time to truly look the kitten over do I realize she's wearing a tiny collar with a golden tag.

And on that tag is a phone number.

Chapter Six

SAMMY

Two days after my ban from The Jewelry Box, I'm distracting myself by working late when I get a text from an unknown number.

> Unknown: Corresponding with you is likely a mistake. But know that I will be quick to block you if you make this weird.

It's her.

Pearl used the number that she found on the kitten's collar.

She's texting me.

I hadn't let myself fully believe that this was a possibility. And because I didn't let myself believe this was a possibility, I don't have a message ready to respond to her.

While my brain is frantically trying to remember words that make sense another message comes in.

> Pearl: What is the situation with this kitten?

Swiveling my chair away from my desk full of drafted blueprints, I focus entirely on this exchange and decide to stick with the topic she brought up. The kitten is a safe zone to focus on, unlike my unending infatuation with her.

> Sammy: Hello, you have reached Sammy Reyes. And the deal with the kitten is that the little fuzzball is yours to keep.

> Sammy: That is if you like kittens.

> Sammy: If you do not like kittens, then please turn the kitten over to Cat. She will then bring the kitten to me. I don't think that Cat necessarily likes kittens simply because her name is Cat.

> Pearl: The kitten is mine.

> Pearl: But I think something is wrong with it.

Panic clinches my chest as I recall the sweet little animal that I found abandoned in a condemned building and kept tucked in my jacket when I snuck it into the strip club. There was no way of knowing if Pearl would immediately fall in love with the scruffy creature. But I knew if the most adorable feline in the world couldn't win her affection, then I— a selfish asshole—had zero chance with the elusive woman.

> Sammy: Is she sick? I'll cover any vet bills. Is she hurt?

> Pearl: It's not a physical issue. It's a mental one.

Then an amazing thing happens.

Pearl sends me a picture.

Not a picture of herself, which would obviously be my first choice. But she does send me an adorable picture of a kitten sitting in a kitchen sink. The cat's fur is wet and sticking up at funny, spiky angles. The damp creature seems to have alien large eyes.

> Pearl: She jumped into the sink while I was washing dishes. The cat likes water. Something is wrong with her.

My heart swells to five times the normal size.
She likes water. Just like her daddy.
I'm so proud.

> Sammy: That's a brave little monster you have.

> Pearl: Funny that you would call her a monster.

> Pearl: I named her Kraken. In tribute to her water-loving soul.

How is it that every interaction I have with this woman makes me fall for her even more? As much as I tried to ignore it, there was a part of my brain that took Rafael's words to heart. That pointed out I might have imagined Pearl to be a different woman than she is, and a single conversation would reveal my delusions.

But these texts are playful, yet dry. I can imagine the dismissive woman from the stage typing these out with no effort. If only I could hear the words spoken in her voice.

What does she sound like? I want to know so bad. But I'm not sure I'll ever get a chance to.

Still, my hopelessness from the last forty-eight hours has diminished greatly from this simple exchange. She's talking to me. I gave her an opening, and Pearl started a conversation. She didn't have to. She could've taken the kitten and run.

Yet here I am, reading words that she has typed out for me. This has to mean something, right? I would think it at least means she has a vague interest in me. And that I don't creep her out. Maybe that she thinks of me as someone potentially more than just a customer.

Unless she messages other customers. The thought comes in a judgmental voice. The same voice that likes to remind me how people are only nice to me because I'm rich and I'll never know if a romantic partner truly likes me.

As much as the lack of clarity about this first true communication makes my nerve endings itch, I don't ask. I don't wanna do anything to make Pearl question the decision to send a message to me.

> Sammy: That name is inspired! I think it should win an award. And I fully expect Kraken will one day demolish entire pirate ships on her whim.

> Pearl: She does demand respect that is for sure.

I watch the three dots of an incoming text message appear and disappear multiple times.

What is she so unsure about?

When Pearl is on stage, she seems to embody confidence, but this hints at hesitation. Eventually, the dots are replaced with an actual message.

> Pearl: Why did you give me a kitten?

This question isn't a surprise. Honestly, it would've made more sense as the first message she sent me.

> Sammy: I hope this doesn't make you feel any less special. But I have to confess that you are not the first person that I have given a kitten to in the past few weeks.

> Pearl: So what? They are leftover party favors you had extras of?

I snort a laugh.

> Sammy: More like a litter discovered on an abandoned construction site. I've been looking for homes for them and thought I might offer you the chance to grab one. You can pat yourself on the back for being a rescue kitten mama.

When I'm not pining for Pearl, I spend my days working as an architect. I went to one of my new build sites last week and heard pitiful meowing. My foreman and I came across a huddled mass of three little kittens that were underfed and too adorable to leave behind. She had two daughters and said that she could take two of the kittens for them, while I decided to keep one for myself. Then I had the inspired idea to offer one to Pearl. Which is probably a good indication that I wouldn't have made a model cat dad in the first place.

> Sammy: I hope she finds a good home with you.

> Pearl: However I feel about you will not affect how I treat this kitten. She is a sea monster princess that I will murder a fleet of bloodthirsty pirates for.

She sends a picture of Kraken eating a big bowl of cat food.

Then one of Kraken napping in a cat bed.

Next is a picture of Kraken nestled on a pair of plump, perfect boobs.

And I lie down on the floor of my office and die a little.

But it's a good death.

Chapter Seven

SAMMY

When I step off my newly purchased plot of land onto the hot sidewalk, I could swear I see a mirage. They aren't uncommon in Phoenix, the intense sunshine reflecting off the ground to make it appear as though there's thirst-quenching water just ahead. But the tempting sight across the street from me promises to sate a different thirst.

But maybe my eyes are tricking me.

I stand still on the side of the street, stare trained across the way where my mirage climbs out of a car she just parked in front of a row of condos. The mirage's pale skin is lit by the late afternoon sun rather than dim club lighting. The mirage's familiar peachy bottom is tucked into a set of high-waisted cut-offs rather than lingerie, and her round tits hide under a tight tank top. Instead of loose, silky curls brushing the mirage's shoulders, she has the white gold strands piled in a messy bun on top of her head. Her feet are in flip-flops, not heels. Her hands grasp cloth grocery bags, not a pole.

And her face is bare. Bare of makeup.

Bare of a mask.

The mirage's strong arms are loaded with her food haul, so she uses her foot to push the car door closed. The slam of it snaps me out of my stupor and makes two things clear.

She's real. I've found her.

I barely remember to check for traffic before jogging across the street.

"Pearl!" I call out, my hand raised to grab her attention. If I wasn't sure before, the way she freezes, body tightening in recognition was the last clue I needed.

She's here. Right here.

We've been texting for two weeks now. Mostly we talk about Kraken, but occasionally topics stray to shows we're watching or food we're eating. When I send flirtatious messages, she responds back with wry humor or outright shit-talk that does it for me for some reason. I haven't stopped falling for her.

This is the real her. I'm about to meet—

Pearl whirls on me, more emotion in her gray eyes than I've ever seen before. Before I have a chance to fully register the sharp glare, she's dropped her bags and shoved me up against the wall of concrete bricks that juts out beside what I assume is her front door.

"Don't. Ever. Call. Me. That." Each word comes with its own punctuation, and I cringe in chagrin, realizing my blunder too late.

I'm dense. She wears a mask while stripping. Obviously Pearl doesn't want anyone outside of the club to know her by that name.

"Sorry. Really. I promise not to do it again." I raise my arms in surrender but don't try to maneuver out of her punishing hold. Honestly, I like it. Knowing that the forearm braced across my chest is hers.

She's touching me. She's pressed close to me. I breathe in deep and catch traces of fresh eucalyptus.

She's looking at me, and I map every newly revealed detail. In the mask, I knew she had a heart-shaped face and pillowy lips. But now I know her cheeks are rounded like sweet apples and her nose has a small, endearing bump on the bridge. Without her makeup and the mask shadowing her eyes, I can admire the pale gold of her lashes.

Even as I hold my hands away, I long to cup her face, to trace my fingers down the slope of her neck where a flush builds under her skin.

I want her so bad my body hurts with it.

She lets out a little gasp, her lids fluttering, then mutters a soft yet distinct, "Gods."

Gods.

Plural.

Could that mean...

"What gods do you pray to?" I rasp, desperate for the answer.

She blinks her eyes open and resumes glaring.

"The same as you, you nosey-ass Squid."

And those are the very same gods I thank because now I know Pearl is a magical woman of some kind. Or at least aware of our world.

"Are you stalking me?" she hisses.

Fuck. Of course that's what she thinks.

"No." I shake my head vigorously, almost hard enough to dislodge my well-worn baseball hat. "Nothing like that. I'm here for that." I cautiously point to the vacant lot across the street. "It was for sale. I bought it."

"You *bought* it?" Pearl shoves away from me, stepping back and leaving my body free even though I don't want to be. "Please tell me that you're not some billionaire who bought the plot of land across from my apartment building just to impress me. I don't need any of that *Fifty Shades of Grey*, *Pretty Woman* bullshit." Her glare burns like molten silver. "I'm not some quiet mouse virgin looking for a BDSM mentor. And I'm not a golden-hearted prostitute in need of saving."

Noted.

"Well, I not a billionaire." But I don't think now is the moment to tell her to change that B to an M. My grandpa was the billionaire. He decided investing in a fruit-themed tech company would be a fun lark. When the eccentric man passed, he left me a portion of his fortune and his favorite harmonica. "And I didn't buy it to impress you. I swear. I didn't know you lived here. I don't even know your real name..."

The woman of my dreams turns her back on me, mouth firmly shut, the silence saying what she doesn't have to.

You're not getting my name.

There's a skittering noise, and I glance to the side to see a fuzzy face in the window. Tiny paws press on the glass, scratching as if wanting out.

"It's Kraken!" I crow, hoping the reminder of the cat we've been texting about will ease the tension of this moment. "She recognizes me. She wants to say hi to her daddy."

Pearl refuses to look at me as she collects her bags off the ground. "I'm a single cat mom. No need for a deadbeat dad."

Are we bantering? This kind of sounds like the joking I do with my friends, and I can't help responding the way I would with them.

"I resent that. I'll be a supportive, loving cat dad. Like right now. I'll give her all the snuggles she requires." *Invite me into your home*, I want to beg. *Anything you want, I'll get it for you*.

"Go away, Sammy."

"You know my name?" I choke out the question, half dead from the way it sounded in her husky voice.

"You wrote it in your note. And sent it in your text. Obviously I know your name." She slips her key into the front door.

"But you remembered it. Because I'm memorable, right?" I let my easy, charming grin settle on my mouth.

Pearl pauses, glancing over her shoulder to give me a raised-brow stare. "Yeah, Sammy. You're memorable. You're the fucking weirdo that handed me a cat while I was in the middle of dancing at a strip club. That's hard to forget."

Nosey. Weirdo.

"I get the feeling that I'm not coming off well in our interactions." I feel when my smile falters and falls away. "That you don't have the highest opinion of me."

Creep. I'm being creepy.

Honestly, I would be perfectly fine with her calling me a creepy, nosey weirdo if she had a touch of affection in her voice as she said the descriptors. Cat lovingly insults Rafael all the time, and it's a joy to watch.

But Pearl—which is the name I have to keep using because I have no other yet—talks to me with a tone of bafflement and distrust.

"You're in front of my home," she points out. "My private home. Where I did not invite you."

I'm freaking her out.

"I'm freaking you out."

She shoves open the front door and sets her groceries inside before facing me again.

"I am *not* Pearl." With her fists on her hips and a glare on her face, she might as well be towering over me on a stage in heels. "I am not whatever fantasy you imagined me to be in your head. I am a real woman with boundaries. And you're crossing them." She jerks her chin toward the construction site across the street. "If that's why you're in my neighborhood—like you claimed—then stay on your side of the street."

In a graceful move, she whirls back to her door and slips inside.

"I'm"—the door slams shut—"sorry."

A whole string of curses plays through my mind, every one of them aimed at myself. I'm the worst guy in the world. For the longest time, I thought I was charming. Funny. Smooth.

But I'm just a creepy asshole.

With a forlorn wave, I bid goodbye to Kraken, where she still sits in the window watching me. I doubt I'll get anymore pictures of her. Her mama is probably blocking my number right now. Maybe calling the cops for good measure.

I shove my hands in my pockets and trudge back to the build site. My magic is a churning tempest in my gut, seeking out nearby water to disturb. The closest liquid I sense in this desert suburb is the water in pipes beneath the ground. I mentally try to tamp down my power as I quicken my pace.

If my sadness-fueled magic floods Pearl's home, I will officially be drowning any shot I have with her.

This morning I was excited about getting to work on a new project. But now I'm dreading working for months so close to, yet so far away from, the woman I want who hates me.

Chapter Eight

AVA

When the door is shut, I press my back against the wood surface and remind myself to breathe normally. Meanwhile, Kraken scrambles off the couch to come twine herself around my legs and let out pitiful meows I've yet to learn the meaning of.

They better not be requests to see her daddy.

Daddy. Ugh.

Sammy Reyes knows what I look like. He knows where I live.

I bet the guy could do a quick search and find out what my real name is.

What would he do with it?

Well, an asshole would find out where I work during the day, realize that my nights at The Jewelry Box would get me fired from said day job, and proceed to blackmail me into doing whatever he wanted.

I won't let him.

But the second after that panicked scenario and furious response play through my head, they drift away.

The idea of Sammy threatening me seems so outlandish.

Is this me giving him a hot guy pass?

Our society tends to go easy on traditionally attractive people when they do shitty things. Like showing up uninvited at the house of a woman he barely knows.

Is that what I'm doing?

No. I don't think so. It's not Sammy's panty-dropping face that has me dismissing blackmail as a possibility.

His actions don't track with that dark response. The way he talks to me, the way he messages me, all come off as light-hearted. I've rejected Sammy plenty, but he's never gotten pissed off about it. Never gotten surly or vindictive.

Maybe a little pouty, but even that has an air of playfulness.

Nothing the guy has done or said up to this point gives me asshole vibes.

But that doesn't mean I'm ready to hand over my social security number to the Squid. I was just starting to get comfortable sharing innocent texts with him about Kraken. Only began to consider making eye contact with him once his ban from the club ran out. I thought I might even be generous and say hello to him in person.

I was *not* prepared to meet him on my front stoop.

Especially not with him dressed in jeans, work boots, and a tight blue Henley. Sammy looked ready to work on the construction site he claimed to own next door.

And damn the gods, that look worked for him as well, or even better than, the business wear he normally has on at the club.

Kraken meows another plaintive wail I decide means, "Feed me, bitch!"

"Fine. Fine," I mutter. "I'll fill your bowl."

For a tiny fluffy ball, she goes through a good chunk of food every day.

After dumping kitty kibble in her dish and refreshing her water, I unpack my groceries and try not to imagine Sammy Reyes sweating in the heat of the day. I definitely don't picture the way his golden-brown hair would drip with perspiration, or how his shirt would cling to his salty, damp skin when he tried to drag it off at the end of the day.

After a few deep inhales, I realize I've been standing at my kitchen sink, staring at the sponge for far too long as my mind made up tantalizing scenarios about the sexy, intrusive Squid.

Fuck the Water Elemental for getting me wet.

The space between my legs suddenly feels achy and tender, and I'm reminded how long it's been since I had sex. A few years now. After college, I kind of lost interest. Once I decided I would fuel my magic without the help of a romantic partner, the urge to search for one faded away.

I still touch myself plenty, but it's been a few days since that, too.

Kraken is wholly focused on her food, so I leave her alone in the kitchen and close the door to my bedroom.

I just need to take the edge off. If I'm not horny, then I won't think about him in any capacity.

I can forget him and get a jumpstart on Monday's emails.

In the bottom drawer beside my bed, I keep a small collection of vibrators. Different kinds to add a little variety to my nonexistent sex life.

Briefly, I consider the large blue one, knowing the clit sucker will get me to a fast explosive orgasm. But I've also screamed a time or two when finishing that way, and I don't want to risk being so loud that a certain Squid across the street hears.

Fucking hell dimensions. He's not even a minute walk away. He can probably see my bedroom window from that vacant lot—though not inside since I have the curtains drawn against the heat of the sun.

Still, knowing he's *right there*, wanting me, spikes the arousal in my body. I grab a simple vibrating wand and toss it on my bed. Stripping fast, I climb onto my mattress and shove a pillow between my legs as I kneel. Then I start my toy, close my eyes, and treat myself to illicit fantasies of Sammy Reyes.

I pretend I forgot to close my curtains. That he wanders over and spies me through the glass. That he braces his hand on the windowsill and unzips his fly with the other, pulling out a hard cock that's leaking for me.

A groan spills out of my throat, and I turn up the speed of the vibrator.

"You love to watch me, don't you?" I whisper to the imaginary man but knowing it's true of the real one. His lust finds its way to me on the stage every Tuesday.

But he doesn't know that I like to watch, too.

My hips rock, and in my mind, I make his hand move faster on his ruddy dick.

Goddess, if he pulled it out in the club while lounging in the VIP section, I wouldn't even think to call security on him. I'd probably forget to dance and crawl to the edge of the stage so I could get a closer look.

I'm fucked up, both wanting him to respect my privacy, but also wanting him panting after me.

But this is my imagination, so I push morals aside.

"Show it to me," I mutter, as if Sammy can hear me, and in my fantasy he does, slipping his other hand into his pants to pull out his balls and palming them along with his hard strokes.

The heated, frustrated need in my body tenses into an almost unbearably tight bundle.

Then I remember his delighted grin when he stood in front of me moments ago.

I break apart with a whimpered moan, pleasure mixed with confusion shuddering through my body.

Why do thoughts of him do this to me?

But I try not to let guilt come into my mind as I ride the last waves of my orgasm. I won't shame myself for what turns me on.

But that doesn't mean I want it to be real.

Right?

Chapter Nine

SAMMY

"You're building a magical, sex-work empire."

Yasmin smirks at my remark, watching me from the opposite side of her glass-top desk. I feel her intent gaze on me as I study the blueprints she passed over the moment I sat down.

I'm currently looking at the floor plan of The Underworld, a BDSM club a few blocks over from The Jewelry Box. I've never visited the place, but I know Cat's sister Harley works there. Apparently, this is Yasmin's latest investment.

"You make it sound like I'm going to war. Don't worry. My jewels are lovers, not fighters."

I snort, knowing that any one of the dancers working the stage at The Jewelry Box could skewer a man. Pearl's done it with her eyes alone.

Thoughts of the blonde beauty I haven't seen in weeks because of my ban have me questioning the point of my presence in this meeting.

"Why am I here?" I ask. "According to you, I'm not allowed to step foot on the premises for two more months."

Is she lifting the ban? Please say yes.

But then I consider what that would mean.

Sure, I could return to my routine of settling into the VIP section on

Tuesday nights to watch Pearl dance. But would I be making her uncomfortable? Now that I've waltzed up to her home?

Having her stroll out onto the stage and ignore me was one thing.

But if I saw her flinch at the sight of me? If I picked up a trace of fear?

Fuck, that would gut me.

With resigned regret, I realize that ban or no, my time patronizing The Jewelry Box is done.

Sensing my sadness, my magic stirs, rocking back and forth in my chest until I can swear Yasmin's office is on a boat. The artistic fountain she has on a shelf behind her desk starts sputtering as the liquid within it rises, threatening to overflow unless I gain control of myself.

With a deep breath, I sooth my melancholy magic. The sadness doesn't leave, I'm not that good at control, but my Squid skills stay in check.

"You're banned from the floor," Yasmin says, unaware of my internal conflict. "Not from my office. And just because I want to hire you for this project doesn't change that. You broke the rules, you pay the consequences." She steeples her long fingers in front of her red-painted lips. "Back to business. I want to completely overhaul the look of The Underworld. Possibly change the name, too. But that'll be for my marketing team to weigh in on."

"Overhaul how?" Work is a welcome distraction. Gods know I don't need the money. I could live my life comfortably off my trust fund.

But I like designing things.

Scratch that. I love it. Architecture gives me purpose and joy, which is why I often use my skills in a volunteer capacity.

Still, Yasmin is a shrewd but fair businesswoman, so I expect this will be a well-paid gig.

She waves at the blueprints. "They have a tantalizing name but go in there and it's like a doctor's office. Predictable layout. Bland waiting room. Hallways with vinyl tiles on the floor." She sneers as if the idea of industrial flooring is offensive. "And the rooms are sad attempts at themes. I want to rethink the spaces. Give them flow. People come for a fantasy. They should be fully immersed from the moment they step in the door."

Yasmin's eyes take on a bright spark of excitement as she lays out her intentions, and the eager energy infusing her words rubs off on me.

"That sounds intriguing. I—" The low thump of music distracts me, and my eyes creep toward a one-way window that overlooks the floor of The Jewelry Box. Customers only see a mirror in an ornate frame hung high on the wall.

Yasmin sees everything.

And now I do too.

"I thought the club was closed on Mondays," I mutter, gaze fastened on a voluptuous, familiar body strutting out on stage.

Pearl.

I haven't seen her since our run-in outside her building. That was two weeks ago.

Today, she's wearing an outfit that would be considered modest compared to her normal costumes. A set of stretchy black shorts and a cropped T-shirt still show off the delicious curves of her body.

"Some of the dancers come in on their off days to practice," Yasmin explains, her voice deceptively casual.

I know I should get back to our business discussion, but I'm having trouble tearing my eyes from Pearl as she leisurely swings herself around the pole. Especially since I decided I'm not going to force my company on her again.

And I find myself particularly interested in the person who joins her on stage.

Someone who looks very much like a man.

"Security guard?" I ask, trying to keep my voice casual. I sound like someone is strangling me.

"Dancer," Yasmin corrects. "I'm broadening the clientele I serve." She taps a wickedly sharp acrylic on the blueprints. "But we're here to talk about redesigning a BDSM club. Not whether my newest hire has a romantic attachment to the woman you have an unhealthy fixation on." That gets me to tear my eyes from Pearl and meet Yasmin's suspicious ones. "Do I need to extend your ban?"

"No." I drag in a deep breath then exhale slow. "But you can if you think that's best. Even when my months are up, I'll still keep my distance. As much as I love what your club has to offer, I think it's time I get over my fixation."

Yasmin narrows her eyes. "What happened?"

I debate not telling her, but if we're going to be doing business together, I'd rather not start with a lie. "We crossed paths outside of the club. Pearl made it clear where her boundaries are, and I want to respect them. Even if..." I clear my throat and try not to look entirely devastated. "Even if that means we don't see much of each other in the future." I gesture at the designs. "But this is a different building. So that shouldn't be a problem, right?" I pull my tablet out of my bag and wake it up, using my stylus to open my digital sketchpad. "I like what you're describing. I want to be a part of it."

I don't need the job for the money. I want it for the challenge. Designing something different. Something edgy and sexual.

Maybe it'll take off the edge of need left by Pearl's absence from my life.

Yasmin's eyes flick from the window to me then to the blueprints between us then back to meet my stare.

Her smile unfurls slowly, but I can tell the expression is genuine. Her eagerness has returned.

"Then it looks like I just hired myself an architect."

Chapter Ten

AVA

While I love my little condo and the comfortable space I've made it into, the place has one glaring flaw.

There's no pool.

For a girl who grew up in the humid northeast, my body has yet to get used to the desert atmosphere even after living here for years. Which is why I finally give into Cat's multiple invites to attend a gathering at her friend's house. Apparently, this guy Damien has people over most weekends. She said I could socialize if I want, but I could also just soak in the refreshing water. Option number two sounded perfect, and I don't regret my decision when I push through the tall gate into a lovely oasis.

Damien Cortez's yard is full of lush greenery that still seems like natural vegetation for our arid climate. The pool is a sprawling blue heaven with two waterfalls feeding it from smaller, elevated pools. People collect in groups around the property and in the pool, drinking from sweating cans as they chat and laugh and fill the space with casual good cheer.

"Ava, hey." The deep voice comes from my right, and I spy the security guard Aspen approaching carrying a cooler. "Didn't know you were coming."

Since I don't spend any time on the floor, I don't chat with the burly bearded man much, but I do know that he's an Earth Elemental. Also, before Yasmin set up gated parking for us, he was always happy to act as a safety escort to my car, which I appreciated.

I smile and shrug, fiddling with my sunglasses. "Cat convinced me. I figure after the tenth invite, she'd think I have something against her if I refused again."

"Cat convinced you, huh?" He sets down the cooler and pops open the top.

"Yeah. I hope it's okay. That I'm here."

The Pyro made it sound like anyone was welcome, but maybe she didn't have the right to expand the guest list?

"It's good," Aspen reassures me. "Damien likes a big group. Want something to drink?" He tilts the cooler toward me so I can browse the offerings.

"What's the fruitiest most basic bitch drink you have in there?"

The Petal Pusher chuckles, riffles through the ice, then pulls out a raspberry hard seltzer.

"Perfect." I crack the can and take a sip, enjoying the cold, sweet, bubbly taste. This outing already has a thumbs-up from me. "Will people think I'm weird if I just chill by myself for a bit?"

"No. Go for it." He closes the cooler then points toward a handsome tan-skinned man working the grill. "That's Damien if you haven't met him. Say hi at some point."

"Will do. Thanks for the welcome. And the drink." I raise my can to him, then enjoy a slow stroll around the massive pool as I sip my beverage, eyes on an empty lounge chair near the deep end. As I'm taking in the gathering, I spot when Aspen joins a group that includes Cat. He bends over—way over since she's a foot or more shorter than him—to whisper in her ear. Her sunglass-covered eyes scan until her face points my way across the water. My coworker grins wide and waves. I wave back, glad she doesn't gesture for me to join her. Maybe later after I enjoy some 'me' time. This week was all meetings and instruction and reference desk hours and more meetings. I barely got to retreat to my office at all. I need to decompress.

Luckily, the chair I snag has a sunshade. My skin does not absorb UV rays well, turning my normally paper pale complexion into painfully red tomato skin. One more small ailment I might not need to worry about if I didn't have to use all my healing magic on my migraines.

Touch of sunburn? Spell it away!

If only.

After tugging off my sundress, I pull out my extra strength sunblock and give myself a good spray coating. Then I unearth my latest read and settle on the thick cushion with a happy sigh. Dressed in a bikini that would give the CFF administration heart palpitations, holding a tasty alcoholic drink in one hand and a historical romance in the other, I'm officially in my happy place.

My can is half-empty, and the rogue is kneeling between his love interest's knees in the carriage, his hand inching up her skirts, when a sound tugs me out of my fictional world.

A laugh. The noise is deep, rich, and ends with a genuine snort that has me smiling before I glance up to see where the joyful sound is coming from.

When I spot the laugher, I'm hit with a full-body shiver.

Samuel Reyes stands on the opposite side of the pool from me, and the sight of him has me thirsty for a lot more than what's left of my seltzer.

He's in a set of swim trunks, the color a royal blue that makes his tan skin look gold in the bright midday sun. The Squid is tall and built, but in a lean way. He has the broad shoulders of a swimmer and a tapered waist that makes a woman want to tug those shorts down. He doesn't have the perfectly defined six-pack of a guy who spends every free minute working out and refuses to touch carbs, but he does have a hint of that naughty V just above his waistband. And the way his arms are casually crossed on his chest makes a set of biceps bulge to the point where I want to bite them to test how firm they arm.

Wait. Hold up. NO.

He's an overeager customer. Not a guy you're going to bite!

Belatedly, I realize the guy Sammy is joking with is an Elemental I've seen at the club a few times, usually talking to Cat. Jade pointed him out as the Squid who caused the notorious sprinkler incident that briefly shut down the club last year.

My mind makes the connection.

Squids. Of course. Cat said Damien is a Squid, too. I should've known there was a chance Sammy would attend this gathering. I hadn't thought to ask the Pyro about the guest list.

Sammy laughs at something else his friend says, and for whatever reason, that earns him a shove. One that sends him straight into the pool.

Unfortunately, it's not until this moment I realize my lounge chair is situated directly in front of one of the pool ladders. The one that Sammy swims toward after he comes up sputtering and chuckling.

There's nowhere for me to hide unless I want to dive behind some nearby shrubbery. And I'm not entirely sure I want to. At least, I know that I don't want to be the one running away.

So I stay seated and watch the live porno that is Samuel Reyes climbing out of the pool.

His long fingers wrap around the metal of the ladder, and his muscles flex as he pulls himself upwards. Water streams over his bare skin and saturates his swimsuit. The material clings to every bit of him, leaving little to the imagination.

Sammy whips his head to the side so his wet hair flicks out of his eyes.

And that's when he spots me.

One foot on the concrete, another on the top rung of the ladder, he freezes. His gaze takes in my face first, then drags over my body. In the wake of his attention, I swallow a decadent rush of magic. Like he held out a rich chocolate peanut butter brownie, and I took a massive bite.

I think I'd like to bite him.

I blink away the thought and try to force my brain back online.

"Ava!" The shout comes from across the pool, and I jerk my head toward my name, shocked when my eyeballs don't topple out of my head in the process, since they were glued to Sammy a second ago.

Cat stands at the opposite edge of the pool and holds up a can. "Do you want another drink?"

I swallow hard, still tasting dessert, and slowly shake my head.

Cat grins. "Okay. Let me know if you change your mind."

"Ava?"

I bite my lip to keep from groaning at the sound of my real name in Sammy's voice. This was one of the many reasons I didn't tell him.

Because I knew the syllables would sound too good in his smooth tone.

When I focus on Sammy again, I spy awe on his slack face. The expression clears, replaced by eagerness, and he takes a step toward me.

Then he stumbles to a stop again, water dripping off his body onto the sun-warmed stones. I watch as his face falls into chagrin, and he rocks back on his heels.

"Sorry," he says. "I...sorry. I didn't know you'd be here." He clears his throat. "Not that I don't want you here. I do. Gods I do. Too much." He grimaces, huffs a dry laugh, and drags a hand through his hair. The movement sets the muscles in his chest and arm to flexing in a whole host of delicious ways. "Shit. I'm sorry. When I see you, I turn into a mess." Sammy rubs a rough hand over his face, as if to wake himself up from a deep sleep. "But that's my problem. You go back to reading. I'll stay on the other side of the pool." He pauses, glancing toward the tall fence that surrounds the yard, then nods as if coming to a decision. "Actually, I can head out."

He's going to leave?

Sammy just got here as far as I can tell, and he's going to fully vacate the party because he thinks that'll make me more comfortable.

As he moves to leave, I find myself making what could be a terrible choice.

"Hey, weirdo," I call out to him, making the Squid pause in his retreat and turn back to me with a wide-eyed expression. I point to the empty chair at my side. "Sit."

Chapter Eleven

AVA

Sammy takes the invitation to sit without hesitation, settling his glistening tan body in an upright chair that's nowhere near as comfortable as my chaise. The Squid clasps his hands in his lap and stares at his fingers, but I could swear he's watching me out of the corner of his eye. With his wet hair dangling into his face and his shoulders bowed, he looks like he's about to be chastised. A tantalizing scent, like fresh air after a summer rain, drifts to me, and I wonder if the pool water dampening Sammy's skin has amplified some enticing cologne. I mark my spot in my book, toss it onto my bag, then sip my drink as I study him.

I let the Squid squirm.

At first, I'm not sure why I asked Sammy to sit down. There's no reason I should give this man the time of day.

Even if I did have a mind-melting orgasm from merely thinking about him.

But a guy can be hot and still be a creep.

So no, it's not Sammy's sex appeal—massive as it is—that had me demanding he stay put.

There are two reasons.

Reason one: Cat Byrne.

My coworker just called out my name within hearing range of Sammy, knowing he'd pick up on it. I know the Pyro doesn't go around sharing dancers' info with whoever asks, and I'm pretty sure she's been keeping her mouth shut about me to Sammy for months now.

I get the feeling that sharing my name was her way of telling me the Squid is nothing to be worried about.

Reason two: Even with my name, and me lying here in a bikini that my magic tells me he likes *very* much, Sammy was fully prepared to vacate the premises. To respect my boundaries even though I've stepped into a space I bet he often occupies.

"Do you come here a lot?" I ask, my voice neutral. "To Damien's house?"

Sammy leans his torso forward, bracing his elbows on his knees, continuing to stare downward rather than at me.

"All the time. I've known Damien since high school. He's a Squid. I'm a Squid. I've wrapped my tentacles around him and refuse to let go." The corner of his mouth curves in a smile.

"So, you're clingy?" I ask.

Sammy barks a laugh before roughly dragging both his hands through his hair. "Yeah. Yeah, I kind of am. I find my people and grab onto them and never let go."

Interesting. Sipping my seltzer, I consider the idea of having someone so devoted to me. When I was growing up, I didn't have many close friends. Not a lot of parents wanted their kids to play with the girl whose mom took her clothes off for a living. Plus, I was the quiet, read-a-book type. Even when I wanted friends, I had trouble figuring out the best way to go about making them. I'm friendly with people. There are some librarians from my master's program I have a group text with. I joke around and gossip with the other dancers at the club. No super-close friends, though, and the only person I would say is devoted to me is my mom. Still, she's devoted at a distance, and that works for us.

But having someone hold onto me sounds...kind of nice.

"You have your slimy Squid arms wrapped around anyone else here?" I'm suddenly curious as to who Sammy metaphorically clutches close.

He chuckles and straightens, eyes scanning the gathering. "Those three." Sammy points across the way to where Cat stands between Aspen and the Squid who shoved him into the pool. The man is closer to the Pyro's height and has sun-touched brown hair and a tan complexion slightly darker than Sammy's. "Cat, Aspen, and Rafael. I'm all up in their business. But they don't seem to mind, since I helped them get together."

"Get together?" I know Cat and Aspen are a thing but—

"Thruple. They need all three to balance it out. Or else Cat would probably kill Rafael. Don't get me wrong, she loves the guy, but it's a Pyro and a Squid. Fire and Water." Sammy snorts out a chuckle. "Things get steamy."

I watch as Cat gazes up at Aspen, laughing as they talk, and the other guy, Rafael, presses a quick, affectionate kiss to her shoulder. She has two devoted partners. Meanwhile, I haven't dated anyone in years because I struggle to figure out if I actually want a romantic connection or if I just want the ease of an immediate power source.

"Who else?" I ask Sammy, needing to be distracted from my thoughts.

He tilts his chin toward a young woman who's appeared beside the grill, poking Damien's shoulder. "Marisol. Merry Berry. She's Damien's little sister, but she feels like mine, too."

"Do you have any siblings?"

Sammy shakes his head, eyes back on the ground. "Only child. A spoiled one, too. But you probably already guessed that."

Oh yeah. I can bet Sammy's parents gave him everything he ever desired. That he never heard the word no.

"Any more?"

Sammy shakes his head again. "Not here. But I've thoroughly tentacled my cousin Auggie and his girlfriend Quinn. My parents. And... that's it."

"What about me?" The question slips out, and I tell myself it's defensive curiosity, and not hope.

Sammy closes his eyes. "If you don't want me around, I won't be. I swear, I'll leave you alone."

I hum a note in the back of my throat. "So only into consensual tentacle-ing then?"

Sammy's eyes fly open and meet mine, though he probably can't tell, since I'm still wearing my sunglasses. Still, he sees my smirk, and he answers with a hesitant grin.

"You're making my affection sound dirty, when I'm keeping this discussion completely innocent," he accuses, delight evident in the curl of his lips.

I don't think anything can be considered innocent when Sammy is shirtless and wet. But I don't tell him that.

"I don't know what you mean," I murmur before going to take another swallow of my hard seltzer, only to realize the can is empty. Sammy must notice too because he holds out his hand.

"Here. I'll recycle that and get you a refill. Want some water, too?"

"Sure," I say, cautiously, worried about softening too much toward him, but also not wanting to get out of my chair yet.

Sammy jogs off with my can and an air of purpose. Meanwhile, I watch the way his wet swim trunks grip his firm backside.

What is wrong with me?

Before I have time to figure out the answer to that question, Sammy is back with two different seltzers and a Solo cup full of water and ice cubes.

"Make sure to stay hydrated." He sets the cup on the table beside my chair. "Which flavor?" Sammy offers a raspberry and mango. I opt for the one I haven't tried.

He cracks open the other, then points to his seat with a brow raised in question. I nod, and he settles beside me again.

"You're not allowed to tentacle me," I tell him and enjoy the way he chokes on his swallow and has to cough to clear the liquid from his throat. I wonder if Squids can drown, or if the water would just reabsorb into his body.

My mother raised me with the knowledge of magic, how different beings in the world can wield it. But I only know the basics, and I'm betting she missed a few mythical beings when she listed them off. Most of our magic lessons focused on healing magic. Every medical spell I know is because of her and our family grimoire.

Once Sammy stops coughing, I continue with what I was trying to tell him.

"But—while I'm at this get-together—you can sit with me. And we can have a normal conversation. If you want."

He nods vigorously. "I do want. I do very much want. That. I want that. To talk to you."

I turn fully on my side to stare at the Squid. From the way Sammy acted at the club—well-dressed, confident stride, cocky smile, handing out hundreds—I figured he'd be a smooth talker.

But the guy can't seem to form a proper sentence.

It's kind of endearing.

"Then we can talk," I say. "Full name and occupation."

"Sammy—Samuel, but people only call me that when they're pissed at me—Reyes. Sexy architect."

I press the cool can against my mouth to hide my smile. "Does that mean you make buildings sexy?"

"Hell yeah." He waggles his brows at me, the hairs a few shades darker than his golden-brown hair. "Everyone wants to fuck my buildings."

My jaw aches from biting down on a laugh. "I don't know if I'm curious or terrified to see what you come up with for the lot across my street."

"Better brace yourself." He fiddles with the tab on his can and keeps his voice casual. "Can I ask your full name?"

This is it. A show of faith.

Please don't let me regret it.

"Ava Bellarose."

He doesn't say my name aloud, but I watch his lips shape the letters.

We're quiet for a stretch until I bravely offer, "And do you want to know my occupation?"

"Oh!" He sits up straight and shifts and inch closer. "Yes. Sorry, I thought..." He thought I was a stripper, but he's probably remembering now I only work one or two shifts a week. "Please tell me about your job, Ava Bellarose."

Sammy smiles as he says my name, and I don't think that should be allowed.

After another sip of my mango alcohol for courage, I say, "Ava Bellarose. Academic Librarian."

Well, that's it. I've given this man all the information he needs to fully fuck up my life. My name, my occupation, plus he knows where I live. Is this how those victims on the true crime podcasts started out? Giving in to the urge to share the identifying details of their life with a nosey, handsome Squid?

"You're...a librarian." There's something odd about Sammy's voice, and when I study his expression, it looks as though he's recovering from an unexpected slap to the face.

"Yes." I double down and frown at the man. "Do you have a problem with librarians? Did the library mob murder your dog?"

A smile cracks through his bafflement.

I swallow hard when I taste peanut butter on my tongue.

"Oh my gods!" I sit up fast and fling my arm out to shove his chest. Not hard, just enough to try shaking him out of whatever thoughts he's currently thinking. "You're turned on. You think librarians are hot!"

Sammy groans and covers his eyes. "I'm sorry. Gods. I just have this mental image of you in a pencil skirt reaching for a book on a high shelf, and when I ask you if you need some help, you shush me for talking too loudly."

Well, that's specific.

"And that does it for you?" I don't need to ask. The lust is spilling off him.

"Yeah." The look he gives me is all wide-eyed and pouty, silently begging for forgiveness. "But I know your job is much more involved than that. Can you tell me about it?"

As Sammy sits in front of me, drenched in lust as the sun dries his honey-brown hair into haphazard curls, I have a sudden urge. A craving to lean in, press my lips against his neck, and whisper that I *do* have a few pencil skirts, and sometimes there *are* books on high shelves I struggle to reach, and there *is* a section of the library that is a quiet zone where he's not allowed to talk.

But there's another part of me that wonders if Sammy Reyes would want anything to do with me if he knew the real me. The woman who isn't always covered in glitter and swinging around a pole. The witch who isn't in a skimpy bathing suit poolside.

Would Ava the book nerd with a preference for tea and introversion have any appeal to the charming Squid?

There's only one way to find out.

"Fine. You want to know about the job of a sexy librarian? Then let me tell you about the sensual topic of information literacy..."

Chapter Twelve

SAMMY

If Ava thinks discussing research databases will turn me off, she misjudged how easily I get a competency boner.

Ava.

Ava Bellarose.

My mind plays her name on repeat in the background like elevator music as I listen to her discuss the online newspaper archive she demos for every Communication 101 class at the college where she works.

As I sit here, poolside, cold drink in my hand, my mystery woman sitting close to me, leaning toward me, speaking with a smile and passionate hand gestures, I'm sure that when Rafael shoved me into the pool, I accidentally traveled through space and time to land in a pleasure dimension.

This is perfection.

"I'm boring you," Ava says, her confident expression faltering and her lovely hands falling into her lap.

"What?" I yelp, scooting my chair forward, closer to her. "No. Not at all. I want to know more. What departments do you work with? Do you like teaching freshmen? How many librarians are on staff? Do you need more water?" I lean over to glance in her cup and realize she's mainly been drinking her hard seltzer. "You're not staying hydrated. You'll get a headache." I nudge the cup toward her.

Her lovely lips twist in a grimace so brief I almost miss it, but then her mouth softens, and she picks up the cup to take a large gulp.

"Fine. I'm hydrating." She tongues a stray drop of water from the corner of her mouth in a move that threatens to kill me on the spot. "And to answer your questions, I'm the liaison to all the departments at the moment, but that'll change whenever the administration hires a new library director. Yes, I enjoy working with first years because I like demystifying the research process so they're less intimidated by higher education. And technically I'm the only librarian on staff. Rodrigo is head of circulation and full-time, but he's considered a library associate."

"What's the difference?"

"Usually, a master's degree." Ava's adorable nose wrinkles with a frown. "And giving him the title of 'Librarian' would mean they'd have to pay him more. Which, by the way, I'm all for. He deserves a raise and works just as hard as I do." She sighs, a defeated noise that has me guessing her bosses don't agree. "Then we usually have ten student workers during the fall and spring semesters. And I guess that sounds like a lot. But we're down to three students for the summer. And I wish we had at least three more full-time librarians. I doubt we'll get the budget approval for it." She lets out another weary sigh. "You know what? I'm tired of talking about my job. I deal with it all week."

Great, I'm poking at her stressful topic. Thinking fast, I glance around for inspiration and my eyes land on her book.

"You like historical romance?" I point to the cover that shows a woman in a flowing blue ballgown that falls halfway off her shoulder.

Ava raises her chin, as if getting ready for a fight. "I do."

"Very cool. I've read a few, but I prefer contemporaries."

"Contemporary...romances?"

I nod. "Yep. It's my favorite genre. Because of the happily ever after. I need that positive ending." I hold up my hand and make a waving motion, coaxing a small bubble of water out of her half-full cup until it floats in the air between us. This simple move takes concentration and willpower because I have zero natural fuel at the moment. "My powers are directly connected to my sadness. If I get mopey, it's hard to keep everything in check," I explain.

"Are you sad now?" Ava asks quietly as she reaches out a finger to fondle the floating water.

I swallow hard before answering. "Not even a little bit."

As if her only goal in the world is to torment me, Ava slips off her sunglasses so I can finally see her gorgeous grey eyes. She holds my gaze as she leans in, presses her lips against the floating orb of liquid, and sucks.

Connected as I am to the water, I can feel the pull on it as well as the way it flows over her tongue and down her throat.

A groan leaves my chest on a ragged breath, and I'm hard as stone in my swim trunks. Ava's lids flutter shut as a flush rushes over her pale skin, making her glow.

Kiss her! The urge shouts in my head, but I refuse to listen. To shatter this delicate chance she's given me to show I'm a decent person.

"Gonna...pool." I grit out the words and cup my hands over my groin as I struggle to my feet. But this position is so much worse because now I'm standing in front of Ava with a hard on and her gazing up at me with wide eyes, her lips still parted slightly and damp from the water she just drank.

Fuuuuuuck.

I stumble back a step, my two goals to get away from her and get into the pool.

Unfortunately, not looking where I'm going is a mistake because I run directly into a Stoner who was passing by, bounce off the guy's massive chest, stumble away from the water and toward a decorative arrangement of plant-filled pots. Before I can regain my balance, the back of my knee meets an urn. In an ungainly flail, I topple over the greenery to plummet toward a stone path on the opposite side. To keep my face from hitting the ground, I fling my arms out, bracing for collision.

I catch myself, but not gracefully.

Over my shout of surprise, I hear the *crack*.

Then comes the pain.

White hot lightning streaks down my right arm, and I try to bite back a groan, only letting out a whimper instead.

"Sammy!" Multiple people call my name, all of them concerned, some scared. If I wasn't in so much pain, I might enjoy the attention. Instead, I stay sprawled on the ground, cradling my arm, panting in bracing breaths as I pray to the gods that the hurt will subside and this will end up just as a bad bruise and a funny story.

But my hand feels wet even though I don't sense pure water.

"Fuck," Damien's muttered curse comes as a shadow blocks out the sun on the inside of my closed eyelids, which I've clenched shut as if that'll relieve some of the agony. "We need an ambulance."

"No," I moan, in part denying the severity of my injury, but also out of the fear every Elemental has.

Discovery.

Sure, there's the possibility humans could learn of our existence and be super cool about it. But humans don't have a history of easily accepting things they consider as "other. " More likely Elementals would be labeled as dangerous. Which is why going to doctors where tests are run is such a risk. Our kind don't get sick, so there's no need to worry about that.

But we can get injured. We bleed like everyone else.

I squint my eyes open and glance down with trepidation. The white splinter of bone poking through bloody flesh turns my guts to water, and I think I pass out for a moment. But something brings me back. A husky sweet voice full of command.

"Let me through. Don't call an ambulance."

I blink up to see Ava in her skimpy blue bikini settling at my side in a cross-legged position.

"He needs a doctor," Damien growls at her, his protective instincts creating a storm on his normally relaxed face.

"He needs me," she says back with utter confidence. "Now hush."

Fuck. If I wasn't suffering, I'd be hard all over again.

"Sammy," Ava croons my name, and I let out another whimper because her affectionate tone sounds so good. "I'm going to touch your arm, okay? I'm going to make you feel better. Will you let me?"

"Yes," I rasp. I'll let this woman do anything to me.

"Good boy," she murmurs.

And I fall in love.

Then I bite down on a scream as Ava carefully lifts my injured arm into her lap.

I can't watch. But her shapely thigh sits only a few inches from my head, so I bend my neck and press my face against the plush part of her, breathing in her refreshing eucalyptus scent as I pant through the pain.

There're touches around the wound, small irritations, like sprinkles on the torment sundae. Then her voice comes again, so lovely, but the stinging ache must be eating at my ability to comprehend words because everything Ava says sounds like gibberish.

Still, hearing her helps. Slowly, a numbness overtakes my arm, eventually overwhelming the limb and granting me glorious relief. I slump in a shaking, worn out mess, face still plastered to Ava's leg.

"By all the gods," Damien mutters, something like awe in his voice.

Much as I don't want to leave off my new face pillow of Ava Bellarose, I want to check how bad my arm is and thank her for finding a way to take away the pain, even if it's for a brief moment.

With a grunt, I roll over and carefully sit up, then clench my jaw and glance down.

My forearm is coated in blood. At first glance, it's terrifying. Only, something is off about the sight.

The skin not coated in gore has strange symbols written in what looks like blue highlighter.

But the weirdest thing is...there's no wound.

I *swore* I saw my own bone. Now there's only blood and what looks like healed scar tissue. My eyes jump from my arm to Ava's hands, where I see she does in fact have a blue highlighter clutched in her fingers. Her hands and legs have smears of my blood, and some of the crimson has speckled on the fabric of her bathing suit. My stare travels up farther to meet hers.

Despite the soothing way she spoke to me moments ago, the woman does not look concerned or caring.

Ava's lips are pinched, and her eyes are narrowed as they meet mine. She tears her gaze away and stands up quickly, leaving me sitting on the ground as I try to comprehend what just happened.

"He should be fine now," Ava announces to the group in a terse voice.

"You healed him." Damien stands, staring at the librarian with excitement, gratitude, and more interest than I'd like on his handsome face. "You're a witch. A healing witch."

A witch. I don't know much about the magic wielders, having only met a few in my life.

"Yes. Well. Yes." She glances down at her red-streaked hands and body. "Thank you for inviting me. I'm going to go."

"Wait." I try to push to my feet, but I'm unsteady. Likely from the blood loss.

"You don't have to." Damien follows her around the plants that attacked me. "You can clean up inside."

"No thank you." Her voice is clipped, and I feel panic rising in me at the thought of her disappearing again.

But she doesn't want to be chased, and I'm in no condition to go after her. Before my muddled brain can figure out what the right course of action is, I watch as Damien pulls out a large orb of water from the pool to float in front of her. A more impressive display of power than what I previously demonstrated.

"For your hands," he explains when Ava looks wary.

She only hesitates a moment before plunging her arms elbow-deep into the floating water, scrubbing her skin.

Getting rid of every trace of me.

Fingers clean, Ava scoops up her towel and bag, slips her sunglasses on, and strolls out of the yard without a backward glance.

All the while I stay seated on the ground in my quickly drying blood, surrounded by gaping partygoers.

"Fuck me," Damien murmurs. "That's some woman."

I couldn't agree more.

Chapter Thirteen

AVA

I don't so much wake up as I become conscious of a sharp pain arising from the base of my skull and streaking across my temples.

With a whimper, I curl into a protective ball in my bed, even though I know that won't do anything. I'm too well-acquainted with this hurt to fool myself.

A migraine.

From under the covers, I extend a hand with fingers that shake, reaching for my bedside table. In the top drawer, there should be a bottle of painkillers. Not that they'll do much. Human medication never seems to work quite right for us magical beings. As if the dosage needs to take our mythical heritage into account.

No, the only thing that truly works is healing magic. *My* healing magic.

The magic I used up yesterday fixing Sammy's arm.

At the time, it seemed worth it. The guy's bone was sticking out and blood was everywhere. I thought my future pain paled in comparison to his immediate suffering.

Okay...fine. The truth is, I didn't even think about it. Didn't stop to consider the consequences.

I watched Sammy fall, unable to stop it from happening, then I heard his whimper, and something flicked off in my brain. Or flicked on.

Whatever the case, my actions were instinctual. My hands snatched the first writing implement I could find in my bag and wrote out the healing runes from memory. My lips formed the words of the spell as easy as breathing, and I felt my hidden stores of magic drain into the torn flesh and fractured bone.

All that lust I'd collected over the week injected as pure healing power into Sammy.

There was none left over for my head, where it normally goes.

My fingers find the handle of the drawer and tug it open. Through the ringing pounding in my ears, I can't hear the rattle of the pill bottle, but I feel the shake as I pick the container up.

After dry swallowing four pills—twice the recommended amount—I concentrate on breathing and willing my thoughts past the razor-filled fog of agony.

Today is Monday.

I work.

There's no way I can go into my job today. I'm not even sure I can walk out to my car without vomiting.

Still, I need to find a way to call in sick.

I let out another groan, this one part from pain and part from frustration. My job isn't easy to simply step away from for a day without preparation. Everyone's schedules will be affected.

Something vibrates against my side, and it takes me a full minute to realize the noise and sensation are coming from my purring cat.

"Breakfast," I mutter. Kraken needs to eat.

That's enough of a motivation to have me crawling out of bed, sweaty and disoriented as spears continue to embed themselves in my skull. I always struggle with balance during my episodes, and with weak fingers, I grasp at doorframes and tabletops as I stumble toward the kitchen. Kraken is kind enough not to weave through my ankles as I move, a habit she has that always threatens to trip me.

After dumping more than the necessary amount of food in her bowl because I can't properly scoop it from the bag, I clutch the kitchen counter and stare at my closed laptop, trying to work up the will to open it and email my colleagues.

A knock at the front door distracts me.

Shit. What time is it?

I try to read the digital numbers on the clock above the stove, but my vision is too blurry to make them out. From the glow around my curtains, I know the sun is up.

How long was I lying in my bed trying to escape the pain? Is it past when I'm expected at work? Did someone come to check on me?

If so, that would be embarrassing but helpful. I could verbally tell them what needs to be done for the day instead of trying to type everything out in a message when I can't see.

With a bracing breath and shaky limbs, I shuffle toward my front door, needing more strength than normal to flip open the deadbolt. In a movement of self-preservation, I slip on my sunglasses before turning the nob and pulling the door open.

Even with the shades, I wince at the overwhelmingly bright day that adds fuel to my brain spikes. I can't even see who's at my front door.

But I can hear them.

"Hey, Ava," comes Sammy's smooth voice. "I'm sorry to show up like this. But I wanted to say thank you. For yesterday."

Goddess. I do *not* need a reminder of why I feel like shit.

And I definitely don't need Sammy Reyes witnessing the pain-twisted, sweaty, queasy version of me. The sun is so bright that I have to close my eyes behind my sunglasses. But I still can't escape the glare.

"You're mad," he says, misinterpreting my silence. "I get it. I'll leave you alone. But I got you this, as a thank you, and didn't want to leave it in the sun all day. Or have you trip on it."

I try to figure out what his words mean. *He got me something.* But that seems much less important than the nauseous churn in my gut that teases at my throat. My skin feels damp and hot, but somehow also cold. The world shifts beneath my feet, and I rock on my heels, thinking I might fall over backwards.

"Ava? Are you okay?"

"I—" The sentence starts with a single word, and it ends with me tilting too far forward and emptying my stomach onto the Squid's legs.

Chapter Fourteen

SAMMY

Is Ava hungover off of two hard seltzers?

That's the thought I have when I realize the beautiful witch looks a touch green and tired.

Then she heaves her guts up, the sick coating my pants and shoes and the steps outside of her condo, and I don't think much at all for the next few seconds. Luckily, some instinct that knew what Ava's clammy face meant, had me holding the gift basket I brought up and out of the way of splatter.

After getting over the initial shock, concern slams into me, and I set my armful on the walkway behind me before gently grasping a swaying Ava by her upper arms.

"You're sick." I point out the obvious.

She rests her forehead against the doorjamb. "The sun. It's too bright. Gods," she groans. "I puked. On you."

"That you did." And I'm trying very hard not to think about it seeping through my slacks. "Great aim. Do you mind if I come inside?"

She offers an exhausted shrug and a nod. "Bathroom is down the hall," she mutters. "You can clean up there."

My need to enter her home has nothing to do with hosing myself off. What I want is to discover what is wrong with Ava and figure out how I can help her fix it. I toe off my bile-covered shoes and step across the threshold, keeping my grip on Ava as I go. Inside, I gently kick the door shut and help her settle on the couch. Kraken lifts her head from a mountain of food, lets out a little meow, then goes back to stuffing herself.

The place is small and cozy, with a warm, desert color palette. There are weaved blankets and rugs, plants suspended in macrame wall hangings next to framed Broadway production posters and colorful art pieces that incorporate interesting symbols. The shapes somehow remind me of the marks Ava made on my arm when she healed me. Maybe the witch's art is magical.

And of course, there are books.

Cracked spines sit in neat lines on shelves made for them, but there are also novels on the low coffee table, in the entertainment system, and on the wide windowsill. I wouldn't be surprised if Kraken has napped on a few of them.

Once I'm sure Ava can sit up on her own, I release my hold, only to set my hand against her forehead. "What's wrong? Is this a hangover? Flu? Food poisoning?"

If Damien served her a contaminated burger, I'll kill him.

Ava's forehead is clammy, but not hot.

She grimaces. "Stop talking so loud." The words are gravel as she mutters them. "It's a migraine. I get them sometimes. Calm down."

This is normal for her?

The knowledge makes my heart ache. "What do you need?"

She sighs. "My laptop."

I don't see how a computer will help this, but Ava knows what she needs most in this situation. Finding the computer on her small kitchen table, I settle the device in her lap, double-check that she's not about to keel over, then retreat to the bathroom to clean myself up. Mainly because I'm starting to smell, and I don't want the reek to bother her when she's obviously in pain.

While in the bathroom, I decide to simply continue to ask Ava what she needs, and whenever she says she needs me to leave, that's when I'll go. Luckily, all of her vomit landed knees down, so even though my pants are saturated, my boxers are untouched.

I wash off my lower legs in the tub, bundle the pants, socks, and shoes together, then stroll back into the main room and open the front door long enough to drop them on the outside step and grab my gift. The professionally decorated basket is full of cat toys and treats and a plush bed. I guessed Ava would be more receptive to a gift for Kraken rather than herself. I place the basket on the kitchen table then return to Ava's side to figure out what my next task is.

She sits where I left her, sunglasses gone, laptop cracked open barely an inch, her entire face scrunched in discomfort.

"Something wrong?" I settle on the coffee table in front of her, not wanting to loom over her.

Ava frowns deeply. "The screen is too bright. And the words are blurry. I can't..." Her next breath catches, and I'm horrified to realize there's tears gathering in the corners of her eyes.

"No, no. Don't cry. What do you need?" I speak softly and ease the laptop out of her hold so it can't hurt her anymore. "Want me to look something up for you?"

Ava slumps back on her couch, body defeated. "I need to tell work I can't come in."

"I can do that. You can guide me through it. But let's get you comfortable first." Setting her computer aside, I reach over to grab a throw pillow and fluff it before setting it against the armrest of the couch. Then I use a few gentle touches to guide Ava to lie back, fully reclining on the couch. "Would something cool on your eyes help?" I keep my voice low, the cadence soothing.

She gives a vague wave toward the kitchen. "Mask in the freezer."

I find it right away, a squishy blue eye mask kept cool next to frozen peas. I wonder how often she has to use it. When I get back to Ava's side, she has an arm thrown over the top half of her face, as if the dim lighting of the condo bothers her too. The sight—half her face obscured —reminds me of the mask she wears when she dances.

As much as I've learned about her, there are still mysteries to solve.

Why does she wear a disguise to dance?

Why does she strip but not care about the money?

Why is a healing witch struggling with a debilitating migraine?

But now is not the right time to ask.

"Here." I gently tug on her arm, which she drops, then I lay the mask over her eyes, hoping the coolness soothes away the pained scrunch of her brow. "Now," I say as I settle on the coffee table again and reclaim her laptop, "do you think you can talk me through the emails you want to send?"

"Yeah." Her voice is tight and quiet, so I scoot closer in order to hear her.

Together we log into the email inbox for her library job. I blink in surprise at the massive number of messages she has but decide not to burden her with the number. Ava can work through the correspondence when her head isn't betraying her.

"Email Rodrigo Alverez—just start typing his name into the address section, and he should pop up. Tell him that I have to take a sick day. And that I don't have any instruction today, so he doesn't need to worry about that. But I'm scheduled for three hours on the reference desk that'll need to be covered." She clutches a pillow hard against her chest. "Tell him that I should be back in tomorrow. And that I'm sorry."

I type all that out, read it back to Ava for final approval, then send.

"Do you have to contact your boss?" I ask, curious about her job. Yesterday, Ava said she was the only full-time librarian, but she didn't talk as though she was in charge. Not as far as I could tell, anyway.

"No," she mutters, arm lying over top of the cool mask as if she wants to mash the thing into her skull. "I am the head. Kind of. Just until we hire a new library director."

"Ah. New boss soon."

Her lips twist in a grimace. "I wish. They've been dragging out the search for months."

That's bullshit. Is this why Ava's got a migraine? The stress? "Why are they taking so long? Didn't you say you were understaffed?"

Ava snorts. "Yeah. And we're supposed to have a hiring committee for another librarian, too. But those are two salaries they don't have to pay as long as the positions are empty." She clenches and unclenches her fists.

I wonder if the reaction is to the pain in her head or the frustration with her administration.

"I'm very rich," I murmur. "Want me to donate a bunch of money to the library? Tell them to bookmark it for library staff salaries?"

Ava's mouth flutters into something like a smile before she tightens her lips to flatten the expression away. "No. Don't pull any of that billionaire shit with me. I'll puke on your pants again."

I bite back a chuckle. "Fair. Need me to send any more emails? I like pretending to be you."

Ava huffs a laugh that turns into a grumble of discomfort. "Do you see my calendar? Could you double check if I have any meetings today?"

I open up the calendar and read through all the colorful blocks that jam pack Ava's day.

Only ten minutes for lunch? What the fuck is up with that?

"Looks like you have two committee meetings in the afternoon."

"Right," she mutters. "No need to email. I'll read the meeting minutes tomorrow."

"Okay." I scroll down. "And then a six o'clock research consultation with a Professor Fellows. Isn't your workday supposed to be done at five?" According to her calendar, she starts working at seven-thirty, which means five is still generous.

A deep frown creases Ava's mouth and the forehead I can see above her mask. Examining her face like this is familiar, after all the nights I've watched her dance in that lacy mask.

"Forgot about that," she says. "He's going to be pissed."

"It's research," I argue, then forcefully gentle my voice. "What does he have to be pissed about?"

"I don't know. It's kind of his personality." She sighs. "We need to email him."

Under her direction I open up another blank message and type out a message that's far more apologetic than I think Ava should feel the need to be. I crack my knuckles in an effort to ease my agitation. She didn't choose to get sick. When I read the missive back to her, she asks me to change multiple phrasings, claiming there's a subtext to academic communications.

But my guess is this guy is an asshole she's trying not to upset.

After that's sent, Ava asks me to put away her laptop. I set it on the kitchen table then return to her side.

"Is there anything I can do to make you feel better?" *Please don't send me away*.

I'm not sure I could function today knowing she's lying here in pain with no one to help her. Kraken, apparently done with her breakfast, struts over to us and rubs her tiny head against my shin. I scratch behind her ears but keep my focus on the woman in front of me.

Ava doesn't answer right away, but she does slip her cooling mask off her eyes to study me through squinted lids. The pain creases deep lines in her face, and I feel an anxious energy in my chest to do *something*.

"You're not attracted to me right now, are you?" Her voice is soft, with a hint of something that sounds like regret.

But that can't be right.

"I'm not trying to hit on you, if that's what you're asking." *Does she think I'm that much of a shit stain?*

Ava sighs, letting her mask drop back into place. "Now is the perfect time for you to hit on me."

"What?" The question bursts forth on a sharp bark that sends Kraken sprinting away. I rein in my volume when I spy Ava's wince. "Sorry. Sorry. But...come on, Ava. I'm not the best guy in the world, but I'm also not pond scum."

Her jaw tenses and relaxes. "I get it. I'm a mess right now, and it does nothing for you. Bravo. You're a standup guy. Pat yourself on the back for being a decent person." She mimes a slow clap then lets her hands fall back onto the pillow in her lap. "Meanwhile I'll lay here in fucking agony because my magic is at a zero."

I'm missing a key piece of information. Trepidation coils in my chest.

"What does that mean?" I ask.

Ava lets out a half growl, half moan. She peels the mask off her face and holds it out for me. "Back in the freezer. Please."

I follow her directions, trying to work out what I did wrong this time. There's no other mask to replace the one that's now warm, so I grab the peas, return to her side, and gently lay them over Ava's eyes. She lets me, with a resigned sigh.

"Can you tell me what you meant?" My voice is careful, getting the sense I'm tiptoeing through a minefield.

"Forget it," she mutters.

"I can't."

"Knowing won't make you feel better. Actually, it'll probably make you feel worse."

Fuck. "I still want to know."

"Fine." Ava presses her fingers into her temples as if she can massage away the pain. "I'm a witch. A healing one, obviously." *Yeah, the fixing of my broken bone made that clear.* "But I'm not *only* a witch. My grandfather was an incubus. Turns out mixing bloodlines can get odd results." She drags in a slow breath, then continues her explanation. "Your magic is in you. Witches direct power that's external. That exists naturally in the world. But I...I have to collect mine. Gather power from the natural world and store it inside me to use." Ava taps a finger against her ribcage. "When people are attracted to me—when they lust after me—I fill up like a battery. I'm a succubus witch. A suck-witch." Ava smirks at her little joke, and I'd find the expression adorably endearing if my mind wasn't currently getting rocked.

As she speaks, things start clicking into place. Why Ava dances while also working full time. Why she seems more focused on the performance than the money at her feet.

She's filling up her magical batteries. So that she can...

Oh no.

"I heal myself," Ava says, confirming my suspicion. "Every evening, I make a preventative brew to stave off the migraines."

Fuck me. Fuck me sideways. Fuck me to every hell dimension in existence.

"But you didn't last night," I rasp, self-loathing stealing my voice. "Because you used all your magic to heal *me*."

Ava stays quiet, but I don't need her to tell me I'm right.

She's in this terrible pain because of me.

Guilt eats holes in my gut, which makes this all worse because every time I try to call up my attraction for the lovely woman, the emotion I previously drowned in spills out the ragged holes. The one time Ava wants me to pant after her, I can't manage it.

And so, she continues to suffer.

Chapter Fifteen

SAMMY

I'd only planned on stopping at Ava's long enough to drop off my thank-you gift basket, but I end up staying the whole day.

She never tells me to go.

Mainly, Ava lays on the couch, and I silently fret and quietly clean her kitchen while Kraken runs around on the tile floor chasing a mouse toy. The kitchen wasn't dirty—no more than an average kitchen—but there are always the hard-to-reach corners and shelves that accumulate dust and grime. I feel better scrubbing that dirt away and knowing Ava won't have to see or deal with it.

This is something I did when I was younger. My parents had a cook, and I liked the way she would sing to herself while she prepared food. When I would wander into the kitchen to listen to her, she put me to work. I didn't mind. Cleaning wasn't hard, and it helped her.

But this isn't the kind of help Ava truly needs.

I wish I could get hard right now, I silently think in frustration.

But every time I try to focus on how ravishing Ava is, my brain trips back into the pit of worry over how she's hurting. And I'm stuck at the bottom, pressed down by the guilt that the witch is in pain because of me. Because she gave her magic to me.

I want to ask her why. If it meant something.

But I refuse to berate her when she's hurting, just so I can have my needy questions answered.

Ava's arm extends from her blanket cocoon to grip her cup of water. She upends the glass and even across the room I can spy the last trickles of liquid slipping past her lips. My hasty internet search of how to ease migraine pain told me hydration might help.

Might is good enough for me, and there's nothing I'm better at than keeping things wet.

"Here," I try to say loud enough for her to catch but soft enough that her head won't hurt any more than it already does. "I'll fill that."

Instead of crossing the room to take it from her, I press the water dispenser on the fridge, and with a flick of my wrist, I send a stream of filtered water through the air to snake down into her cup until I sense the container is full.

Ava tugs down her blanket enough to stare at me with unfocused eyes. "Magical water fountain."

I offer her a sheepish grin. "That's me. How are you feeling?"

Ava sets her glass down, and with a groan, she presses herself into a seated position. "There's less stabbing. Now it's pounding ache and dizziness."

I can see the way she sways in her seat as if the couch is moving underneath her.

"What can I do?" I come to her side, kneel, and fight the urge to scoop up her hand and clasp it to my chest. But I don't need to reach for her because Ava reaches for me. She extends both her arms and rests her hands on my shoulders. Then her storm-cloud eyes claim mine, doing their best to focus.

"I feel gross," she mutters. "I want a warm bath."

"Water always makes everything better," I agree.

"Could you get it started for me?" She waves toward the hallway. "There's eucalyptus oil under the sink. That helps. Just add a few drops. And don't let Kraken jump in because eucalyptus is bad for cats."

"Got it." This is the perfect task for me. "I will make you the best bath you've ever had."

"That's some big talk, Squid." Ava tries to smirk, but it comes out as a pained grimace. "Help me up. I'm going to lean on you and hopefully not puke."

"Puke your heart out if you need to." I cup my hands under Ava's arms as I straighten to my feet, and she rises with me, fingers fisting in the shoulders of my shirt. No issues yet.

Ava drags in a few breaths through her nose then lets go, only to lean into my side. I slip an arm around her waist, then walk in a slow shuffle to the bathroom, where I settle her on the closed toilet lid. We keep the lights off, working only by the daylight creeping through the frosted window set up above the tub/shower combo.

The water comes out of the faucet warm, the sun on the pipes easing the job of the water heater. I make sure the temperature doesn't go too far in either direction as I let a few eucalyptus droplets fall into the quickly filling tub.

As if called to the water, Kraken comes scampering in, but I catch the kitten before she can climb into the tub. After carrying her out to a cactus-shaped cat tree by the front window, I return to the bathroom, shutting the door behind me.

"Do you need..." My words disappear when I turn to discover Ava has already peeled off her shirt, leaving her topless. As much as I try to be a stronger man, my eyes demand to drop lower and catalogue the blush pink of her nipples.

Gods, I want to taste them. Feel them tighten on my tongue.

Ava shivers as she stands. Then her fingers hook in her waistband and the shorts slip to the floor, and I learn the witch has trimmed her intimate curls into a perfect triangle on her pubic bone.

"Fuck," I mutter.

A slight flush starts to creep over her skin in response to my staring. I shake my head and tear my gaze away.

"Sorry. I'll leave you—"

"Stay," Ava says in a firmer voice than she's managed up to this point. "In case I need you."

The idea that Ava might need me has me ready to do anything. If this witch asked me to carve out one of my kidneys with a spoon, I'd be rummaging through her utensil drawer in the next breath.

Ava maneuvers past me on unsteady feet and reaches out to clutch my arm. I press my hand over hers, feeling the smooth heat of her skin against my palm and biting back a groan as her tits sway when she leans down to grab the side of the tub. Ava lets me go a moment before slipping into the fragrant water that does nothing to cover her luscious, bare curves.

If only she had some bubble bath.

But would that really help at this point? Now that I've seen her nude body, my brain is tattooing the image into my gray matter.

"You can sit down," she murmurs, eyes closed, head reclined on the sloping side of the tub. The caretaker rises in me again, and I'm able to get my mind out of the gutter long enough to grab the hand towel hanging by her sink and roll it into a pillow shape. Then I gently cradle her head, raising her skull off the hard porcelain so I can slip the terrycloth underneath. Ava stares up at me as I guide her head back.

"You're full of surprises, Samuel Reyes," she murmurs before closing her eyes again.

"Not really. I'm a simple man. Not even a man really. More of a pig. But a pig that's nice to you. Like a teacup pig."

I want to be your teacup pig.

Ava's plush lips twitch toward a smile, but I still see the strain in the tense muscles of her face and shoulders. I mean to settle on the toilet seat. Put a few feet of distance between us. Instead, my legs end up dropping me on the lip of the tub. Still, I use every fiber of will in my body to keep my gaze collarbones and up.

"Does anything else help?" I whisper the words eager for more tasks, no matter how inconsequential.

Ava cracks one eyelid to study me. Then her glistening hand lifts from the water.

"Ever tried giving a palm massage before?"

"I'm a palm massage virgin," I admit. "But I'm ready to pop my cherry." Despite how eagerly I say the lighthearted words, I'm careful as I cradle her limb with both my hands.

I start by pressing my thumbs into the center of her palm and making circular motions.

"Harder," Ava directs, and my cock twitches in response.

I dig deeper. She gasps and my briefs start to feel tight.

I should've known Ava would want a firm touch. Her skin is covered in calluses, I'm guessing from all the time she spends on the pole. The rough skin taunts me. I want to press the rough areas against my lips. Tongue them.

"Goddess," Ava moans, twisting in the water, a flush coloring her skin like a desert rose. "Just like that."

I'm so close to pointing out how sexual her words sound, but I refuse to do anything that will have her retreating into her pain when it seems like this might be helping.

I pay attention to each finger, making sure to massage each joint and muscle and tendon. I only stop when she lifts her other hand to balance the attention. All the while, Ava's boobs crest the warm water like little floatation devices, and she whimpers noises that have me fully hard.

"Sammy," she whispers my name when I'm working her thumb and thinking about how much I want to slip it into my mouth and suck.

"Yeah?" My voice is a strained rasp.

"Take your dick out."

My hands pause. "What?"

"Do you want to make me feel better?" the witch asks, her eyes more focused now as she watches me.

"Yes. More than anything."

Ava slips her hand from mine and settles it around the bottom curve of her boob, thumbing the nipple.

"Then take your dick out and show me how you fuck your hand."

Her words from earlier come back to me.

"Get horny for me."

When she'd been sweating and shaking from pain, eyes clouded with sharp agony, my brain couldn't fathom sexualizing her.

But now Ava is pliant, more relaxed than before, naked body wet and on display. I can still see signs of the pain in her gaze, and I have to battle the internal voice that tells me I'm a shitty person to lust after her when she's hurting.

Lust helps her. She's asking me for this.

"You're sure?"

Her thumb swipes over her pebbled nipple again. "Positive." Then the temptress tilts her lips in a smirk. "Put on a show for me. It's only fair."

I feel a responding grin spreading across my face. "Good point. But I'm a novice performer. You'll have to go easy on me."

Ava narrows her eyes with a snort. "Really? You look like a showboater to me."

She's not wrong. I'm ashamed to think back on my early twenties when I convinced myself my body—and dick—was a gift to anyone who unwrapped it. Took a few years for me to realize that while my partners might have thought I was hot, they wanted more than sex from me.

And I'm not talking a loving relationship.

To them, I was a good lay and a black credit card.

"Sammy." Ava saying my name tugs me out of those toxic thoughts and back into this moment.

This moment where the woman of my dreams wants my body. Kind of.

Any hesitation seeps out of my mind when her cloudy gaze holds mine and she murmurs, "Please."

Fuck. I'd hand over everything I own to hear that single word from her lips again. But I have a more important task than liquidating my life savings.

I've got to jerk off.

Since my puke-covered pants are still outside, all that covers my rigid cock are my form-fitting underwear that leave nothing to the imagination. *Yeah, buddy. I'm not going to ignore you anymore. Ava's orders.* With a well-practiced slip of my briefs, I've got my hard cock out, the steel length ready for action. When I wrap my fingers around my shaft, a grunt sneaks out from deep in my throat.

"Mhmm." Ava watches me, a pleased murmur telling me I'm doing well.

And that works for me. I want her approval. I want her to tell me I'm a good boy in her husky voice like when she healed me.

"Show me," she says.

I start low and drag upward, milking myself until a bead of precum leaks out of the tip. "Like this?" I ask, my breath heavy as I ease my stare over her bare body and imagine parting her legs and spreading my liquid on her pink pussy.

"Are you thinking about fucking me, Sammy?" she asks, voice purring. "How tight I'd be? I haven't had sex in a while. You'd have to get me so wet." Ava shifts and the water slaps at the sides of the tub. "But you could do that, right? Get me soaked before you slip inside me?" As the needy, filthy water-themed descriptions flow off her tongue, Ava's eyes stay fixated on my pumping hand.

Meanwhile, I gape down at the woman who is a fantasy come to life. What she describes plays in my mind, vivid enough to have me groaning, my balls tightening.

What in all the hell dimensions?

I never come this fast. Not anymore.

But Ava has me on the edge with only her throaty voice and detailed words.

And she's not done.

"Last time I came," she says, "I was thinking about you."

My entire body stills, hand included, at her confession.

"What?" I rasp, trying to meet her stare.

But she's gazing at my cock with something like rapture.

"I was in my bed. Naked, legs wide, using my favorite vibrator and imagining you watching me." Her dangerous eyes flick up to my bewildered ones, but immediately return to my cock. "I want to see you make a mess."

Fuck all the gods.

My hand squeezes reflexively, my hips jerk, and I erupt, cum fountaining out of my tip, splattering on my T-shirt that I didn't think to strip off. The sound that comes from my throat is more animal than man, and I grip the side of the tub to keep from sliding to the tiled floor or into the pool of warm water.

But damn, do I want to sink into the tub with Ava. The urge to wrap myself around her and claim her as mine is so strong, I know I need to keep it to myself or else scare her away.

Ava relaxes back with a sigh, and when the haze of ecstasy clears from my eyes, I notice a healthy glow to her skin. Or that's how it appears anyway.

"Did that help?" There's a desperate edge to my words. I need to know that tsunami of an orgasm meant something to her, even if it was only a relief from pain.

Ava smiles up at me, but I still see the strain around her mouth and eyes.

"That was...thank you. It did help. My magic is charged up."

"But do you feel better?" I press.

She sighs, the water rippling with the movement of her chest. "That's not how it works for witches. We need assists to utilize our magic. For bigger things, anyway."

I think back on the way she healed my arm.

"Those symbols you drew," I say, and she nods. "I can get you a marker." I'm already on my feet, tucking my soft dick into my briefs and ignoring my sticky shirt. Ava said she wanted a mess, and I definitely made one.

Her voice stops me. "It's not that simple. Not for my migraine, anyway. I brew a tea for the spell."

"Okay." I kneel beside the tub. "Tell me how to make it. I'll brew it. You say the magic words and shotgun it. You'll be back to berating me for being a creep in no time."

Despite laying out my perfect plan, Ava doesn't start rattling off ingredients. Instead, she stares at me with a bemused expression.

"Take your clothes off," she says.

"You need more power?" I straighten and palm my cock, hoping I can manage a fast recovery time. If Ava starts that dirty talk again, it shouldn't be a problem.

But she flaps a staying hand. "No. I'm good on fuel. But you're covered in squid juice. I don't want to get smeared with it when you help me out of the tub."

Once again, I glance down at my cum-coated clothes.

"You wanted me to make a mess," I remind her, even as I tug my shirt over my head and toss it onto the floor. I stand in the middle of the bathroom in my mostly unscathed briefs. "You can stay in the tub. I know how to make tea. When half the ingredients are water, you can't go wrong with a Squid."

Ava points behind me, and I turn to find a turquoise terrycloth robe hanging from a hook.

"I need to be the one who makes it," she explains. Then the witch pushes herself to standing, water cascading off her mind-imploding body. But I don't gape, instead rushing to wrap her in the robe when her knees wobble.

With my assistance, we make it to the kitchen, and I stay close by, waiting as she heats water and grinds different herbs and spices in a pestle. While observing, I'm ready to lunge forward with a supportive arm if her balance falters. As the witch pours the tea into a pot to steep, I hear her mutter words under her breath and watch as a glow radiates from her hands and transfers to the beverage.

Her power. Fueled by my lust.

Is that all she wants me for?

I try not to explore the tender pain in my chest at the thought, distracting myself by seeking out Kraken. The kitten crouches in the middle of the living room, looking ready to pounce. In front of her is a tiny, dull-yellow scorpion. The pests aren't uncommon, but I doubt the cat should be tangling with it, no matter how fierce Kraken is. With a flick of my fingers, I draw water from the faucet and send the mini wave across the floor. The scorpion tries to scuttle away, but I scoop it up in a magical current as I stroll to the front door and wash the stinging creature outside where it belongs. Kraken tries to chase after, but I shut the door, scoop her up, and rejoin the witch.

"Thank you," Ava murmurs, eyeing me with my fuzzy armful.

"Got to protect our monster." I grin and scratch the little beast under her chin as she purrs.

When Ava pours the green-brown brew into an 'I ♥ Banned Books' mug, she takes a moment to breathe in the steam. Even that simple move has a relaxed note entering her features. Then she blows to dispel some of the heat, and my stare fixates on her pursed lips.

That tea isn't the only thing that's hot in this kitchen.

As if sensing my thought, Ava flicks her attention up to me. "I guess it's only fair to tell you I always know when you're turned on," she murmurs. "You think steaming beverages are sexy?" The witch sips her drink, and a smile plumps her cheeks. For the first time since she puked on me, I feel like I can relax.

"What can I say?" I shrug. "I like the idea of you swallowing warm liquid."

She snorts and rolls her eyes at my dirty joke, then drinks deeper, letting out a sigh.

"Do you feel better now?" I ask.

"Loads." Her gaze meets mine, then drops to my crotch.

And I can tell we're both thinking about a particular load. I don't bother to bite back my smile, thoroughly enjoying sharing immature jokes with the captivating witch.

I'd like to share more with her. Share everything.

But for now, this is enough.

Chapter Sixteen

AVA

Sammy asks me to go out for ice cream the weekend after our...whatever it was. I agree, figuring it's the least I can do after the guy acted as my personal assistant and nursemaid, then pleasured himself in my bathroom at my request.

I don't know what's going on between us, but I do know I haven't been able to get the image of him standing shirtless in my kitchen while cradling my kitten out of my mind. Maybe I just need to spend more time around him for his latent playboy douchebag personality to reemerge, and then I can go back to ignoring him without a hint of guilt.

After insisting on driving myself, I arrive at the address Sammy sent me and stare up at the intriguing wood-carved sign.

Land of Ice Cream & Snow.

I smile at the play on words. As a librarian, I appreciate a quality pun. And I can't remember the last time I treated myself to an ice cream cone. Or too much of anything now that I think about it.

The realization has me frowning.

With the depleted library staff, it's not uncommon for me to work late multiple nights a week just to keep my email inbox from exploding in a passive-aggressive, professor-request mess. When I get home, I'm exhausted, but I still have to brew a cup of my healing tea, which I now make a dose of morning *and* night to stave off stress migraines. Used to be that I only needed a cup of the elixir once or twice a week.

With my magic running out faster, I'm dancing more at The Jewelry Box to keep my well full. Not that Yasmin minds my request for extra shifts, but I don't know that I want to be there as often as I am. Or, at least, I don't want to *need* to be there.

When I'm not on the stage, I try to treat myself to a book, but more often than not, I can't get into the story with the next day's to-do list scrolling through my head.

Damien's backyard pool party was supposed to be a treat, but then it turned into another magic drain. Not that I blame Sammy. He didn't mean to shove his bone outside of his skin.

The memory has me rubbing my chest where a tight panicked ball forms.

Much as I hate the aftereffects, I'm glad I was there. That the Squid didn't have to go to a hospital. That he didn't have to spend more than a few minutes in pain.

As I walk across the hot parking lot toward the door of the shop, I quicken my step. The urge to see Sammy and check on his arm washes through me. When he showed up during my migraine spell, I was too steeped in my own pain to remember his.

When I push the door open, a tingling chill races over my skin, but I'm used to that after living here for so long. In Phoenix, I don't need a jacket outside, but sometimes I wish I brought one when I step into the businesses that pump up their AC to the max. Though, I have to admit, after the initial shock, this coldness is pleasant. Mild and refreshing after the sweltering day.

Everything about this shop is pleasantly surprising. I expected cutesy colors and a handful of small tables only large enough to support a few cups of ice cream. The classic ice cream parlor decor.

Instead, I enter a mountain man's wet dream.

The place is full of heavy wooden furniture and glows with warm lighting from simple, rustic fixtures.

It's like the abominable snowman opened an ice cream shop in the Rocky Mountains.

"Ava!"

I glance toward the sound of my name and spy Sammy dodging around a group of teenagers who loiter in the middle of the shop.

"Sammy." I say his name in a more subdued tone than he used with mine, but it doesn't dim his grin as he comes to a stop in front of me.

"You came." Somehow, he manages to smile wider. "Quinn bet Auggie twenty bucks you'd stand me up."

"You're saying the names of people I don't know." And I'm not sure how I feel about people betting on me.

"Sorry." A light blush stains the top of his cheeks, but that grin keeps on grinning. "Auggie—August—is my cousin. Well, second cousin, I think. His grandfather and my grandmother were siblings. Anyway, he owns this shop." The Squid waves to take in the log-cabin decorated place. "Quinn is his girlfriend."

"Ah." Still not sure how I feel about it. "Show me your arm."

Sammy's brows quirk.

"The one I...fixed," I clarify, using the vague word, since we're in public.

"Right." Sammy extends his right arm to me, the limb bare since he's wearing a short-sleeved gray Henley. I try not to notice how the material strains over his bicep. Instead, I cradle his forearm, tilting it to search for any sign of lingering injury. There's a light pink scar tracing through his golden-tinted arm hair. Other than that, there's nothing to indicate he was severely injured only a week ago.

Despite establishing this, I don't immediately release him. My fingers require more exploration to be satisfied. Tracing the blue veins from his inner elbow to his wrist, where I find a surprisingly callused palm. I wouldn't expect a pretty boy with more money than he knows what to do with to have hands that look used to manual labor. But maybe that's what he thought when he saw the rough patches on my librarian's hands.

My mind brings up the memory of Sammy massaging my fingers with the perfect amount of pressure. Then I recall how his forearm tensed and flexed as he stroked himself.

For me.

A bell rings, and I jerk my head up, remembering I'm in public, and that was the sound of another customer entering the ice cream parlor.

Also, I've been fondling Sammy's forearm for an undetermined amount of time. My gaze flicks up to meet his, and I see a hunger in his eyes that I doubt is for frozen treats. Not with the way my skin is flushed with the sparkle of magic and the taste of peanuts tickles my tongue.

"How do I look?" When he asks, Sammy's voice is more serious than I've ever heard him.

"All healed." I drop his arm as if burned and shove my fists into the pockets of my loose linen shorts. "So, your cousin makes the ice cream here?" A change of subject I need. "Is it any good?"

The Squid's smile is slow and entirely too self-satisfied. But he doesn't push me. "It's the best." He tilts his head toward the line, and I follow him. "I wanted to invest in the place, but he adamantly refused. Auggie *never* takes my money." He practically whines the words, and I bite my lip to keep from smiling. "So now I spend all that potential investment cash buying myself endless ice cream."

There's something in his voice that catches my attention. The glow of pride. But I don't feel like it's for himself. I get the sense that Sammy is genuinely proud of his cousin for making this place a success.

"I haven't had ice cream in ages," I admit.

Sammy turns a horrified look on me. "Gods. Why not?"

I shrug. "I never buy it from the grocery store because I'm worried it'll melt on the drive home and get everywhere. And I don't go out for it."

He nods, face somber. "Maybe that's for the best. Because this ice cream will shame all other frozen desserts you've ever consumed. It's not fair to compare them."

"Oh really?" Now I bite the inside of my cheek to fight off a smile.

He sends me a mischievous smirk. "You'll see."

Just then, the couple in front of us step to the side, clutching their desserts, and reveal the man behind the counter.

A mountain of a man.

A big, bearded mammoth dressed in a blue apron.

"Ava, meet my cousin August. Auggie, meet Ava." Sammy grins between the two of us like this is some momentous occasion. Like he's been eager to introduce me to his family member for a while now, and finally the event is upon us.

What does Sammy want from me?

I keep that question to myself and offer a nod to the wall of a man. "Nice to meet you."

August's beard crinkles as the corners of his mouth curve up. "You too, Ava. Sammy talks about you a lot."

"A normal amount," Sammy amends.

"All the time." August rumbles.

"Only some of the time."

"If you're here against your will"—the ice cream maker holds my gaze —"blink twice."

"That's it!" Sammy huffs, throwing his arms in the air. "We don't want any ice cream from you."

"I still want ice cream," I chime in, stifling a chuckle at their familial banter. "You need to keep your hostages well fed."

Sammy gapes at me and August grins wider. "What'll it be?" He jerks a thumb over his shoulder toward a chalkboard with flavors. "Feel free to sample."

Sammy steps in closer, his chest brushing my shoulder, and his fresh rain scent teasing my nose. "The Peach Gobbler is my favorite."

"Good for you." I place a hand flat on his chest intending to push him away, but then I forget to follow through and end up fiddling with a button on his collar while I read over the offerings and enjoy the buzz of a magical refill trickling through me. "Could I sample the Campfire S'mores and the Death by Minty Chocolate?"

August nods, his eyes twinkling as he turns to the freezer to spoon out my choices.

"You're not even going to *try* the peach?" Sammy's question sounds breathless, and I glance up to find him staring at me, pupils dilated. My fingers continue to play with his button, and I can't fully understand why this man's intense attraction doesn't have me running in the opposite direction.

Maybe it has something to do with the fact that he took care of me when I needed someone to, and he did it in the *way* I needed him to.

"You're getting the peach, right?"

He nods.

"Well then, I assume you'll be willing to share some with the woman who made sure you have two working arms."

The Squid's eyes go wide, but he doesn't have time to respond before August is offering me my tastings while grinning at something over my shoulder.

"Thanks for that, by the way," a husky voice says at my back. Next I know, a bombshell of a redhead is leaning against the counter beside me, a welcoming expression on her face. "You can't imagine how much whining we'd have to put up with if Sammy were in a cast for months." She offers a small wave. "I'm Quinn. I think you know my sister, Cat."

Ah, yes. It's all coming together in my head now. The web of interconnected magic wielders in Phoenix.

"I would *not* have whined," Sammy announces. "I would have suffered in silent dignity."

Quinn snorts. "You mean like I did the one time we slept together?" She throws out the comment the same time I slip the S'mores scoop onto my tongue, and suddenly my entire body is cold.

That's some potent ice cream.

"Quinn," Sammy groans.

"What?" The redhead shrugs. "It's best to air this stuff in the beginning." Quinn fixes me with her warm hazel gaze. "I'm in a committed relationship with this one." She jabs a finger at August, who silently watches the exchange, wearing a small smile like he's enjoying the show. "Years ago, Sammy and I slept together once. It was bad. Never wanted a repeat."

"Is this supposed to help me in some way?" The handsome Squid at my side huffs as the chill under my skin quickly dissipates. "I think it's important that we—as a group—acknowledge people can change and grow and get much better at figuring out where, exactly, the clit is located *and* how much attention it should be given!" Sammy's voice is a touch too loud at the end of his rant, and I swear I hear a gasp from the table of teenagers.

Well, he's not wrong. And it's information they should keep in mind.

Quinn appears delighted, her eyes practically glowing as she flicks them between my irate companion and me. "Look at you! I think Sammy has a *crush*." Quinn sings the last word in a taunting note, then leans in close and pretends to whisper to me. "Even though I lost, I'm glad you showed. This is amazing." She slips her hand into her back pocket and pulls out a twenty, then circles the counter to tuck the bill into August's apron.

Then she helps her boyfriend scoop our orders, despite Sammy glaring at her the whole time. I let him pay because he seems to enjoy giving his cousin money, including a large tip in the jar on the counter, which has August rolling his eyes.

We settle in a booth, him with a cup of Peach Gobbler flavor and me with a waffle cone of Death by Minty Chocolate. The freshness of the mint paired with the rich chocolate is decadent, and I stifle a moan as I take a long lick.

Magic prickles through me, tightening my nipples, and I lift my gaze to find Sammy's eyes on me. He drops them quickly, but it's no use.

His lust is a constant force between us.

Is the physical all he feels for me?

Is that a problem?

He's an attractive guy, and the simple act of him coming in front of me gave me more magic reserves than I can ever remember having.

And more dirty dreams too.

Would it be so bad if we did it again? Maybe when my head isn't threatening to split in two?

"You promised you'd try," Sammy says, and I'm about to snap at him in defense that I promised him no part of me.

But then I realize he's extending his spoon across the table, with a mound of creamy treat. Without a word, I lean forward and let the spoon slip past my lips, noting how his pupils dilate as he watches.

The taste is ambrosia, peach mixed with his peanut butter lust. The flood of magic is invigorating after what's felt like years of living on the edge of exhaustion.

And I decide this man is too tempting not to sample.

After the spoon slips from my mouth, licked clean, and I swallow the offering, I hold Sammy's stare.

"Come over tonight."

Chapter Seventeen

AVA

After he checked multiple times that I was serious, Sammy agreed to come to my place at nine. I figured that would make it clear this is just a hook-up.

Which is what I want.

Right?

My body is fully on board with getting the Squid between my legs.

But my mind keeps trying to remind me that relying on any one person risks screwing me over and leaving me in pain.

I'm not relying on him, I reason. *I'm enjoying him.*

This—whatever it is with Sammy—will be like a magical vacation. I'm knowingly giving myself a break from having to work a stage for every drop of magic. No one books a round-trip ticket to a tropical resort and then is surprised when they have to go home. That's how it can be with the handsome Squid. A brief reprieve.

But what if he doesn't want it to end?

What if...I don't want it to end?

My laptop dings, and I push the tangle of thoughts to the back of my brain as I wait for the video call to connect. There's another chime, then my mother's face appears on my screen.

"Hey, sweetheart." Her face is slightly flushed, and I can hear the smack of her feet on the treadmill. Mom is the type of woman that needs to be in constant motion. Meanwhile, I'm reclined on my couch, piles of pillows behind me as I try to relax in the few hours before my evening sex date.

"Hey Mom. How's life?"

"Life is good. Danica got a raise last week and wants to celebrate with a trip to Amsterdam. We're thinking next month."

I'm sure my mom and her partner will have a wild time. Fanny Bellarose may be my mother, and a generously loving person, but she's not what society would label as the classic 'mom.' When most mothers were driving their kids to soccer practice, mine was sneaking me into Broadway shows and encouraging my adolescent crush on the Phantom of the Opera. Lots of parents paid for dance lessons, but Mom didn't bother shelling out hard earned money when I could learn the same skills and more from her nipple-pasty-wearing burlesque co-workers. I'd practice my moves then work on my homework when the ladies went on stage.

Becoming a masked, stripping librarian makes a little more sense now, right?

"That sounds fun." Any vacation sounds amazing at this point. I can't remember the last time I took off. The sick day with Sammy doesn't count. "Take a lot of pictures."

"You could come with us if you wanted. Danica loves talking books with you."

I try not to grimace. It's not the offer that fouls my mood. Danica is great, especially for my mother. What has me pouting is the immediate knowledge that I'll have to turn Mom down. "Sorry. The library is swamped. I'm not sure I can take off more than a day until we get the director position filled." Whenever the hell that'll happen. "I'll just have to live vicariously through you."

"Hmm. We'll plan a trip then. When your schedule frees up. But tell me more. How's the job? And I need to see my fluffy grandkitty."

I spend the next half hour detailing the good and bad about the library and The Jewelry Box, then I show Mom how Kraken chases a laser pointer and loves her new water fountain bowl I found in Sammy's thank you gift basket.

All the while, I consider if I want to make a mention of the Squid.

But what would I even say?

Hey Mom, there's this guy that loves to watch me strip, gave me a cat, fed me ice cream, and will hopefully bang my brains out tonight.

She wouldn't blink at any of that, having had plenty of wild romances in her day.

But that's the problem. I'm worried about what this thing with Sammy is, and if it'll end up being like one of her past lust-fuel relationships.

Mom has a similar situation to me. Chronic pain, only hers is in her joints rather than migraines. We don't know if it's our mixed witch/succubus linage, or if the pain is a normal burden we each got stuck with and lust magic is a solution where human treatments fail. Either way, mom spent years jumping through emotionless relationships to make sure she always had a bed partner to fuel her magic and keep her pain free. She danced burlesque like I strip, but she wanted the extra boost of a partner.

Whenever a breakup came, I could see the panic in her eyes. The worry that dancing wouldn't be enough, and the pain would come back worse than before. The need for lust like the craving for pain pills.

Now Mom has Danica, a relationship that is real and provides her relief. I'm happy she has the best of both worlds, but I'm also befuddled by the idea of putting that much trust in another person.

What if I sleep with Sammy on the regular? What if I get used to him and decide to stop my stripping to free up all my evenings?

And what if he gets tired of the arrangement, and I have to go crawling back to Yasmin for an open spot, my head in agony because my reserves are gone, all because I relied on a man?

"So, things between you and Danica are good?" I ask my mom after showing her the bird feeder I placed outside the window to entertain Kraken.

Mom's smile goes all dreamy on my computer screen, still wildly in love even after five years. "They are perfection. Well, she still snores. But other than that, we're great."

I breathe easy on my mom's behalf.

"Tell her that I said hi. And that I'll have a stack of books waiting for her by the Solstice." Mom and Danica always make sure to visit me during the winter holiday.

Mom grins wide, and I hear the slowing of the treadmill, reflecting the winding down of our chat. "I will. Text me when they finally fill the director position. I'll send you a bottle of champagne." I laugh and exchange goodbyes, then sit quietly on my couch, letting my mother's love sink into my bones, even if she had to send it to me from hundreds of miles away.

Then I put all thoughts of my mother out of my brain as I dive into my lingerie and seek out an outfit to make a Squid melt on sight.

Time to fill my cauldron.

Chapter Eighteen

SAMMY

Ava's invite sent me swirling down the drain of self-doubt. People think because flirting is a language I speak fluently that I must hook up constantly. That my bed is never cold. Never empty. That I'm happy in the life of a playboy.

But I haven't lived like that for years, as much as my personality would indicate differently. Sleeping with someone lost its appeal when I realized there was an angle to it. That however much they liked my body, what really mattered was my money. I started to see the same silent question in everyone's eyes: How much could they get from the encounter?

And if I didn't give them anything, how much could they take from me on their way out?

Still, I have a lot of experience.

So, why are my hands so sweaty as I walk up to Ava's front door? Why is my heart pounding hard enough to hear, like the crashing of ocean waves in my ears?

I'm nervous.

About a hook up.

Of course I am. Ava Bellarose is different. What happens between us matters to me. I want to sleep with her, but I don't want us to end there.

If we have sex, will she be done with me?

The thought comes at the same time I knock on her door, meaning I have no time to retreat.

Then she opens the door, and I can't remember how to walk away from her. Ava stands on the threshold wearing a silky blue set of sleep shorts and a camisole edged with black lace. The color choice is so different than the white she normally wears at the club, and I gape at the way the shimmering material drapes over her curves.

"I wore blue because you're a Squid," she says, the words abrupt, and I realize that while Ava teases and tantalizes audiences with her body, her words are never coy. "You're welcome."

"Thank you," I rasp.

Her plump lips curve in a smile. "Do you want something to drink?"

All the water in your house, please. I need something to revive myself. "I'll drink whatever."

Ava rolls her eyes as she grabs my wrist, towing me inside her place before shutting the door. "I'm not about to waste my good wine on you because you're trying to be polite." She leads me into her kitchen, and I follow happily, loving the possessive nature of her hold on me. Ava stands on her tiptoes to reach a bottle on top of the fridge, and the move reminds me of the nights she dances on the pole in bare feet.

"Why do you wear heels some nights and not others?" I ask, wanting to solve one of the many mysteries of this woman.

Ava settles back on her heels, bottle of amber liquid in one hand, my wrist still in her other.

Never let go of me.

"I'm an instruction librarian. Some days I have a lot of classes, which means I'm standing all day. My feet would stage a rebellion if I tried to force them into heels after that." She holds up the bottle so I can see the label. "You drink whiskey, right? That's what you order at the club?"

She knows my drink.

"I do."

"Is this any good? I asked the store clerk, but they kept trying to sell me tequila, so he was no help. I picked the one that had a cool label."

"You bought whiskey for me?"

"Yeah. Did I have it wrong?" Her skin flushes a delectable pink, but I don't think it's from embarrassment. "I was kidding before. If you want some of my wine, you can have a glass." Her breaths come a touch faster, and a confused expression flits across her face as she licks her lips. "You just got turned on. Like *super* horny. Even more than when I first opened the door." Ava studies me. "Do you have a kink involving whiskey? No judgement. But I like my sheets, so we might have to put a few towels down."

This evil, perfect witch.

"No," I choke out. "No whiskey kink." But apparently, I have an *Ava went out of her way to get something she thought I'd like* kink. "A glass would be great though." I'm distracted by pinpricks on my shin, and I glance down to find Kraken using my designer slacks as a scratching post.

"I think she missed you." Ava lets go of me to seek out a glass, and I deal with missing her touch by scooping up my feline child.

"Of course she missed me." I cradle her against my chest and scratch the white tuft of fur under her tiny chin. "I'm her daddy. This split parenting isn't healthy for her. We should move in together."

Luckily, Ava snorts as if what I said was a joke instead of hearing the desperately sincere note in my voice and shoving me out the door for getting clingy.

"Let's sit on the couch. Come on, Daddy," Ava says, then smirks when her skin turns pink from another wave of my lust fueling her magic.

I get off on the silly, suggestive nickname paired with the fact that I can make Ava feel good simply by wanting her. She leads me through the small condo to the living space, carrying a glass of whiskey for me and a glass of chilled white wine for herself. When we settle side-by-side on the cushions, Kraken leaps from my arms and sprints to her cactus cat tower where she disappears into a cave-like hidey hole.

With no kitten between us, Ava and I stare at each other. All my flirting game evaporates in the face of panic. I worry that I'll say something wrong and Ava will cut me out of the small space in her life I've started to ease into.

Flirting comes easily when you don't care.

"I like your cousin," she says.

Ava's comment smashes a fist into my gut. I swipe up my whiskey and drink half the pour in one go.

She likes August? She invited me over to talk about how she likes my cousin? And wore a sexy nighty to torture me during the process?

"Sorry, but he's taken. By Quinn. Who you met. They're in love." That doesn't seem like enough, so my panicked mouth keeps going. "Also, I don't have proof, but I'm pretty sure he's a serial killer. And he hates cats. And spits in his ice cream. Not the scoop he gave you, of course—I made sure of that. But in general, he's a terrible person inside and out. And that beard is fake."

Ava stares at me, eyes wide, mouth open in an O, and I try not to feel like a terrible person for making up a bunch of insulting lies about the guy I love like a brother.

Suddenly, a wonderful noise fills the small space, and I realize Ava is laughing.

Gods, I thought she couldn't get any more gorgeous.

She wraps her arms around her middle, bending at the waist as the humor bubbles from her throat in a rich stream. Even if I wanted to hold onto my surly attitude, I can't with this wonderful music I'm submerged in.

"Oh my goddess," she gasps, wiping tears from her eyes. "I meant I liked him as a person. As your friend. Not that I wanted to get with him." More giggles spill out as she watches me with sparkling eyes.

"Of course. I knew that." I did not know that. "And I may have exaggerated a few details. August can be a decent guy."

"When he's not murdering people and cats?"

"Now wait." I hold up a staying finger. "I said he didn't *like* cats. Not that he murdered them. Careful about spreading that false information."

Ava shakes her head, then her expression settles into something more contemplative, and I'm not sure how I feel about the scrutiny. "I like August. I like Quinn. And Damien and Cat." She taps a fingernail against her glass. "Do you remember the first time you saw me dance?"

"Impossible to forget. You were in a lace bra and panties—white of course—and heels that night, glitter on your skin. Your hair was in a high ponytail, curled and bouncing around every time you moved. And you did some kind of superman move where you planked while holding onto the pole with only your thighs."

Ava blinks, and I realize how obsessed that made me sound.

I clear my throat and take another sip of my whiskey. "I mean, yeah. I guess I sort of remember."

Ava gives me a smirk, then her face fades into a slightly far off look. "You came with a few guys."

Now that I think about it, pushing past the overwhelming memory of the first time I set eyes on Ava, I recall I did bring some people with me. Guys I went to college with. They were from my party days. Social climbers who envied how I could set down a black card and control the room.

"I haven't spoken to them in over a year," I tell her.

"I figured you spent most of your time with people like them." Ava tilts her head. "They were assholes. Jade throat punched the one with the goatee when he tried to stick his hand past her waistband."

Marty. He *is* a major dick now that I think about it. Didn't know about the throat punching incident though.

"He deserved it," I say. "And like I said, I don't talk to him anymore." I shift to face Ava on the couch. "I've definitely been an asshole. Not a *grope women without their permission* asshole, but still. There were a lot of years I was a self-important douchebag. And I hate I was like that. That I still probably slip into it from time to time. But for a while now, I've been trying to be at least tolerable. To be someone people like having around." For my personality and not my wallet.

Ava picks up her wine for a quick sip, then sets it down on her coaster. Then she crawls across the small space between us and leans in to place a gentle kiss on the pounding pulse in my neck. "You can tell a lot about a person by the people they surround themselves with," she whispers against my hot skin.

I draw in a ragged breath. "I'd like to surround myself with you."

That earns me a chuckle and another press of lips on the corner of my chin. Meanwhile, I stay completely still, afraid even the rise and fall of my ribcage will somehow shatter this dream.

"Sammy?" she murmurs before kissing the lobe of my ear.

"Hmm?"

"Do you have a statue kink? Because if not, I'm getting the sense you're not into this."

Shit. I'm messing this up by trying *not* to mess this up.

I've gone through life affecting complete and utter confidence. But I guess that's easy to do when I knew I could have whatever I wanted. All the world has a price tag, and because of my inheritance, I can afford to buy almost anything.

But not Ava. She's never asked for a cent from me. There's no way to pay for a path into her life.

And that's terrifying.

In a quick move, I set my drink aside, wrap a hand around one of Ava's muscular thighs, and drag her over to straddle my lap.

"I'm into this." And I emphasize the claim by gripping her ample ass.

Ava rocks into me, and I groan as the pressure on my hardening dick threatens to melt my brain. Her fingers comb into my hair, and I want her to mess up the careful styling I agonized over before arriving. She continues to press her body against mine, kissing my neck and making happy noises in the back of her throat.

Like she likes this.

Like she likes me.

"You're not interested in my money?" The insecure boy in my chest needs an answer to the question.

I want Ava to say *no*.

But I also want her to say *yes* because paying for things is all I know. It's safe.

Ava rears back, brow furrowing as her hands still. "Did you come over here expecting I'd charge you?"

The end of her petting devastates me, and I try to press my head into her strong hands, so she'll start again. "No...I...no."

Her frown deepens. "Then why are you bringing money up right now?"

Frantic to keep her from slipping away, the truth falls from my tongue. "It's usually what people find most attractive about me."

Ava lets out the most adorable noise, like a little growl, and she curls her fingers in my hair until her nails drag against my scalp in an erotic sting.

"Sammy, you dense-as-hell Squid. You are sexy. Just you. I mean, you know that, right? You have to. You're more lick-able than a double scoop of Death by Minty Chocolate Chip. And you saw how I licked that, right?"

"You devoured it." And I saved the image in my memory to bring up on a bad day.

"Exactly. And I want you more than that." Ava gives my hair a tug. "And your money means nothing here. Nothing to me. The most expensive hobby I have is buying special edition, sprayed-edge copies of my favorite books. But I get those for myself. With my own money. And, admittedly, I am probably in a slight amount of credit card debt because of that. But I'm not looking for a book sugar daddy."

"I could get you books," I pant. "All the books you want."

Ava sets her forehead against mine, gazing deep into my eyes. "Okay...I admit those sentences out of your mouth were *very* hot."

So hot that she finally dips in and kisses me, full on the mouth, licking me like she promised. Our tongues tangle, and I wonder why I ever said any words at all. Why I cared if Ava might be using me for my bank account when I could have this heady, delicious witch consuming me.

She breaks off, and I groan a protest.

"But I'm not fucking you for books," Ava says, as if our conversation wasn't interrupted by the best kiss of my life. "Currently, I'm not fucking you at all because you're being weird. So tell me, Sammy. Why are you here? Do you want to have sex?"

"Yes." I nod and try to follow her mouth with mine, slipping my arms around her waist to hold her close. "That's why I'm here. I want to have sex." I want more than that, but we can talk about it later. Once I show Ava I can be everything she needs.

Once I prove to myself I'm more than a thick wallet.

"Good." Her frustration slips away, replaced with a smile that stabs me straight through the ribcage. "Do you know what I need you to do, Sammy?"

"Tell me," I beg.

"I need you"—she leans in until her warm breath caresses my ear—"to wash your hands."

"Huh?"

Ava straightens in my lap and purses her lips in a scolding expression that almost has me spilling in my pants.

"You were holding my cat. Now you want to touch *my* pussy? You better wash your hands." She tugs my arms away from her perfect waist and slips off my lap. "Then meet me in the bedroom."

Chapter Nineteen

AVA

Want him for his money?

I scoff to myself as I listen to the gush of water coming from the kitchen sink.

Money has never been a big deal in my life. Not because Mom and I had a lot. In fact, we lived relatively close to the poverty line by most standards when I was growing up. But my mother never let that become a stressor in our lives. She was an expert at getting us everything we needed, even if it was from bargain racks and favors from friends. Backstage at burlesque shows, I saw how flimsy displays of wealth were.

And how quickly cash could be earned with the right tease of your body.

Plus, Mom always knew how to find us the cheapest tickets to Broadway shows, and we spent a lot of our time at public libraries, where I could explore thousands of different worlds for free. When I was rich with stories, I didn't need money.

The only currency Fanny Bellarose taught me to covet—to save up and horde—was power.

Magic.

And that's how Sammy will pay me tonight. But I refuse to feel bad about the fact. It's not like I can stop my body from absorbing what he offers, and the Squid knows what I get from his lust. Besides, this doesn't feel transactional to me because I know that even if there was no magical exchange, I would still want him here.

Despite this being the easiest channel to spell fuel, I don't sleep with just anyone. In fact, I rarely hook up at all. I invited Sammy over because his body turns me on. And yes, his personality too. The sincere—slightly vulnerable—goofball he's revealed himself to be underneath that cocky playboy persona he wears most days does something for me.

I thought Sammy Reyes was pure confidence.

Turns out, the guy has his own insecurities.

"I washed all the way up to my elbows," he announces, appearing in my bedroom doorway with his hands held up as if he's about to go into surgery.

I raise an eyebrow. "I hope you don't plan on being *in* me elbow deep. Pretty sure I'm too tight for fisting."

With suppressed glee, I watch Sammy's throat bob in a hard swallow and experience another wave of lust magic. Goddess, my skin is tender like a ripe fruit from all the power he's giving me, and I swallow the rich taste of his wanting.

"Noted," Sammy rasps.

Climbing onto my bed, I stand on the mattress, towering over him the way I do on stage when he's in the VIP section. Then I peel off my top and push down my bottoms. Sammy saw all this before, but that was when I was sick, and he was trying to be a decent guy taking care of me. I doubt he noticed the white ink design on my hip. I'm not sure he sees it now, his eyes too busy dragging up and down my exposed body.

"Come here, Squid." I tap my hip. "I want to show you something."

He stumbles closer, eyes following my finger.

"I know a binding witch," I say. "She's got this neat little birth control spell. Inked it on me when I was eighteen."

Sammy grins up at me, and at first, I think he's delighted by the fact that we can forgo condoms if he'd prefer. But then the Squid undoes his belt and pulls down his own pants to show the same symbol on his skin. Only his is inked in black instead of white.

"I got one too. Binding witch in Denver," he explains. "We match."

A warm tingle sneaks through my chest. A touch of ease and

happiness, knowing that Sammy took responsibility for his own birth control. Too many partners have assumed I would be solely in charge of contraception. One guy was almost *inside* me before I stopped him to ask if he wanted to know about birth control.

"We do match," I murmur. Then I reach out and comb my fingers through his hair, loving how the silky strands tease against my skin. "But maybe you should kiss it. Just to make sure it's real."

Sammy's stare flares with heat and humor. "I do like to use my mouth to test the authenticity of things."

I'm giggling when he licks my hip bone, then squealing with laughter as he bears me to the bed and buries his head between my legs.

Despite the eager energy thrumming off of Sammy, he takes his time, slowing down once I'm prone before him. The sounds he makes, wet licks mixed with pleased hums, should be banned for the way they drown my brain. Thoughts slip under the surface of an ocean of lust.

It's been so long since I've been with someone, I forgot how good sex could be. Or maybe I didn't forget, and it never was this decadent. We've only just started and already my legs—which I thought were strong before—quiver as if void of all muscles. But even as my body weakens under Sammy's enthusiastic tonguing, the core part of my being, the internal cauldron of magic, fills steadily, until I envision my magic as a luminescent liquid filled with stars and sparks, spilling over the brim.

I've never had to wonder what might happen if I got too much magic.

Protect me Dark One, I pray to the witch goddess, finding myself suddenly giggly again as I realize I'm afraid this orgasm will be so good, I need divine help through it.

"Am I that bad?"

I gasp, less from Sammy's unexpected question and more from the fact that he was sucking on my clit *so good* a second before he stopped.

"Goddess," I pant, pressing a hand against my flushed chest and staring down my body to where Sammy stares at me, his lips glistening with my arousal. "Why in all the hell dimensions did you stop?"

He presses a kiss to my inner thigh, which twitches in response. "You were laughing." He doesn't sound upset, only curious. "If you want me to do something differently, I will enthusiastically accept feedback."

"Fucking Squid," I mutter as I place my foot on his chest and press him backward.

He pouts, fingers briefly digging into my ass before he lets me go and sits back on his haunches. Then he lands on his ass when I slip off the bed straight into straddling his lap.

"What I want," I purr while fisting my fingers in his hair, "is for you to be a good boy and finish what you started." Then I grind down hard on his lap and take his mouth in a punishing kiss. He groans, and I taste myself on him. Reaching down, I carefully unzip his fly so I can pull out his rigid dick. He's already seeping from the tip, and I thumb the liquid around his sensitive head. "I laughed," I mutter against his panting mouth, "because I thought I needed a goddess's protection from how good you were making me feel."

I ring my hand around the base of him and give a firm squeeze. Sammy lets out an animalistic sound, his hips thrusting upward. As I meet his eyes, the normally dark blue is hazy with awe and arousal. His mouth hangs open. Feeling playful again, I lean in to nip at his bottom lip.

Then I press closer, my mouth against his ear as my hand guides his member between my legs. The man whimpers when he slips against my folds.

"Do you want me to take you deep?" I ask, smiling when he shudders, and his hands clasp my hips. "Do you want me to come on your cock and squeeze you tight?"

"Gods," he breathes. "Yes. Fuck yes. Please, Ava. Please, put me in."

Maybe other women like to be dominated, to give up power to a partner they trust. I think if Sammy wanted to fuck that way I'd be down to try.

But this, me in charge with him begging, is so delicious, it's dangerous.

And from the power spilling from him, the Squid gets off on being teased and tormented. He wants me on top. Earlier I called him Daddy, but that's not right.

He wants to be my Good Boy.

I sink down, claiming him inch by inch. Sammy writhes and grunts but doesn't try to take control back from me.

But he keeps begging. "More. Please, Ava. I'm going to die if I don't get all of you."

With my hands tangled in his hair, I tilt Sammy's head back and grin down at him. "You're so dramatic." I soften the chiding words with a teasing kiss to his lips, then another to the tip of his nose because I like the way his eyes widen.

When I settle fully in his lap, his cock buried and his balls cradled against the cheeks of my ass, Sammy's lids flutter and I worry his eyes might roll fully back into his head.

Meanwhile, I'm the fullest I've ever been. Not just of his physical penetration—though that seems to be exactly the right size for me—but of magic. Maybe I have a whole collection of internal cauldrons, and finally the rest are getting filled.

All I know is I haven't orgasmed yet, and this is still the best sex I've had in my life.

Still...I *do* want an orgasm.

"You feel so good," I croon to Sammy, and when I'm swamped with another wave of lust power, I conclude I was right about his love of praise. Untangling my fingers from his hair, I let my hands set to work on unbuttoning his shirt as I lean back. "Look at how well we fit."

We both stare down, met with the erotic sight of Sammy's thick cock stretching the lips of my vulva. I can feel him jerk inside me, and my body clenches in response, which has him moaning and digging his fingers into my waist.

"I never want to leave," he whispers, his eyes still on where we're joined.

The words sound heavier than sexy talk, and I guess mine did, too.

Look at how well we fit.

I never thought I could fit with a guy like Sammy. But what does a guy like Sammy even mean anymore? He's different than I thought.

But I'm too turned on to dive deep into the tumult of thoughts and emotions and revelations swirling through my consciousness. Right now, I just want a night of pleasure with a guy I can't get off my mind.

I flex my legs, letting Sammy slide almost all the way out before slipping back down, the wet noise of our combined pleasure mixing with our ragged breaths. He reaches to spread my intimate lips further until his sure thumb finds and massages my clit.

"Goddess. Don't stop. Don't stop." I chant the words as I continue to ride him.

Sammy bites his lip as his brow furrows in concentration. As if stoking my pleasure is a serious business. Seeing the normally silly man go so serious is the last push I need, and I surge into my orgasm, crying out and clutching the Squid's shoulders as my body tightens around his.

Sammy wraps his arms tight around my torso, pulling me flush against his chest as he drags me up and down his cock, using my shuddering release to milk his own body while groaning into my neck.

"I'll never stop," he promises with each thrust. "Never stop."

Then his body stiffens against mine and he mutters my name with curses as a warm wetness spills inside me. So much that it drips down my legs.

Overflowing just like everything else inside me.

Chapter Twenty

SAMMY

After the first night spent with Ava, I'm determined to find a way to mix our lives together. I can't fathom only experiencing that level of pleasure and connection and joy once. She's become imperative to my happiness. Without her, I'll become the ultimate mopey, heartbroken mess and forever flood whatever room I walk into.

But claiming Ava's time requires some strategic maneuvering with her busy schedule and energy-draining job.

I make it work.

Like today, she had to stay until seven at the library because of some maintenance issue. I coaxed her into letting me pick her up from her place to grab food. It helps that the build site of my latest project is right across the street. I stayed late myself, going over the blueprints and reviewing progress so far to make sure the project is progressing the way I envisioned.

First, I offered to cook dinner for her, which I've done a couple of times in the past few weeks. But Ava said she wanted to stretch her legs and be somewhere that wasn't the college, the club, or her condo. So now we stand in line at my favorite street taco stand. I wrap my arm around her waist and lift her up to my mouth, wanting a kiss but also wanting to give her feet a break. The sultry witch kisses me back with a smile on her lips, and when we break apart there's a flush on the apples of her cheeks.

"If this food tastes as good as it smells, I might die."

"Death by taco is a noble way to go."

Luckily, despite the inappropriate groans Ava makes while munching on her al pastor taco, she does not perish. The seats outside the shop are all spoken for, so we meander as we eat. A few blocks over, Latin club music drifts through the air from the door of a nightclub.

As if unaware of what she's doing, Ava does a basic cha-cha dance step while she walks.

A thought occurs to me. "Do you like dancing?" I ask. "Outside of The Jewelry Box?"

Ava's cheeks are puffed out from her bite of flavorful pork, but she nods, and I wait patiently as she finishes chewing and swallowing for her to expound upon her answer.

"My mom performed in burlesque shows in New York City for most of my life. I grew up around dancers. Even went to college for it, but I changed my major after freshman year."

She doesn't sound regretful about the information, and I let curiosity drive my next question.

"Why the change?" From what I've seen on stage, she's spectacular.

Ava tongues a drop of sauce off her thumb, and I almost forget to listen to her response.

"The program was really competitive. A lot of people were friends to your face while hoping you broke an ankle behind your back. Add that with the body shape expectations—it got toxic sometimes." She shrugs. "Maybe it's better now. Or maybe other schools are different. But I realized that I didn't want to rely on dancing to support myself. Didn't want to stress over how I looked and performed every minute of the day. I wanted to keep it as a fun thing, like it felt at the burlesque club." She smiles sweetly. "So I majored in business sophomore year. Then switched to English my junior year and stuck with it. Not that an English degree opens up a lot of doors, but I worked as a tutor and realized I liked helping students figure out their research. Which is why I went on to study library science."

"But you kept the love for dancing?"

"I did." She grins, then takes another bite. As the witch finishes her meal, I formulate a plan. Once our trash is in a can, hands wiped clean, and Ava is looking full and satisfied, I voice my thoughts.

"Let's go dancing."

Her brow curves up. "Sure."

"Right now." I tilt my head down the street where we can still hear the strains of music.

Ava snorts, then her eyes widen when she realizes I'm serious.

"We can't go now."

"Why not? Are you tired?"

She plants her fists on her hips and studies me. "No. But I'm not exactly dressed for clubbing."

I run my eyes over her voluptuous body, clad in a black sports bra and a pair of soft shorts that grip her right under her belly button and flare at her hips only to end short enough that the under curve of her ass cheeks have been constantly teasing me.

"One, you look sexy as fuck. Two"—I lean in close and slip an arm around her waist—"who are you wanting to get dressed up for? You've already got me here, ready to drop on my knees for you."

Ava wrinkles her nose, but I can tell she's fighting a smile. "Fine. But I don't want to stand in line all night. If it's long, then we're leaving."

"Lines. Ha. You're cute."

My hand in hers, fingers laced together, I guide her up the street and past a decent-length line of club goers dressed to impress. But Ava isn't alone in her casual attire: I've got on a set of jeans and a T-shirt, the get-up I opt for whenever I'm on the build site. We'll be underdressed together. As we approach the bouncer, I can see the way he eyes my determined steps and lack of high-ticket clothes. The beefy man squares his shoulders, ready to send me to the back of the line.

Ava's fingers tighten in mine, probably spying the same body language I do.

But I slip my free hand into my back pocket and tug a few bills out of my money clip. Some guys would leave it at that—reach out their hand to try for a smooth, sneaky exchange of cash to bribe the guy.

But no one would ever claim that I'm subtle.

"Good evening, my fine sir." I offer him a wide smile, tug Ava to my side, and settle an arm around her shoulders. "This amazing woman has had a shit day at work, and I'm hoping to treat her to a dance." Now I hold up the money, flared so he can see there are multiple hundreds. "Any way my name is on that list?"

The thing is, my name *could* have been on that list easily, if I'd known we were going to come here. The only club in this city I'm not allowed in is The Jewelry Box—for now.

He doesn't answer right away, eyeing me, then glancing at Ava. Eventually, he speaks.

"Bad day, huh?" He grunts.

She lifts a shoulder. "I'm a librarian. Sometimes things go to shit."

The blockish man's mouth twitches. "Love a good book." He plucks the money from my fingers. "Hope you left yourself some to treat her to a drink." Then he jerks his chin, a silent *Get inside before I change my mind.*

There's some grumbling from the people in the line, but it fades as we step into the club.

It's nothing fancy—not like The Jewelry Box—just an open floor with a DJ booth on one side and a bar on the other, with a dance floor full of writhing bodies in the middle. The place is easy to get lost in, which I think is exactly what Ava needs.

To move to music but not be on display.

"Do you want a drink?" I call out over the thumping beat.

She shakes her head, hips already rocking along with the rhythm. "Let's dance." Ava takes the lead, and I follow along behind her, one hand still in hers, the other resting on her hip. Bodies press in on us from all sides, and when we're in the thick of it she turns to face me with a hazy expression of happiness.

With a gentle tug, I pull her flush against my body and let the music melt into my muscles.

Then I move along with her.

Ava gasps in delight when she realizes I can keep up. Here I can, at least. I would not trust myself near a pole. With one hand clasping hers and the other pressed into her lower back, I lead us in a basic salsa as the Spanish words fill the air around us.

We flow together, two currents meeting and melding. I duck my head to press my nose against her hair, better to breathe in the salty scent of sweat mixed with the tang of eucalyptus. With the volume so high, I can't hear her breath, but each of her inhales presses her ribcage against my chest, and each exhale is a warm rush against my damp skin. Unable to stop myself, I lick the sweat from her neck, wanting her moisture inside me.

My witch's fingers tighten, pressing imprints into my flesh as we continue to flow with the intoxicating beat. Latin music was made for dancing.

And Ava Bellarose was made for me.

Chapter Twenty-One

AVA

After another stressful week of working late at the understaffed library, I eagerly accept Sammy's invite to attend a poolside gathering at Damien's house. The Squid asked me out, leaving the day open ended for me to choose. But I was too exhausted to do anything more than ask him to swing by my place to check on Kraken when I had to go straight from the library to The Jewelry Box. He's still working on the other side of the street anyway.

It wasn't until I was strolling out onto the stage—eyes immediately scanning the VIP section—that I considered how easily Sammy chose helping me with cat care over watching me make love to a pole. When I got home that night, the Squid was passed out on my couch, Kraken curled up on his chest with her green eyes focused on the TV screen. Apparently, my cat is a fan of action movies about prehistoric sharks the size of skyscrapers.

"I'm sorry. I didn't mean to stay so long," Sammy had rasped when I nudged his shoulder to wake him up.

"Kraken appreciated the company." The kitten leaped off him to attack the strap on my duffle bag.

"I'll get going," he said, sitting up and rubbing sleep from his eyes.

But I had a leftover buzz from performing and a strong craving for a taste of him.

Sammy reconsidered leaving right away when I kneeled between his legs, unzipped his pants, and took him in my mouth.

"Fuck, Ava," he panted my name, staring down at me with an expression of lust and disbelief. "I'll cat sit whenever you want."

That had me chuckling, which must've felt nice on his dick because he let out a guttural groan and only lasted another minute.

That was the only night this week we kind of spent together. Maybe Sammy didn't want me to think he expected a blow job for checking in on Kraken, because he never stayed late after that first time. What he did do was stock my fridge with some delicious, easy-to-reheat food. I would've thought the guy was hiring a personal chef to stop by my place, but the cat spy cam I installed showed him arriving in my home with bags of groceries and leaving the place spotless after cooking and wearing out my cat. If I didn't have to work, I might've watched him all evening.

When the weekend rolled around, and I examined the slight aching discomfort in my chest, I realized something odd.

I missed him.

I missed Sammy Reyes with his teasing grins, and earnest affection, and strong hands, and dirty jokes. Missed the way my kitchen looked with him standing shirtless, cradling my cat. There were times in the morning and evening I'd see Kraken sitting at the window, gazing across the street toward the build site, as if she wanted to catch a glimpse of the Squid, too.

I saw his texts Thursday during the few minutes I had to scarf down my lunch.

Damien is having a get together Saturday, wanna go?

With me?

Some of your JB coworkers will probably be there too.

My thumbs typed out an immediate *Yes*, and now I'm trying not to stare out my front window as I wait for my ride to arrive.

That's right, I agreed to carpool.

This is not keeping things casual, the self-preserving part of my brain points out. *Wasn't this just supposed to be a hot hook-up?*

But that's the thing. I don't know that I figured out *what* I wanted this to be in the beginning, and I don't think I know now. All that I'm sure of is I don't want to fall into the habit of relying on Sammy. Not for my supply of lust. Because if I do, he has the power to take it away.

Though I have trouble imagining him doing that.

There's a knock on my front door, and I definitely don't sprint to open it. Kraken is at my heels, and I scoop her up before she can sneak out, then I turn the knob.

Temptation per-Squid-ified stands on my front stoop.

Sammy really is conventionally good looking. Tall, tan, defined muscles, and a head of golden-brown hair. But all of that could sour if he was the douche bag I originally assumed he was. Instead, he wears an eager smile and leans down to plant a kiss on Kraken's fuzzy head.

"My ladies," he says, tilting his chin up to meet my eyes from under his beat-up baseball hat. Our faces are inches from each other, and he could easily claim a kiss.

But he waits for my move.

I tilt my head, so I don't bonk myself on the rim of his cap, then give him the kiss I know he craves. The same one I want.

Sammy rumbles a pleased noise in the back of his throat when I swipe my tongue along his lower lip, but just as he steps closer to deepen the contact, Kraken lets out a pitiful meow.

I huff a laugh and step back, leading Sammy into my apartment. "Let me hide some treats for her and then we can go."

"Do you have a bag? I can put it in my car."

I point to a bulky tote where I stuck my towel and sunscreen, then proceed to hide a handful of cat treats around my living area, hoping the hunt will entertain Kraken for a little while. After locking up and turning toward the small parking lot in front of my home, I pause and gape.

Sammy leans against a beautiful, royal blue Mustang convertible.

I wouldn't call myself a car fanatic, but after years living among outrageous stage performers, I've come to love colorful, outrageous things.

Like gorgeous blue cars that promise to mess up my hair and make my pulse pound.

"What do you think?" He rests a hand on the door. "I can put the roof up if you'd prefer."

"No way." I stroll up to the beauty and realize the sunshine on the paint job gives the car an almost rainbow sheen. "Can I drive?"

Some guys—most guys—get protective of their precious, expensive cars.

Meanwhile, Sammy holds out the keys and says, "Fuck yeah."

But when I go to grab them, he holds them up, just out of my reach. I scowl and consider giving him a purple nurple through his T-shirt. But then he wraps an arm around my waist and pulls my body flush against his. "Sorry. To get these keys, you gotta pay the kissing toll."

"Oh really?" I press my lips into a firm line to keep from smiling at his corny seduction technique.

"Yep. It's a steep toll. Government issued. I don't make the laws. But I do follow them as a standup citizen."

"I'm going to kiss you," I tell him. "But mainly to shut you up."

"I'll take it!" Sammy slips the keys into my hand the same time he claims my mouth, tasting like fresh rain and lust.

My skin tingles, my nipples tighten, and I try not to fall into the deep end of the infatuation pool.

When Sammy deems the toll has been paid, he opens the driver's side door and points out how to adjust the seat for my slightly shorter legs.

The drive to Damien's place is invigorating, with the sun on my skin and the wind tugging at my ponytail and the loose fabric of my sun dress. I feel Sammy's eyes on me, especially when I'm shifting gears. I guess he likes watching me handle the stick shift.

When I park on the street outside of Damien's house, the air feels too hot without the constant wind and because my body is flush with magic from the Squid beside me. I need to submerge myself in some cool water.

Luckily, this is the perfect place to do that.

"I can carry my stuff," I tell Sammy when he drapes the strap of the floral print bag over his shoulder.

"I put my towel in here, too. How about you carry this?"

He hands me a massive reusable Yeti mug. The cup is cute, light blue with a handle and a straw. There are some stickers on the side, and I study them closer.

An image of Evelyn from the movie *The Mummy* with the quote *"I am a librarian."*

A cat wearing a witch's hat sitting on a stack of books.

One that simply says *Easily distracted by cats and books.*

"Is this yours?" The cup looks more like something I'd have. In fact, I kind of want to steal it from him.

"It's yours. I got it for you."

"You did?" I blink between him and the cup that is perfect for me. "Is there booze in it?"

Sammy's teeth shine bright against his sun-kissed skin as he grins wide. "Damien will provide plenty of alcohol. That's full of ice water. Hydration is important. Here, you can also carry this." He slips his hand into my free one and laces our fingers together, then tows me and my fancy new mug toward the pool party.

And I try not to let my brain melt into happy, grateful goo. But it's really hard because he got me this small, yet wildly thoughtful gift, and he even took the time to put stickers I'd like on it. Goddess, I can see in my mind him cradling the cup in his long fingers as he carefully places each one.

Damn it. Sammy Reyes is one suave Squid.

I let my eyes drag over him as we walk a stone path toward the gated yard. He has on a set of flower-patterned swim shorts that sit low on his hips and hug his round ass. A loose tank top shows off his lean, muscular arms, and I find the golden fuzz of hair on his forearms tantalizing. Especially when the muscles beneath flex as he rubs his thumb over my knuckles.

When we're done with this gathering, he's totally getting laid.

As if hearing the thought, Sammy glances back at me when his free hand settles on the latch. Luckily, I have my sunglasses on, and the large, tinted frames should be hiding my ravenous eyes.

Still, he smiles again, then tugs me inside, and I follow willingly. Eagerly. And I take a long drag from the straw of my mug, hoping the chill water will put my libido on ice.

No luck. Especially not when we claim two lounge chairs and Sammy tugs off his shirt. The move reveals more sun-drenched skin with a light coating of golden-brown hair I want to rake my fingers through.

"You need to put sunscreen on me," I tell him, my voice coming out in a stern demand. There are too many people here for me to mount the Squid, so I need another—more socially acceptable—reason to feel his hands all over my body.

Sammy's face glows with eagerness, and he digs through my bag until he locates the bottle of SPF 70.

Yes, I have the skin of a ghost.

Sammy makes no comment, only squirts a large amount into his palms as I tug my ankle-length, flowy dress over my head and give him my back.

"Gods," he groans, probably at the sight of my black string bikini, then mutters more curses and compliments under his breath as he rubs the lotion into my back. I shiver when he slips his warm fingers under my straps to cover every bit of my back. Eventually, his touch drops away. "You're good. Perfect. Fucking perfection," he tells me.

I turn to face him. "Good? That wasn't even fifty percent of my body."

Sammy gapes at me, then swallows. "Do you want me to put it on *all* of you?"

There's no legitimate reason for him to put the SPF on the front of my body, which I can reach perfectly well on my own. But again, I'm feeling needy.

"I think that's best." I nod. "You're an architect, after all."

Sammy's brows raise so high they almost disappear under his baseball hat. "That's...true."

"And as an architect," I say, bullshitting like a pro, "you know how to account for every part of a structure. Therefore, you won't miss any spots. And I won't get sunburned."

When Sammy smiles this time, the curve of his lips is slow and so satisfied I feel a clench in my lower belly. "That is irrefutable logic. I will be thorough."

And bless the Goddess of Darkness, he is. Sammy coats his broad palms in the white cream and makes sure to massage the protection into every inch of exposed skin I have. He pays particularly close attention to the vulnerable skin of the inner thighs, leaving my legs so shaky I have to plop down on my lounge chair. A position he takes advantage of, insisting—as an architect— he needs to cover me even to the tip of my pinky toe.

By the time he finishes, I'm not sure I'll ever need to dance at The Jewelry Box again, I'm so full of magic. Sammy has to arrange a balled-up towel on his lap so no one else sees the rigid shape of him in his swim shorts.

"I don't know if I can get this to go down," he mutters. "Not when you're wearing that."

Sammy tips his head toward the swimsuit I chose, the black bottoms cut high on my hips and the strings of the top straining to hold two triangles of fabric over my boobs.

"I'm too hot to cover up," I tell him before pursing my lips around the thick straw of my mug and sucking hard.

Sammy presses knuckles against his mouth and lets out a muffled, pained sound.

"What if I give you a moment to yourself?" I ask, setting my drink to the side. "This heat is brutal. I need to get wet."

"Fuck, Ava," he mutters, burying his face in his hands.

"Sorry." I slip off my chair. "I honestly didn't mean that to sound suggestive." Leaning down, I kiss his sweat-damp neck, then let my lips brush his ear. "Thank you for the sunscreen. Why don't you relax here, think about unsexy things for a bit, then join me in the pool when you're not about to bust a hole in your swim trunks."

"Okay," he mutters, sounding pouty, which makes me smile as I give his neck another kiss. The stretch of skin is one of my favorite spots. It tastes good, and I enjoy the jump of his pulse against the sensitive skin of my lips.

As Sammy tries to redirect the blood flow in his body, I stroll over the textured concrete toward the pool steps. Normally, I enjoy cannonballing in, but this suit is not built for athletic endeavors. It was fashioned to bring a certain Squid to his knees. Mission accomplished.

At the first brush of cool water against my toes, I let out a happy hum. Last time I was here, I didn't get a chance to swim before the drama went down. Now I ease into the pool and sigh happily as the water surrounds me in a gentle embrace, gifting me with weightlessness and a refreshing chill. Reaching up, I tug the hair band out of my ponytail and slip my sunglasses off to hold as I dunk my head under water.

The sounds of the gathering disappear, replaced by the soothing noise of water against my ear drums. Resurfacing, I slip my sunglasses into place and ease through the water toward what I realize is a pool bar, equipped with submerged seats.

Damien has a nice setup.

And as I think of the Squid, he appears on the other side of the bar just as I take a seat.

"Ava!" He greets me with a grin and passes over a sweating can of hard seltzer. "I'm glad you came back."

Damien could rival Sammy for the devilish smile and sultry voice, but this Squid doesn't affect me the same way his friend does. I also like the fact that I get the barest flicker of magic fuel from him. Only enough to indicate he thinks I'm attractive, but not that he's having active horny fantasies about me as we share smiles.

"Sammy won me over. Don't tell him that. It might go to his head."

The guy smirks. "Never. I love seeing him squirm on your hook." Damien braces his elbows on the bar top, leaning toward me, his head close enough that we could have a private conversation.

The man is bronze as sand at sunset with midnight eyes and messy dark hair to match. Yasmin has started to hire male performers, and I bet she'd love to get a man like Damien on the stage. He moves in a way that you know he's a good dancer.

"Cheers to torturing Sammy with love." I raise my can and take a sip, only realizing the heavy word I spoke once I swallow the mango-flavored drink.

He knows I was joking, right? I don't love Sammy.

I don't.

Whatever Damien thinks, he keeps to himself. But his topic change isn't much better.

"So, you're a healing witch?"

My stomach drops.

Chapter Twenty-Two

SAMMY

I should've jerked off before picking Ava up. I'd considered it, but eventually decided to abstain, knowing that she'd receive a larger dose of magic this way.

But I also don't want to walk around this get-together with a raging hard-on.

Gods, that witch will send me to an early, sex-induced grave.

I drag in deep breaths through my nose and think about taxes. Having to fill out all those boxes, and gathering all my receipts, and knowing I did everything above board but still worrying the IRS will audit me because I might have accidentally filled out one of their endless forms incorrectly.

My dick softens, and I let my hands drop away from my face. And despite spending the last few minutes trying to clear thoughts of her from my mind, my eyes immediately search for Ava among the gathering.

A decent number of Elementals are here today. I spy plenty of Squids, and the fiery Byrne sisters linger by the cornhole boards along with my cousin August. He lifts his hand when our eyes meet, and I wave back. As far as I know, he's the only Ice Elemental—or Snow Cone—in all of Phoenix. There are Airheads and Stoners and Petal Pushers drinking and laughing and relaxing as the afternoon sun shines down on us.

Damien lets so many of us into his home.

I haven't even invited Ava back to my place.

Why haven't I?

A double knot tightens in my chest. One from the idea of having someone in my house who's not related to me.

But the other from the worry that Ava might read into the lack of invite. She has more reason to worry about me, and yet she told me where she hides her spare key and asked me to check on her kitten.

Ava continues to let me into her safe space, but I haven't shown her the same vulnerability.

I search with an edge of urgency now, wanting her in my view. Wanting to reassure her that I'm not trying to keep any of myself from her.

Any part of me she wants, she can have.

The black of her bikini strap stretched over a pale shoulder catches my attention. Her blonde hair appears a shade darker as the strands hang in a wet curtain down her back.

While I watch, she raises a can to her lips.

And across the pool bar from her, Damien leans forward, as if the guy only wants to get closer.

I'm off the lounge chair and diving into the pool before I remember to take off my hat and shoes. As I paddle toward my witch, I send a wave behind me to carry my sandals and baseball hat to settle on the side of the pool. Maybe they get there, maybe they don't. Doesn't matter as long as I reach Ava before my friend woos her with his charm and handsome face and responsible personality.

I rise from the water like a surprise sea monster right beside Ava's seat and let out a not-at-all-breathless, "Hey guys! What're you talking about?" as I attempt to lean a casual elbow on the bar.

Ava's eyes are hidden by her opaque sunglasses, but her plush mouth pops open in a surprised O. I'm so tempted to dive in and kiss the fuck out of that soft mouth, but I'm trying not to be too desperate and overbearing.

Just a little bit needy.

"Sammy," Damien says with a smirk. "Where'd you come from?"

"You invited me," I point out, knowing he's trying to draw attention to my awkward entrance. We've been friends far too long for him to let things slide. "Are you losing your memory in your old age? What are you now? Eighty?"

Damien's smirk deepens, and I can see him coming up with exactly the right words to reveal to Ava how immature I truly am, which will have her reconsidering things.

Things like letting me rub sunscreen onto every inch of her body. Things like asking me to watch after Kraken when she has to work late. Things like climbing behind the wheel of my car and letting me believe that wherever she goes, the witch will take me with her.

I head him off. "What did I miss? What's the hot Elemental gossip?"

Damien's thick black brows creep up, but he lets my topic change slide. "Actually, you two are. Well, Ava specifically." He re-trains his attention on the witch at my side, and she shifts on her watery seat. "People are buzzing about the stunt you pulled here with Sammy's arm."

In response to his comment, a small zing goes through my forearm, as if the limb remembers how magic mended it back together. I'd still be in a cast today if Ava hadn't intervened.

"That was pretty spectacular," I agree as I wrap my perfectly functioning arm around Ava's waist.

"You all have magic, too," Ava mutters before taking a long drag of her drink. I can't help thinking this conversation makes her uncomfortable. But before I can do another abrupt topic change, Damien continues talking.

"We can play with the elements, sure." To emphasize his point, Damien waves his hand, and the pool water at his side swirls and rises, a thin column twisting in the air before it falls down with a slap. "But you healed a man. And that break was nasty. Your magic is useful."

"My magic is finite," she grinds out.

Damien leans forward. "That can't be right. There's always fuel for magic. And you can use yours to keep us safe." He tilts his head toward the gathering, the group of mythical beings surrounding us. "You could be our on-call healer. So no one has to risk a human doctor. We don't get sick, but we do get hurt."

"That must be nice," Ava mutters so low I almost don't hear. But I do, and my memory brings up the pained expression on her tightly drawn face as a migraine ravaged her head and body.

Damien doesn't know about how Ava paid for healing me. There's a thrumming eagerness in my friend's voice, and I realize he's been planning this. This conversation with Ava. Maybe the guy is attracted to her. Maybe he's not.

But one thing I can tell for certain is he wants to use her.

"Damien," I snap, my voice taking on a harsh note I never use.

Two sets of surprised eyes flick to me.

"Ava is a witch." I glare at him. "Not an Elemental. Things work differently for her."

"But—"

"You will not guilt her into being your on-call doctor," I inform him. "You don't know what it costs her."

He frowns, his attention returning to Ava. "You're not fueled by your emotions?"

Tight-lipped, she shakes her head, not going on to explain how she needs to draw from others.

And that she needs her magic for herself.

Damien sighs and straightens, combing a frustrated hand through his hair. "That's..." He sighs again. "I just want our kind to have options. Safe ones."

From my angle, I watch as guilt tightens Ava's face. I press closer to her, tightening my hold and trying to convey support for whatever response she wants to give.

Ava leans a shoulder into me, then, after unclenching her rigid jaw, she mutters, "If it's serious—like Sammy's arm bad or worse—you can call me. But I'm not a doctor. I'm not a healer. I'm a librarian."

Damien's expression softens and he gives Ava a hint of his charming smile, which has me crowding even closer to her side, holding her warm wet body flush against mine.

"Thank you," he says. "I promise only to get in touch if it's an emergency. Can I grab your number before you leave?"

Ava rattles off a string of digits I had to wait months and gift her a cat for. Damien climbs out of the pool, presumably to add Ava as a contact on his cell.

"Let me know if he tries to sext you," I growl against the smooth skin of her shoulder before tracing kisses up her neck.

She chuckles, and I relax at the sound.

"I don't think that's his plan." Her tone shifts mournful on the last word.

"You don't have to heal anyone." I wrap my arms tighter. "You need to take care of yourself first."

Ava nods. "My mom always liked the saying don't set yourself on fire to keep others warm. That's what I reminded myself of whenever people asked me to heal them in the past."

I cup her cheek and push her sunglasses to the top of her head so I can gaze into her liquid silver eyes. "You set yourself on fire for me."

She offers me a sad smile and a shrug. "I didn't think about it. You were hurt. I didn't want you to be, so I did something about it."

"Don't do that again," I tell her. "I can go to the hospital. If something weird comes up on my charts, I've got enough money to make the forms disappear."

Her mouth twists in a sardonic expression. "Your money is another form of magic, huh?"

"Basically." I lean in to pepper her snarky mouth with worshipful kisses. "Promise me."

Ava reaches up to trace a finger over the line of my jaw until she reaches the point of my chin. "No."

"Ava." I try to make my tone scolding. But I've never had a good intimidation face.

"I promise," she whispers, and I think I managed it, but then she keeps going, "only to heal you when you're topping off my tank." Then the evil witch palms me through my swim trunks. My hips rock into her touch, and I swear I can feel magic infusing her skin where I hold tight to her.

"I want you to keep that magic for yourself," I groan against her neck.

Maybe I should be concerned about this situation. I've worked hard to distance myself from people who use me for my money, and now here is a woman in my arms who is literally part succubus. She's not after my wealth, but Ava is still using me for my lust.

But she's offering to give it back if I need it.

I don't want her to, though. And I don't care if she *does* use me. Uses every last drop of power she can glean from me.

All I want is for her to want me along with the using.

Her hand slips away, and I let out a grumbled protest.

"There's at least thirty other people around this pool, and while I may dance in next to nothing, I'm not an exhibitionist," Ava tells me, a teasing note in her voice. "Let's see if we can behave ourselves."

I half forgot we weren't alone. The only way I can hope to keep some composure is by releasing my tentacle-tight hold and slipping onto the underwater stool beside Ava's.

"Fine." I steal a sip from her seltzer, and she flicks water at me in laughing revenge. Then I ask her about her extra-long days at the library and try not to get pissed off at her unsupportive administration or turned on by how she eagerly gestures when she talks about finding sources for a particularly tricky research question.

"I'm hoping now that the summer break has started for most colleges there will be more applicants for the director position." Ava leans back in the water to wet her hair again, and I could swear I feel the moisture tracing through the strands.

The word *summer* catches my attention, and before I consider if it's a good idea, I ask "Would you want to come to my parents' house for the summer solstice?"

The witch's sunglasses are back in place, but I can feel her slow blink at me.

I clear my throat and sit tall. It's only weird if I make it weird.

"They love the holiday. Go all out for it. Get way too much food and have a massive party at their house." And though I had fun during the solstice when I was younger, the past few years have felt like going through the motions.

But if Ava came with me, everything would be new.

Ava tilts her head. "You want me to meet your parents and their friends?"

"Yes." *I want to introduce you to every corner of my life.*

"They won't mind if I'm there?"

"Not at all. Honestly, they won't even realize you're there until I introduce you. That's how packed it gets."

And even after I introduce her, it won't be long until she slips from their minds.

I love my parents, but they're like fast-moving rivers, constantly rushing through life and moving onto new things.

Ava gives a slow nod. "Okay. I'll spend the holiday with your family."

Chapter Twenty-Three

AVA

The summer solstice ends up being on a weekday, which means I have to work the hours before going to the Reyes's house. I expected the next few months at the library to be low-key, but there are still students on campus for a summer semester, and when we have less than half the necessary staff, every day is still full. Today though, I don't mind staying busy. This way I don't have time to fret about what meeting Sammy's family will be like.

Unluckily, my last hour on the job has me at the reference desk and Abraham Fellows strolling into the library, planning to take up all my time and then some. It's fifteen minutes past when I planned to be in the parking lot to meet Sammy, and Fellows is still insisting I brainstorm more search avenues for his exploration into historic river uses.

"How about I finish the search on Monday and send you the sources I find," I offer through the cheeriest smile I can manage when all I want is to drop-kick him out of my library.

"Why can't you have them to me by tomorrow?" he asks, brows furrowing.

"Tomorrow is Saturday. I don't work weekends." Not officially anyway. I've had to come in sometimes to cover circulation desk hours—again because we're understaffed.

"It won't take much of your time. You can finish it up tonight," Fellows says with a confident nod, like he's my boss, and I'm a slacking subordinate.

"That won't be possible," I grit out through my fake smile. "I'm about to leave."

His frown digs deep trenches into his normally smooth forehead. "You're ducking out early because it's Friday?"

How have I not murdered this man, yet? Seriously, I deserve an award.

"It's six-fifteen. Technically, my day ends at five, but I stayed later because the reference desk needed coverage, and I wanted to be here if students needed help." *Not that I was able to help students with you hovering at my desk for the last forty-five minutes, you arrogant asshole.*

Just as he opens his mouth, most likely to make another comment on my work ethic, movement at the doorway catches my eye, and the handsome man I've wanted to see all day wanders into the library.

Sammy Reyes is here.

And I missed him.

Our eyes catch, and he grins wide, offering a small wave.

"And look at that," I say with an easier smile than before. "My ride is here." I nod toward Sammy, and when Fellows turns to look, I quickly shut down the computer at the reference desk.

He will not claim another minute of my weekend.

The professor turns back to me with a tight smile that's as genuine as the one I give him each day.

"Your husband?"

Gods, with the amount of time he spends hovering around me, you'd think the man would notice the lack of a ring on my finger.

"No," I say in response and offer nothing else. He doesn't deserve anything more, having never tried to get to know me as a person. The guy is too self-involved to think of me as anything more than a means to an end. But there is also the fact that I don't know exactly what label to use for Sammy, and I bet calling him my "fuck buddy" would be a violation of the morality clause in my contract.

"You ready to go?" Sammy asks as he sidles up to the reference desk.

"I am," I announce before Fellows can argue that I need to give up my evening to finish his research. And when the professor looks away, I bug out my eyes in a way that I hope conveys my message of *please get me out of the hell dimension that is this man's presence.*

"Are you a student here?" Fellows asks, studying Sammy down the slope of his sharp nose.

I bristle at the unspoken implication, that I might be going out with a student.

Sammy wears an easy grin. "Never had the pleasure. I attended a university on the other side of town."

"Strangers aren't allowed to wander into campus buildings." Fellows sneers.

I roll my eyes behind his back, then take great pleasure in correcting him. "Actually, community members are allowed in the library. They can even apply for a library card, since we participate in a consortium with the city's public libraries. And Samuel Reyes is an upstanding member of the community."

Delight sparkles in Sammy's eyes at the description, and I'm thankful for the padding in my bra that hides the tightening of my nipples.

"You know," Sammy says, "Ava has told me about a few of the faculty here. The most avid supporters of the library." I'm going to murder him. "Am I right in guessing that you're Professor Abraham Fellows?"

Yep. He's definitely dead.

Fellows stands straighter and slides me a glance that has a touch of leer to it. "I am. Not surprised she's mentioned me."

And much to my disgust, a rush of magic flushes through me, sickly sweet chocolate rushing down my throat. Because of course the guy is turned on by the idea of me talking about him, unaware that I was lamenting to Sammy about how he's the bane of my professional existence.

"Always glad to put a face to the name." Sammy is suddenly at my side, gazing down at me. "My parents are expecting us soon. You want to drive?" He holds up the keys to his beautiful blue mustang, and I decide I can always murder him another day. It's like the Squid knew that after such a long stretch of being condescended to, I'd need to be in control for a little while.

"You bet I do." I snatch the keys dangling off his finger, grab my bag from under the reference desk, and arrow toward the exit. "Have a good weekend," I say to Fellows as I pass.

"I'll expect your email first thing on Monday," he calls out after me.

I grind my teeth and suck in a calming breath through my nose.

You don't have to talk to or think about him for the next couple of days.

If only it were for the rest of my life.

The blue sports car is a siren call in the parking lot, and I give in to the urge to jog to it, overwhelmed with the irrational fear that someone will catch me leaving and drag me back.

And suddenly, I'm not angry anymore.

I'm sad.

When did I start dreading my job like this?

Used to be I was excited for work. I looked forward to arriving early in the morning, brewing myself a cup of tea in the staff room, then settling in my office to map out my day. I'd look at the colorful calendar that identified which classes I'd be visiting and eagerly await the moment I could stroll across campus to meet a new crop of students and demystify information literacy for them. I'd create fun games to go along with my lessons, and I'd pin thank you cards from professors on my corkboard, glancing up at the notes with pride.

But somewhere along the way, academic politics and budget cuts started putting pressure on the library. A pressure that's largely falling on my shoulders as the only full-time professional librarian.

"Ava." The sound of my name has me blinking, and I glance over to find Sammy watching me. I don't know how long I've been sitting in the driver's seat with the engine running, staring out the windshield at the exterior of the library I don't want to go back to even after a few days of relief.

"Sorry," I mutter. "Got lost in thought."

"Here." He holds my insulated mug out to me. I must have left it on the reference desk, forgetting it in my hurry to leave. "I filled it at the water fountain on the way out. Are you thirsty?" Sammy watches me with such sincerity, concerned once again for my hydration, that something melts inside me.

I lean across the consul and rest my forehead against his shoulder, breathing in his clean rain scent and acknowledging that sitting here next to him has made my crappy day exponentially better.

"We don't have to go to my parents' party," Sammy says, and I feel the gentle press of his kiss on the crown of my head. "We can go back to your place. And I can make us something tasty like Chile Colorado with rice and beans. And I'll rub your feet. And call a guy I know to make that asshole suspiciously disappear, so you never have to see him again."

I huff a laugh and my heart squeezes in a totally inappropriate way in response to his offer to fund a hitman to get an aggravating professor out of my life.

"That all sounds amazing," I admit. "But I still want to go. I think I need a little solstice magic to reinvigorate my spirit."

Sammy lets out an unhappy grumble in his throat that has me smiling wider. "What's the use of being rich if I can't use my money to fix all your problems? I want to make him disappear," he complains.

I chuckle and straighten in my seat, then lean fully over to press a quick kiss on his pouting mouth. "I'll consider it." Then I pick up my mug and take a long draw from the straw.

Sammy's eyes go hot as he watches me suck the water, and when I feel the rush of power from him, I enjoy the pure shot of energy.

From Sammy, the tingles remind me of a cleansing rain, refreshing and delightful.

Who knew that a playboy would be so good at taking care of me?

Chapter Twenty-Four

AVA

I've never met a man's parents before. That's not to say that I haven't been in a relationship. I've had relationship-type situations. Things that have gone on for close to a handful of months.

But thinking back on those situations, none of them have been too serious. I never gave much of myself other than my body. I wouldn't say any of those relationships were bad. But they weren't memorable either. I recall faces, and, after a moment of pondering, names. But there is no loss of love. There is no regret for things that ended, even if he was the one to call it off.

So, this is the first time that I am meeting the people who gave birth to someone that I am sleeping with.

That is a weird way to put it, and I don't think I'll ever say that out loud.

"What are you thinking? Is it something weird? Is it something naughty? Tell me." Sammy stares at my face as we walk up a beautifully paved path to what can only be described as a mansion. Sammy has mentioned that he has money, but this display of his family's wealth makes it real in a way it wasn't before.

"It's weird. Not exactly naughty. I'm gonna keep it to myself."

"Damn you, you temptress. You torturous being. But I won't pester you because you're already being amazing by agreeing to come here." Sammy steps in close and wraps his arm around my waist tucking me into his side. The Squid loves holding me close, and despite the Phoenix heat, I find I don't mind. "You're not nervous, are you?"

Nervous. Is that what the nauseous clenching in the bottom of my gut is?

Oh goddess, I'm nervous. When did this happen? Why is this happening?

I am a pro at meeting people and putting on whatever face I want them to see. Funnily enough, that's a skill I've mastered both as a librarian and a stripper.

But maybe I don't want to have to put on a face for these two people.

Maybe I want to wear the face that comes most naturally and have them like it.

But why?

If I dig too deeply into that then it means I have to explore certain emotions I may be having about the man that is slipping his hand into the pocket of my sundress. There's nothing in the pocket, I think he just wants to get close.

I'm thoroughly tentacled.

"I would say I'm cautious," I say finally. "Anyone should be cautious when approaching those that made Sammy Reyes."

"You make me sound like a dramatic event." His lips brush my ear. "I like that."

He presses his face against my neck. The Squid likes to tuck his face into the crevice. Maybe the bright sun is hurting his eyes, and I am his moving, talking, sexy, smell-good sunshade.

"You're tickling me." I don't tell him to move away though. It's more an observation than a complaint.

As if knowing that, Sammy doesn't retreat. He only presses closer and sneaks his tongue out to lick the thrum of my pulse.

"Is this the best thing to be doing moments before I meet your parents?" My voice is breathy, and my skin feels tender and tingly with lust magic.

Sammy sighs deeply, then straightens. And I regret the gentle chastisement.

"I can promise to be on my best behavior. But I'm going to be

honest, my parents probably won't be on *their* best behavior." He frowns thoughtfully. "Correction, they will be on their best behavior, but their best behavior is someone else's worst behavior. But a good kind of worst.
"

I pause on the front step and stare up at the confusing man. "What did any of that just mean?"

He offers me a charming grimace.

"It's hard to explain. I think you're just gonna have to meet them. And hopefully, you still want to associate with me afterwards." Sammy opens the door without a key, but we had to pass through two gates to get this far so I guess leaving the door unlocked is not a big deal. Especially since a party is going on.

Beautiful, well-dressed people fill the Reyes's home. I get ready for Sammy to start introducing me around, but he doesn't even make eye contact as we weave through huge, dramatically decorated rooms. This is a place I could see *Architectural Digest* doing a tour of while some starlet describes each artistic piece.

It's gorgeous.

It's also...cold.

I much prefer my second-hand couch and handmade decorations and the funky cat towers Sammy keeps showing up with.

"You grew up here?" I ask Sammy, trying to sound curious instead of worried. What would a wild, young Squid do in a house like this? Everything looks so breakable and expensive.

Although, I guess the Reyes parents could replace anything their son damaged.

"We moved here when I was sixteen. From LA. We lived in New York when I was younger." He throws a wistful smile my way. "I wonder if we ever crossed paths?"

I narrow my eyes. "You were even more incorrigible as a teenager, weren't you?"

Sammy laughs and pauses to cup my face in his hands. "I was a pigheaded asshole. I thank the gods you didn't meet me then." He lightly brushes his lips over mine. "You would have hit me with a witchy curse just to shut me up." Since his mouth is so close to mine, I can hear his whispered words. The joke needs to be spoken quietly. Sammy warned me this party has humans in attendance.

So much for an openly magical solstice.

"Samuel!" A sweet voice calls out, and we both turn to discover an ethereal beauty strolling toward us in a flowy dress that makes it look like she's floating. The woman is white-skinned with golden hair and a towering, willowy build. Following behind her is a man with bronze skin and a devilish grin that reminds me of the man at my side.

"Hi Mom." He lets me go to wrap the woman in a tight hug. "Papa." Sammy holds his father just as tightly. Both parents hug him back, but I can't help thinking the affection lacks the genuine intensity of their son's. Still, they offer him eager smiles that transfer to me. "Ava, these are my parents, Louisa and Jose Reyes." Before we got here, Sammy told me his dad is the Water Elemental, and his mom is a human in-the-know. "And this is Ava Bellarose. My..." He trails off, and I realize we never discussed this.

A label. What we are. What we're doing.

And I see the smallest dimming in Sammy's expression that I'm almost certain is because he wants to say a word I haven't given him permission to use.

And damn the goddess, my heart hurts at the sight.

"Friend," he finishes after an awkward beat.

I huff a sigh and hold out my hand for a shake. "I'm Sammy's girlfriend." And because I decided to be the most honest version of myself, I let all the truth out. "We met at a strip club. I work as a stripper some evenings and as a college librarian during the day. It's really nice to meet you both. Thank you for the invite."

There's a beat of silence as my words sink in.

Sammy's mom recovers first.

"This. Is. Perfect!" Mrs. Reyes squeals and clutches my hand, but not to shake it. She whirls on her heel and proceeds to drag me through her designer house. "I just had it installed." *Just had* what *installed?* "The timing!"

"Mom!" Sammy chases after us. "Where are you taking Ava?"

"To my studio!" the blonde calls back.

By 'studio' Louisa means personal dance studio. The space has wooden floors and mirrors along one wall. In the corner sits a wide range of workout equipment, but plenty of space is left open. And in that space is a shiny new pole.

"*Please*, show me some of your moves!" She claps her hands and hops in place and generally reminds me of a butterfly.

Sammy bursts in a few steps behind us, his eyes going wide when he sees the pole. He groans. "Mom, no. Ava isn't here to teach you how to strip."

His mother ignores him and waves me forward.

Since I *do* want to make a good impression, I step up to inspect the pole. "I don't mind." It spins, so I decide to do a simple rotation with an air walk.

Louisa laughs in delight. "Another! This is fantastic." Jose walks in then, moving at an easier pace than his wife and son.

Under my sundress, I have a swimsuit on, but it's not as secure as the outfits I wear on stage, so I keep to non-inverted moves. Don't want to give the Reyes's too much of a show.

The shoulder mount hang.

The stag spin and the reverse stag spin.

A few different sitting positions.

The Titanic is a graceful position, and unlike the name, I hope it's helping me keep this first impression from sinking. I name each move as I go when I remember what they're called. Working in a strip club, we usually just do what feels sexy and learn on the job. Pole classes are where you get the terminology, and I've only gone to a handful over the years just to see what they were about.

"You are a vision." Louisa sweeps up to me and presses a kiss against my cheek. "A stripping librarian. Just what we need in our family. Samuel!" She shines a bright smile at her son. "You should take her next week. To your alma mater." Her attention flits back to me. "We're just making a little donation. And to the library, no less! This must be the work of the gods." Louisa holds her hands up in the air, as if the Elemental gods are peeking into this party. I guess on the solstice, anything is possible.

"The gods bless our family," Jose agrees, a besot expression on his face as he watches his wife. The hint of his devotion is adorable. I wonder if he shows his son the same level of affection.

"But look at me, ignoring my guests." Louisa drops her pious pose and pats my cheek before she dances to her husband's side. "You two have fun. All the blessings of the solstice!"

"Nice to meet you." Jose tilts his head, smiling all the while. And I decide he doesn't look like his son. At least not as much as I first thought.

Sammy's smile is a million times more approachable.

Then, as quick as they arrived, they're gone.

The room seems to echo with silence after their departure. Sammy and I stare at each other, his eyes tracing over my face.

He clears his throat. "Sorry. That they left so quickly. They're...I want to say they're not always like that. But they get distracted easily."

Louisa Reyes seemed charming and joyful. Jose appeared to have a quiet charisma.

Neither seemed to truly acknowledge their son. They didn't even ask a simple 'How are you?'

They're always like that?

No wonder the man seems starved for attention. With parents that step in and out of his life so easily. They don't appear to see him even when he stands directly in front of them.

"I'm glad I got to meet them," I say. It's the truth. I feel like I understand him better now.

Sammy glances away and nods.

I use the moment to slip in close and wrap my arms tight around his waist. This time I'm the one with tentacles.

Sammy sucks in a breath and stares down at me, and I watch his pupils widen.

I fake a glare. "I'm *just* your friend?"

"What?" he yelps. "No. No way. Who said that? Not me." He dips to press a smattering of kisses across my cheeks. "You are my girlfriend. Definitely. I'm your boyfriend. I'm going to get a necklace with your name spelled out in diamonds and wear it around, so everyone knows."

"Oh, gods," I groan, but I can't complain anymore because his kissing has moved to my mouth, and I'm drowning in an onslaught of peanut butter-flavored magic.

After a good five minutes of making out—and Sammy telling me how he's going to be the best boyfriend—he begs me to teach him a move on the pole. The Squid commits, putting his full body into the fireman hold that has him spinning in an almost cross-legged position. After I save him from faceplanting, he scoops me into another kiss. Eventually, we decide to rejoin the party.

A party I'm pretty sure is full of people Sammy doesn't know.

That is until we navigate to the massive pool, and I spot a familiar face. Quinn Byrne reclines on a swinging mattress that's partially shaded from the sun. She wears a crimson swimsuit that sets off the color of her hair and has me wondering if Yasmin ever offered her a job. The freckled Pyro would make a killing on stage.

As I head her way, Sammy breaks off to grab us drinks.

"Thank the goddess. Someone who isn't a super-rich Squid or a super-rich human." Quinn grins at me and pats the wide seat next to her. "Everyone here is talking about buying their fifth home. Or the summer Olympics and some big water polo match and a shit ton of other water-based topics. I really hope I don't discuss fire as much as they do water."

"Not that I've noticed." I settle beside her with a sigh. Another sore feet day, this time because I was carrying stacks of books to the shelves. Our last surviving shelving cart lost a wheel, and we're still waiting on maintenance to come fix it. "And I rather you don't start now that it's getting hotter than a hell dimension outside." My sundress clings to the beads of sweat forming on my skin, and I eye the glittering water eagerly.

Quinn quirks a smile. "Is it? Can't really tell. I'm always at a simmer." She laughs when I scowl at her. "You need help with that?" She waves at the sunscreen I pull out of my bag.

"If you could get my back, that would be great."

I stand and slip off my cover-up. "Is August here?"

"He's coming later. Once his manager starts her shift at the shop. I'm planning to be at least three drinks in by then."

"Is this a gathering I'm going to need to be tipsy to get through?"

More chuckles as Quinn's strong hands smooth the cool lotion onto my shoulders.

"I'd say yes, but only if you don't get too chatty." She lowers her voice. "You know most of the people here are humans, right?"

"I don't make a habit of chatting about magic, even when I'm tipsy," I murmur over my shoulder. "And I wasn't planning on shooting sparks from my fingers." Though I easily could. Not because pyrotechnics are my specialty, but because the energy from the solstice shimmers in the air. The magical holiday fuels every witch, making this a common day to cast spells. I set up an altar in my condo before work this morning, and Sammy swore Kraken hadn't demolished it when he checked on my kitten before picking me up at the library.

"That would level up your stage performance," the Pyro jokes.

I smirk. "Would be more impressive if I shot them from my tits."

Quinn lets out a sharp bark of laughter that draws the attention of some people who look like they're about to board a million-dollar yacht.

"Hey!" My Squid appears in front of me, holding two fruity cocktails and wearing a deep frown. "That's my job. Why is Quinn doing my job?"

It takes me a moment to realize he's referring to applying sunscreen to my back. I roll my eyes and Quinn snorts.

"Sorry, Sammy." Quinn doesn't sound sorry at all. "You were too slow. And Ava said she wanted a skilled set of hands. Someone who knew what they were doing."

The Squid gasps in outrage as Quinn resettles on her rocking mattress with an evil grin.

I smile, pleasantly surprised that I enjoy their teasing rather than feel intimidated by it, knowing their past sexual history. Clearly, neither one holds a flame for the other. Which is great because it means I can become best friends with the fiery woman.

"Don't get your tentacles in a twist," I chide Sammy as I rub sunscreen on the parts of my body I can reach. "I'll need to reapply in an hour. You can help me then."

In response, Sammy sets one of the drinks down on a low table, pulls his phone out of his pocket, swipes a few times, then turns the screen to show me he's literally set a timer for sixty minutes.

"I'm holding you to that." Brief petulant mood evaporated, he hands me the cocktail and throws a question Quinn's way. "Where's Auggie?"

"He's scooping till two. Then he'll be here."

"Is he going to bring any ice cream when he comes?" I ask, thinking how good a cone would taste right now.

"Ooo. Good idea. I'll text him." Quinn slips a phone out of her bag, and while she's busy typing, Sammy guides me to a nearby lounge chair.

"Do you want shade?" He tilts his head toward a folded umbrella.

"Yes, please." The Phoenix sun is brutal, and I can feel the intense rays already trying to turn my skin pink through my SPF 70. Sammy makes sure my chair is comfortable, and the sun can't touch me unless I want it to. He arranges a table within reaching distance where I can set my drink down. He also places my newly filled water mug on the table, a silent nudge to stay hydrated.

Then, when I expect him to pull up his own chair, Sammy instead sits on the end of mine and lifts my feet only to set them in his lap, where he proceeds to massage them.

I barely stifle a horny-sounding moan.

"I'm glad you came," Sammy says, staring at me across the length of my body. Our eyes hold, and the words between us feel weighted.

"I'm glad I came, too." Even though this day is something of a shift. We're not casual anymore.

But I think I'm okay with that.

People don't think of Sammy as a serious guy.

But I think I might be serious about him.

Chapter Twenty-Five

SAMMY

Reluctantly, I leave Ava in the pool, where she and Quinn are sampling the five different custom solstice cocktails Mom had a mixologist prepare for the party. My witch's giggling is hard to walk away from, but I need to use the bathroom. That's one liquid my body doesn't have much control over.

When I come out of the restroom next to the kitchen, I spy August in front of the open freezer. He has a large cooler at his feet and looks to be transferring cartons of his delicious ice cream into the massive fridge.

Sneaking up beside him, I pause when my eyes slip toward the glass doors, and through a part in the crowd, I have the perfect view of Ava sitting on the lip of the pool. Her long legs dangle in the water as she chats with Quinn, who floats around in a unicorn inner tube.

I bet she brought that. The rainbow mane doesn't match the party's aesthetic.

For a moment, I'm mesmerized by the sight of my witch. The sun shines off her skin, making her appear to be a luminescent moon in the middle of the longest, sunniest day of the year. When she laughs at something the Pyro says, she presses her fingers to her mouth as if to suppress the moment of joy. I wonder what has her thinking she needs to hold anything back.

Maybe it's that restrictive school she works for. Just the thought of the place, which I imagine has a pretentious vibe much like the professor I encountered, causes an unfamiliar anger to boil in my veins.

Being pissed off is not a common state for me.

"Never should have doubted you." A deep voice knocks me out of my whirlpool of thoughts, and I find August at my side with an understanding smile. "She's the one."

"The one?" I ask.

"For you." He drops an arm over my shoulder and gives me a firm hug.

"You make that sound like I was destined to find her." I keep my voice light even as I feel a twinge of panic at his words. Not because I think my cousin might be right.

But because he might be giving me too much credit. He's counting Ava as mine when I'm not certain I can.

She said I'm her boyfriend. That has to mean something, right?

"Maybe the gods help a bit with love. I don't know." August squeezes me again, then lets go. "Look at me and Quinn. Hard to believe there wasn't a touch of fate, me moving here and finding her." He scratches his beard, expression thoughtful. "You're not still trying to buy her love, are you?"

"What?" I scoff. "No."

Even I hear the overcompensation in my voice. August raises a brow and waits, his stoic silence hard to argue with.

"I only buy her things she likes. Toys for Kraken. You're going to tell me I should stop spoiling a kitten? Are you a monster?"

The Snow Cone rolls his eyes. "Money isn't what convinced Ava to give you a chance. More gifts aren't going to make her love you."

Maybe not impersonal gifts like cash and jewelry. But thoughtful gifts have to show how much I care. Right?

"I'm worried I'm going to mess it up," I confess. "That she'll realize she can do way better."

August hums a low note as he opens a few drawers until he discovers a spoon. A moment later he's handing me a massive scoop of Peach Gobbler. As I lick the delicious ice cream, I watch Ava sip a pink drink and lick her lips.

I wish she swallowed my love with equal reverence.

"Maybe I'm biased," August says, his blue eyes holding mine when I glance his way. "But I think you're pretty great."

"Auggie—" Embarrassment has me ready to make a joke, but he talks over me.

"You're loyal. And smart." He crosses his arms and wears a hard expression, daring me to contradict him. "You're fun, too. You have a big mouth and like to tease, but you're never mean or cruel. You're kind, Sammy. And the people you care about get a hell of a lot of you. As far as I'm concerned, Ava should count herself lucky to be loved by you." He sets heavy hands on my shoulders, making it impossible for me to dance away from his intensity. "Keep showing her the real you. Don't hide behind your money."

I'm rarely lost for words, but I have no idea how to respond to what he just said. My cousin gives a firm nod, as if setting his statements in stone, then lets his hands fall away.

"I'm going to change into my suit. See you out there."

The Snow Cone strolls out of the kitchen, leaving me reeling.

Did he mean all that?

Those words he used to describe me: loyal, smart, fun, kind. I'd like for all of them to apply to me.

But he can't be right.

People like me because I'm handsome and could buy a private island if I have the urge. I learned that early on.

August might as well have been describing himself. I'm not surprised in the slightest Quinn fell for him.

Ava...I still feel like I'm tricking her into this relationship.

And I'm too selfish and self-centered to explain she should stay away from me.

After dropping my spoon in the sink, I head outside, suddenly anxious that my witch will have used the potent magic of the holiday to make herself disappear.

But she's still by the pool, flicking her feet in the water. As I move toward her, I let my magic flow through me, feeling it rock like waves in my chest until I sway with each step. Since there are humans here, I keep my manipulations subtle. I make a gesture with my hand, imagining little droplets of water pressing into her thighs like my fingers. I watch as the water does my bidding, indenting Ava's bare skin ever so slightly. The witch gasps, staring down at her legs with wide eyes. She's so distracted, she doesn't realize I'm beside her until I kiss the curve of her neck.

Ava blinks up at me, a slow smile unfurling. I stay crouched beside her and lean in for a quick kiss, then whisper three words against her soft lips.

"Happy summer solstice."

Ava lifts her cocktail in a toast, takes a sip, then pulls me in for a deeper kiss that tastes of lemon, sugar, and sunshine.

For now, I have her.

Chapter Twenty-Six

AVA

Turns out when you have the kind of money that the Reyeses have, you give hefty chunks of it away on occasion. And not only to strippers. Sometimes you offer a tidy sum to academic institutions.

Which is how I find myself at the massive university that counts Sammy Reyes as one of their illustrious alumni. When his mother mentioned a donation at the solstice party, my minimum wage mind did not properly fathom the quantity they might pen on a check. Apparently, "a little donation" equates to paying for an entire new wing of the library.

The Reyes Wing.

When I asked Sammy why the library—not that I disagreed with their choice—he admitted his mom hadn't been specific about where she wanted the money to go, so he'd made the recommendation.

Is he funding academic libraries because he knows it brings me joy?

Admittedly, I also find it entertaining to watch Sammy dress up in a sexy-as-hell suit and be greeted like a visiting prince by the board of the university. They shake his hand, they take pictures, they stare at his perfect ass—probably considering if they should kiss it or bite it.

Or at least that's what I tend to do when I see his butt.

When his fawning fans finally leave us to explore on our own, I take the lead, heading into the beautiful library. I got to tour the place a couple of years ago during an academic conference that was held here. I texted Veronica—an old school buddy—to let her know that I would be stopping by. I find her at the reception desk chatting with one of the student workers.

"Ava! I can't believe how long it's been since I saw you." She grins wide at my approach. "It's like we don't even live in the same city."

Guilt curls in my gut. Veronica is not the one to blame for our lack of quality time, it's me. Every time she sent me a text about meeting up, I had to turn her down because of the workload sitting on my desk and in my inbox. Or because I had a shift at The Jewelry Box—a pastime I have not shared with my human library friend. I never know how someone is going to react to my stripping, so I tend to keep the fact close to my chest.

"I know. I'm sorry." My apologies come with a tight hug. "But here I am, ready to drool in envy at your library."

"Please no. We just got the carpets redone. If drooling could wait until the fall semester when the students overrun us, that would be fantastic." We share a chuckle, and then I watch Veronica's eyes flick over my shoulder. Her stare widens when she takes in the man at my back.

"Oh, yes." I turn and wave the Squid forward. "Veronica, this is Sammy Reyes. Sammy, this is Veronica Martin. We did our library science degree together. And Sammy is here because his family is making a donation."

"Reyes? You're the money behind our new archival wing." The librarian's curiosity morphs into giddiness. "Oh my gosh, I am so happy to meet you! Thank you so much for that donation." My friend eagerly holds out her hand to shake his.

Sammy accepts and offers her his charming smile. The one that makes everyone in a fifty-foot radius swoon. I smirk.

"You can thank my parents," he says. "I am simply the pretty face delivering the check."

"And how do you know Ava?" Veronica's eyes flip between the two of us, interest clear in the uptick of her voice.

I have no idea what response Sammy was planning for this question. I don't think that he would out the fact that he met me at a strip club.

But knowing that Veronica is my friend, he might accidentally let slip a mention of The Jewelry Box—saying he met me at my second job or something like that. The confidence I had sharing the info with his family evaporates in the face of someone in my professional field knowing.

Unfortunately, in my hurry to field the query, I accidentally word vomit.

"We're seeing each other," I announce. "Not because he's rich. Or because he's good in bed. Although he is both those things."

Oh my goddess, did I just say that out loud?

Sammy stares at me with a baffled yet slightly delighted expression. "Is that what we're telling people now?"

My friend presses her fingers against her lips, laughter evident in her eyes.

"No. We're not," I growl at Sammy. "That was...I didn't mean it like that." I turn my back on him, concluding it's the sexy suit that has muddled my brain briefly. "Anyway, let's ignore what I just said. Veronica, you said the carpets were just redone. Anything else new in the library?"

My friend is grinning as she waves for us to follow her. She takes Sammy and me on a tour of the building, pointing out the renovations they've started over the summer, including where the Reyes Archival Wing will soon be located. I'm not sure how interesting Sammy finds any of this, but I find it fascinating. One of the reasons that I gravitated towards working at the college where I do now was the look and the feel of the library. When I first visited, it seemed like a cozy, warm place. It was a smaller institution, and I thought that was why the library was also small. It was respected and a comforting place for the students to be.

After working there for multiple years, I now see that the cozy shabbiness was actually lack of funding and my predecessor's inability to put a shine on something that hadn't been replaced in decades. Things that likely won't be replaced in decades to come.

What would it be like to work at an institution like this?

True, this library is bigger than what I originally thought I would prefer. But this is a place that is getting funding and is obviously utilized by the university as a whole.

I recall the enthusiastic way other librarians from well-funded institutions discussed their workday when I attended the conference here. How they described the support that they received from the administration and faculty. No one claimed that their institution was perfect, but on a scale of positive work environment to step above a hellscape, I think mine fell on the lower end. Veronica points out the twenty new computer stations on the second floor, and I can't help remembering the sight of Rodrigo sweating through his dress shirt as he struggled to fix our ancient printer for the third time in a single week.

"This place is gorgeous." I sigh out the confession as we descend the main staircase. "I'm not ashamed to say that I'm jealous."

Veronica gives me a cheeky smile. "And it is causing me physical pain not to say I told you so."

I roll my eyes. "Well technically you did just say it, so I hope that was a relief for you."

"Told Ava what?" This comment comes from Sammy, who hasn't said much up to this point, simply wearing a small smile and letting the librarians geek out.

Veronica glances over her shoulder at him. "I told Ava that there was more job growth and more funding at larger universities than at small private colleges that don't care so much about their libraries. But she wanted to be a big fish in a small pond." She turns to me with a scheming sparkle in her eye. "But if you would like to take a swim in larger waters, one of our instruction librarians is going to be going on maternity leave in a few months. You could always put in your résumé for consideration as a temporary replacement." She digs a gentle elbow into my side. "Give it a try. See what you think."

There's a tug in my chest. A longing. The offer is more tempting than I ever expected it could be.

But there was a very important word in her offer: temporary.

"That sounds like you want me to quit my job for one that would only last for a short time," I point out. "Doesn't sound like the smartest decision to me."

"I know it seems that way, but it could turn into a full-time gig." Veronica leads us back to the front desk. "Or, if you like it, you could just apply at other large institutions. Don't pretend like working at CFF isn't draining you dry. I've heard from other librarians who worked there, and

I know how they treat you." All teasing has fallen away when she meets my stare this time. "You deserve better than that."

I can feel a flush pooling under my cheeks, but I hold Veronica's gaze. "Thank you for letting me know. But I'm making it work."

She heaves out a sigh, then checks her watch and frowns. "Crap. I have a meeting in ten minutes, and I need to grab some things from my office." When her eyes lift again, they're a touch sad but also hopeful. "It was really good to see you, Ava. And I'm not trying to pressure you. But if you change your mind, and you do want to put your name in for that temporary position, let me know. I will back you up with my boss." She pokes my arm. "And we need to get drinks soon. I have a feeling that you want to unload some major library-related frustration, and you *know* that I would be the best person to understand everything that you're going through."

She's right. One of the problems of being the only full-time librarian at CFF is that I have no one to commiserate with. Rodrigo isn't really the chatty, gossiping type.

And even if unloading all this shit to Veronica would give her more ammo for pressing me to leave my job, it would still be nice to tell it to someone who fully understands the fuckery of working in academia.

"Okay. Yes. Drinks. I will text you the nights that I'm free."

Veronica grins wide and waves. "I'll hold you to that. It was great to meet you, Sammy. I'm glad that Ava likes you despite you being super rich and really good in bed!" The student worker at the desk giggles, and I reconsider getting drinks.

Maybe I'll murder her instead.

Chapter Twenty-Seven

SAMMY

"We explored your domain. Now it's time to enter mine." I lace my fingers with Ava's as I tow her out of the library toward a building that thankfully does not have my family's name on the side.

When she heard the amount of money my parents were donating for the new library wing, the witch's eyes went wide as full moons, and she needed a full minute of rapid blinking to recover.

It's one thing to see a string of pearls. Another to visit a large house.

But when someone gives away multiple millions of dollars, the level of wealth cannot be ignored. And I get the feeling that my family's money, at best, disinterests Ava and, at worst, dissuades her from wanting any kind of future with me.

"So, this is where all the architecture nerds hung out?" she asks in a dry voice as I lead her through the department. I can't recall a time in my life I've been called a nerd.

I kind of love it.

"You bet. A bunch of us just sat around comparing the quality of our protractors and graphite pencils."

"Oh baby." Her voice goes breathy. "Save that dirty talk for when we get home."

Even though she's teasing me, my cock twitches, and I lock on the way Ava sounds when she says "home." The word is all warmth and promise.

But she's not talking about my house, a place she hasn't even visited yet. Ava has her little condo, with its colorful witch language pictures, piles of books, and menace of a kitten in mind.

I want to be on her mind when she says "home."

We meander down hallways, studying student projects set out for display and peering into classrooms as I regale Ava with stories about my successes, and maybe a few failures, while I worked for my degree.

"Here are some faculty offices." I tug her down a side hallway lined with doors. Every one is closed, lights off. I bet most of the faculty take advantage of the summer break to work from home if they aren't traveling. Reading the name plates, I pause in front of a familiar one and smile.

"Eliza Fernandez. Her work is inspired. And she's such a good teacher. I was her favorite student."

"She said that?" Ava asks with a smirk.

I shrug, returning her expression. "There are certain things that don't need to be spoken aloud. And we keep in touch. We should have dinner, and she can tell you herself." I wish Eliza was here now so I could let Ava into her office. There are some beautiful blueprints framed on the walls.

Unfortunately, when I turn my back on the door, my eyes catch on another name, familiar for a different reason.

"Meanwhile, that asshole is the reason I almost didn't graduate." I point across the hall to an office I visited once and never again after.

Ava follows the track of my finger and studies the entrance with a frown. "What do you mean?"

"Anders Dreyer. *Doctor* Dreyer." I emphasize the word the man always insisted we used when addressing him. "Fantastic architect. Terrible human being." I fight the urge to grit my teeth. "He was the master of microaggressions. Especially against students of color. The moment he heard my last name, my worth became zero in his eyes. On the first test, I missed a few questions and didn't understand why, so I came to his office hours. He didn't outright call me lazy and dumb, but it was a close thing. Said I might be better relying on my family money than trying to learn concepts that were above me." I can hear the disgust dripping in my voice at the memory. The condescending tone he used and the judgmental sneer on his face. "I realized he wasn't going to help me. So I helped myself. Showed him that as much as he didn't want me in his classes, he couldn't get rid of me. If it weren't for him, I would've graduated with a 4.0." My glare threatens to burn through the thick wood of the door. "Bet there were others though, who weren't as stubborn as me, that took his words in. Believed them like they were truth."

"Asshole," Ava mutters, and I recall the professor I ran into when coming to pick her up. He gave me the same self-important vibes as Dr. Dreyer.

I wonder how many stuck-up pricks Ava has to deal with on a daily basis. On her own, since she's the only librarian. At least I had other students to rage with about Dreyer.

Makes me want to drive over to the college and burst a pipe in the ceiling above that asshole professor's office.

As I imagine the petty act, Ava steps away from me and up to Dreyer's door. She slips her hand into her bag, pulls out a paperclip, and whispers, "Let me know if someone is coming," before crouching down and sticking one end of the metal into the keyhole.

I have no idea what I'm watching, only that a moment later, when the lock clicks and the knob turns, I'm suddenly *very* turned on.

"Come on." The sneaky witch disappears into the office. "Hurry up, Squid."

I stride after her, and Ava shuts us in the dark space once I clear the door.

"Did you just pick that lock?" I ask, wonder in my voice. "Where did you learn that?"

"I told you my mom worked with some interesting women. One had a locksmith for a father, and she taught me how." In the dim light, I can make out her wide smile. "I've never gotten locked out of anywhere. Not for long anyway."

Fuck. I'm half hard hearing about my witch's not-so-legal skillset.

Then she presses me back against the door and drops to her knees again, only this time her focus is on unlocking my belt buckle.

"Ava—"

"I'm going to suck you off in this prick's office. He tried to hurt you in here." She gazes up at me, gray eyes wide and so gods damn lovely. "But you didn't let him. And I'm going to make you feel *so* good."

My lungs seize in my chest, forced to stop working as my heart swells to ten times its original size.

I love you, I want to say. Want to drop to my knees in front of her and beg her to never leave me.

But Ava already has my fly down, her skilled fingers finding and cupping me until all I can do is groan. When the hot wet cradle of her mouth envelopes me, I forget where I am.

All that matters is who I'm with and that she never stops.

With my shoulder blades digging into the hard wood of the door, I brace my feet wide and cradle the back of Ava's head as she bobs on my cock. When the pleasure builds to a point I'm about to spill down her throat, I pull Ava off me and drag her to stand.

"Sammy," she growls, her face flushed, eyes bright. "I want to finish you."

Don't you realize you already have? I'm fucking done with any kind of life that doesn't have Ava Bellarose in it.

Instead of answering, I spin her around and move us across the few feet to Dreyer's ridiculously large desk. The same one he sat on the opposite side of years ago when he tried to make me feel worthless.

The man didn't know what I had coming.

I didn't know either.

But now she's here, her hips in my grasp, her palms landing on the surface of the desk and staying there. Ava braces herself, understanding my intention as I drag up the skirt of her flirty sundress and reveal a set of sky-blue silk panties. I tug the lovely scrap of material down only far enough to reveal her glistening pussy.

"I love when my witch is wet for me," I mutter.

I revel in the sound—slick—as I drag the head of my cock around her dripping entrance, then slide deep with a quick thrust. We both gasp out prayers and curses to the gods.

"Fuck me hard, Samuel Reyes." Ava's words are raw, dirty, and beautiful.

I follow orders, slamming into her repeatedly until I've driven her thighs into the edge of the desk. Each thrust sends the furniture sliding a few inches across the floor, our fucking rearranging the asshole's room. Reaching around, I press the heel of my hand against Ava's mound, grinding her hood into her clit. Ava's cries grow sharp and needy, and my dick sinks inside even easier as her lust soaks me.

Wrapping an arm around her torso, I drag Ava upright, clutching her against my chest as I drive into her relentlessly. She reaches back to tangle her fingers in my hair and tugs.

I love the sting.

"I'm so close, Sammy. Please," she rasps, and her begging almost does me in. But even more than I want to spill into her glorious pussy, I want Ava falling to pieces in my arms.

There's so much moisture between us, and my mind snags on an idea. With a flick of my fingers, I call up my power and coax Ava's wetness to follow my lead—to flow over her vulva in rhythmic waves, massaging the sensitive skin around the intrusion of my cock.

"Goddess! What—" Her question is choked off by the start of a shrieking orgasm which is then muffled by my hand pressed over her mouth.

Don't want a custodian busting in here thinking someone is getting murdered.

Thought bleeds from my mind as Ava's body shudders and clenches around me, her cunt bearing down hard on my member. My balls tighten, and I feel the heat racing down my length just as my eyes land on the desk nameplate.

Doctor Dreyer, it reads.

I grin in triumphant self-satisfaction as my huge cock gushes waves of cum into the intelligent, beautiful, devious woman I love.

A literal *fuck you*.

Chapter Twenty-Eight

SAMMY

My temporary ban from The Jewelry Box is officially over, and I celebrate by treating myself to a glass of top shelf whiskey on a Tuesday night. Only, unlike my former routine, I don't immediately head to the VIP section.

Instead, I hang out by the bar to trade jokes with Cat and talk to Mia —the club's head mixologist—about her plans to renovate her house. Aspen claps me on the shoulder when he's making his security rounds, and after a half hour, Rafael shows up. My best friend isn't wearing his aquarium uniform, but I still catch the slight scent of salt water from him.

"Look at you." He grins and waves at Mia, who sets a glass of tequila in front of him. "They let you back in. You're lucky Yasmin likes you."

"I *am* feeling quite lucky lately." I clink the rim of my glass against Rafael's and enjoy the delicious burn as I replay the encounter with Ava from last week's campus visit. How her pale ass had pooled on the surface of that pretentious desk during our second round of revenge sex. How my pounding strokes rattled the customized fountain pens until they rolled out of place. How the wicked witch held me deep inside her when I finished for a second time and crooned that I was a good Squid.

Those sweet words had me coming so hard my eyes crossed, and I swore my balls were drained dry.

Praise from Ava is my sexual kryptonite. I get destroyed in the best way.

Blinking away the erotic thoughts, I refocus on my friend. "And I wouldn't go so far as to say Yasmin *likes* me. I think she's more interested in my architecture brain than being buddy-buddy."

I don't hold it against the Airhead. In fact, I enjoy how the club owner wants me for a skill I worked to cultivate. That's a kind of wanting I enjoy.

We've met twice more about renovating The Underworld, and it is officially happening. I'm the architect in charge of redesigning the kinky club. And despite Yasmin providing the funding, she's decided to hand off the major aesthetic decisions to Harley Byrne. I knew the Pyro was a dominatrix at the club, but this is a different kind of work. Harley and I have only ever interacted at Elemental parties where we tease and taunt each other. But this is business, where we could potentially build something great, I'm excited for the challenge.

And I'm also hoping that Ava and I could possibly use one of the rooms when everything is finished.

Warmth envelopes my left side, and I glance over to find Cat smirking at me as she settles her serving tray on the bar. "So Pearl is really giving you a chance, huh? You found a way to charm her?"

I sip my whiskey as I think about Cat's comment. Charm comes naturally to me but maneuvering my way into Ava's good graces was anything but that.

"Don't think it was my charm," I admit.

"So, what then?" The redhead braces her elbows on the bar top, and I watch her boyfriend's eyes drop to her metal-covered cleavage. The guy is gone for her, and I like that she's not setting him on fire for the move.

"I think she warmed up to me around the time she vomited on my pants."

Cat's mouth pops open, and Rafael coughs out the tequila he inhaled instead of swallowed.

"You annoyed her so much she *puked* on you?" The Pyro asks the question through delighted giggles.

I pout. "No. It wasn't because she was annoyed. She had a migraine."

Cat sobers with a wince. "Oof. Poor Pearl. I've heard those can be rough."

Recalling the sweaty, drawn nature of her face when I arrived, and how every move she made appeared laced with pain, *rough* is too mild in my opinion.

But I nod. "She let me take care of her. I must have done a good enough job that she decided I wasn't a total asshole."

"That's the goal," Rafael declares, clinking his glass against mine while Cat smirks at her own charming former-playboy.

As the pair trade flirtatious quips, I slide off my stool, drawn to a spot with a better view of the stage. But I still don't go up to the VIP section, or even where Ava might spot me. Now that she acknowledges me outside of The Jewelry Box, I don't have the desperate urge to capture every second of her attention here.

Ava has on an outfit with tassels, and the little strings sway with every one of her skilled movements. The muscles in her arms flex when she hoists herself higher and rolls her body like a wave on the pole.

Magnificent.

"Does this bother you?" Cat pauses at my side, holding a tray full of drinks.

"You stepping out on me by serving other people cocktails? Yes. I'm wounded. I thought we had something special my little red menace."

The Pyro rolls her eyes. "Don't make me set your pants on fire. I meant, does her dancing for all these guys? All of them lusting after her, does that bother you?"

"Gods no." When Cat raises a skeptical brow at me, I stand by my statement. "It doesn't. For one, she pays them as much attention as she did me. But more than that, all this lust"—I sweep my arm to take in the room of spectators—"it fuels her magic. She's not like us, with it always under her skin. She needs an outside source."

"Wow." The redhead glances toward the stage. "That's how witches work?"

I shrug. "How she does, anyway. And when she has power, she can hold off the migraines. That guy"—I tilt my head toward a middle-aged white man with a receding hairline, expensive suit, and prominent boner

—"is pure magic fuel. Filling up her battery. So tomorrow, she can wake up pain-free." I lean my shoulder against a column and watch in wonder as my woman fully inverts herself on the pole, arching her back as she slowly spins. "Anything that makes her feel good, I want her to do. Anything that keeps her healthy and happy."

"That's progressive of you, Sammy." Cat gives my arm and affectionate knuckle tap. "I think you might not screw this up."

"I'm honored by your confidence." My voice is thick with sarcasm, but I can't help grinning at Cat.

She thinks I can make this last with Ava. That's all I want.

As the Pyro strolls away to serve more drinks, I attach my eyes to the masked dancer on stage. The song speeds up, and Ava's body flows with the melody, pure temptation until I'm adjusting myself to keep an erection slightly more discrete than the man I pointed out to Cat. He's not the only one salivating over my witch, and every stare trained her way eases the tight anxiety I didn't realize was in my chest. The worry that Ava will find herself without magic again and have to experience more of the wretched pain I saw painted all over her body.

Guys sit around the edge of the stage, tossing bills at her feet or holding them up in an attempt to draw her closer. They don't have any luck, not that I expected them to.

She doesn't care about the money.

Ever since I realized how empty the friendships I bought were, I've longed for someone to want me for more than my bank account. I've hoped a person might get to know me and decide there's a drop or more of substance to me beneath the surface. That I have more to give than my Amex card.

That was one of the reasons I worked so hard to coax Cat, Rafael, and Aspen together again after years of fission. Because they're the kind of people who will be my friend no matter how much I'm worth. For that, I would've done *anything* to make them happy. And since I couldn't buy their happiness, I had to figure out another plan. Good thing I knew the three of them wanted each other, and I was the right kind of pushy to make that happen.

Now the Pyro, Squid, and Petal Pusher are in love, and Cat is my friend.

If Cat can get over her animosity toward me enough to count me among her trusted companions, then maybe a spectacular woman like Ava could find something real to love about me.

A Squid can hope.

Chapter Twenty-Nine

SAMMY

As I reach out to type in the gate code while Ava sits in the passenger seat of my Mustang, I have to acknowledge how big a deal inviting her here is.

I've lived in this house for three years now. My friends and plenty of other people cycled through the luxury condo I lived in before this. I had guests over almost every day, and parties almost nonstop. I worked, sure, but then my coworkers would come over for drinks after hours. And that's when they found out that I didn't have to work if I didn't want to. Because I was flush with cash.

Everyone who came to where I lived could tell just how much money I had.

And for some reason, the fact that I had what they considered an impressive number in my bank account, that suddenly changed who I was to them. I became less of a person in their mind. More like a caricature of life. The things that they saw in my home suddenly became up for grabs.

Who cares if you walk away with something? Sammy can buy fifty more of whatever you take.

I got used to people taking things from me. Convinced myself that that meant they liked me.

But I couldn't tell myself that lie anymore when they took things that mattered.

Specifically, my grandfather's harmonica.

I had it on my bedside table.

Who just takes a harmonica?

When I realized it was missing, I didn't even know who had done it. There'd been upwards of fifty people in my home the night before. I asked around, but no one admitted to the theft.

That night I went home alone. Sat in my penthouse alone. And realized that I felt violated.

But not just that. I felt...

Empty.

Meaningless.

Useless.

The next day, I called my realtor and put my penthouse on the market. I had them send me listings for plots of land far from where I'd been living. Places where I could start from scratch.

I spent some time by myself, trying to figure out what I liked about me. What I liked in general. And it was mortifying to realize how much of myself I had crafted based off of what others thought of me.

I went to therapy. I focused on spending time with people who knew all facets of me—shallow as I am—and still wanted to be in my life. People who weren't afraid to insult me to my face.

Most people don't like to be insulted. *I* don't like to be insulted either if the comment is said with hurtful intentions. But when someone who cares about me points out a flaw with a playful smile and a snarky laugh, it's one of my favorite things in the world.

I don't think Cat Byrne realized how highly I held her as a friend all the while she hated me.

With good reason.

We've mended fences, but she is still the best person to go to when my ego needs a caring punch to the gut.

And now I have this house that is full of things that I like. It is crafted for me, and I keep it for myself. No one takes anything I don't freely offer.

But now Ava is here, and I am sweating as I wonder if she'll like anything that is from the truest version of me.

"Goddess, I'm surprised you were willing to stay over at my tiny apartment. Your house is *huge*." Ava gazes out the window as I pull up the front drive and into my garage. Kraken sets her little paws on the door, also staring out as if fascinated with my house.

The kitten is probably just excited for her first road trip since the day she went to the club with me.

"I like your place," I say. Every inch of it feels like her, which makes every inch of it perfect.

Ava snorts and climbs out of the car with Kraken cradled in her arms. The cat tries to escape, but Ava keeps a firm hold. "Can we head inside so I can set her down?"

"Of course." I lead the way through a door that takes us from the attached garage to a large entryway. Ava follows, then lets Kraken leap from her arms onto the wooden floor. The kitten scampers off, and I hope she doesn't get lost in the place. We could spend a day looking for her in here and still not run out of hiding spots.

"Would you like a tour?" I offer.

Ava nods. I take her hand, lacing our fingers together, and walk us through my home. We cover living areas, my office, home gym, and the kitchen before she says anything.

"It's weird."

I freeze in the act of opening the fridge to grab her a drink. "My house?"

Gods, please don't let her hate it.

I want Ava to come back. To want to spend time here.

"Yeah. This place is huge." She tilts her head to glance at the tall ceilings. "But it's also...warm. In a good way." The witch steps past me to grab a bottle of sparkling water from the fridge. She lets go of my hand to screw the top off.

Since I'm needy, I step in close and wrap my arm around her waist. I watch her throat work as she swallows, wanting her to say more nice words.

"Did you design it?" she asks after screwing the cap back on. "Your house?"

I nod.

She smirks. "Maybe that's it. The house is like you."

"Like me how?" I rasp.

"You know...showy at first. Sitting on top of its hill saying, 'Look at me, I'm a fancy ass house.'" Ava wiggles her shoulders, which brushes one against my chest, since I'm standing so close. "And I see it and think, 'Well maybe it's gorgeous on the outside, but I bet it's all cold, sharp angles on the inside. Not somewhere I'd want to live.'" The witch smiles up at me. "But then you come inside, and it *is* big and showy and kind of fancy. But it's also warm and soft and somewhere I might want to stay a while." She taps my chest. "You're showy, charming, and you *should* be an asshole. But I stepped through your front door, and I think I'd like to stay a while."

Words rise and fall in my chest, none of them reaching my tongue.

I love you, I think very hard at her as my witch gives me a sassy smirk.

"So does this place have a pool?"

After a bracing breath, I step back enough to twine my fingers with hers again. I raise Ava's hand to my mouth where I can press and hold my lips against her knuckles as I lead her to the backyard.

Words still aren't available to me right now. Only kisses.

"I should've known." She laughs when we step through the sliding glass door. "You're a Squid, through and through."

The pool is rather large, with multiple levels and four waterfalls.

"It's bigger than Damien's. Your whole place is!" Instead of moving forward to explore the swimming area, Ava leans into my chest and relaxes as I twine my arms around her waist. "Why aren't you the one having Elemental parties?"

I brush my mouth against her bare shoulder and re-learn how to speak.

"I used to have parties. At my old place." I drag my lips along the curve of her neck. "People stole stuff." I kiss the corner of her jaw. "It wasn't a big deal at first. But my grandpa left me his harmonica when he died. After that was taken, I decided I wanted my own space."

Ava's body stiffens before she turns to face me. Her expression is thunderous, bordering on terrifying.

"People stole from you?" she growls.

Is she ready to defend me?

Gods, that's hot.

But I also want this to be a happy tour, not a pity party.

"It's in the past." I press a quick peck to her frowning mouth, then aim us toward another entrance to the house across the stone patio.

The next room is my ace. The one I'm buzzing and fidgeting about. The room I expect Ava will see, then shove me up against the wall and give me the same treatment as she did in my asshole professor's office.

Maybe she'll beg me to make a mess again like when she was in the bath.

"Oh, hey. How about we go in here?" I say super casually.

Ava glances at me with a crinkle between her brows.

Okay, maybe that didn't come out as *super casual* as I meant it to be. Maybe my voice went up a few too many octaves, and I waved my arm in a much-too-broad arc toward the doorway.

Whatever. She'll forget my weird behavior in a moment. Soon she will be overcome with lust—and maybe love—and the world will be full of only rainbows and unicorns and orgasms.

"Sure," she says, the word coming out in a slow draw.

Eagerly, I step forward, turn the handle on the glass door, then sweep the entrance open and usher her inside.

Straight into my library.

I've had a trusted set of workers in here for a month perfecting the place. Hardwood floors scattered with plush rugs compliment a turquoise water-patterned wallpaper and are illuminated by a sparkling chandelier with warm lighting. Cozy seating is available in every corner. Windows come equipped with three different kinds of shades depending on how much light you want to let in. A sprawling view of the Phoenix desert is visible through the glass.

And of course, shelves. Shelves and shelves and more shelves reaching to the ceilings, equipped with rolling ladders. One of them is even a secret passageway, but I'll let Ava figure that one out on her own.

Or I'll tell her in a fit of passion—the jury is still out.

"So..." I say after a full minute has passed with Ava standing in what must be rapturous silence. "What do you think?"

She turns to me. Instead of looking ecstatic, Ava appears confused.

"I thought you said you've been living here for three years," she says, voice holding a question.

"Uh, yes. I have." *Where's the erotic shoving and the kissing?* I want to make out with my sassy witch in the library I designed for her.

"Well then, where are all your books?" She points at the walls, and I realize my misstep.

All the shelves are empty. And I haven't told her why.

"Right. Sorry. That's the best part." Slipping up behind her, I rest my hands on Ava's shoulders and slowly turn her so she can take in the full potential of the room. "I want you to give me a list, all your favorite books. All the ones you look forward to reading. Every new release that catches your eye. No limit. Don't think about cost, just about what you want to read." I murmur the words in her ear. A teasing temptation. "And I'll have them all here, waiting for you."

Now for the book-inspired sex-fest.

But Ava doesn't maul me with love. She tilts her head to meet my eyes over her shoulder, expression still confused. "But it's your house. Your library. You should fill it with books you read."

I firm my jaw to keep away a grimace, disappointed this isn't turning out how I expected. I know I can't *make* Ava fall in love with me with expensive trinkets and jewels and designer clothes.

But I thought *books* was a sure thing.

Maybe you should stop trying to win affection by purchasing things, a voice that sounds a lot like my therapist's speaks from the back of my head.

I know I've fallen back on a habit, one I swore I would move on from: buying affection.

But I get panicky whenever I think of Ava moving on from me, and I end up making desperate ill-advised decisions. And now I have to admit a fact that will knock off whatever attractive points I've managed to scrape together up to this moment.

"I don't read," I mutter, so low that I hope my lovely librarian doesn't hear.

Success. Only not really, because she turns around and pokes my stomach. "Speak up."

I sigh and sneakily tentacle my arms around my witch's waist so maybe I can stop her from immediately fleeing from me in horror. "I don't read," I repeat, this time loud enough so she can hear.

"Oh." Ava stares up into my face, and I search for signs of devastation or disappointment or disgust. But there's only another confused brow wrinkle. "You're not a fan of books? I thought you mentioned a few you liked."

"I listened to those. Audiobooks. I can listen while I'm working out or cooking or driving. But I can't sit down and concentrate on words for more than five minutes. So...I don't read."

And now it comes, the twisting of her lips and piercing glare. My librarian knows that I'm not worthy of her.

"Excuse me," she snaps. "Listening to audiobooks *is* reading. I don't ever want to hear that bullshit take again," she growls and grips the back of my neck to drag my face down, our eyes locked. "If you listen to audiobooks, then you're a reader."

"But—" I stutter, and her nails dig into my skin in a way that maybe is supposed to be punishing but just makes me hard.

"You are comprehending a story in the way that works for you. If you were blind and listened to thousands of stories, would you say you'd never read a book before?"

"I..." I'd never thought of it like that. "You're right. I'm sorry."

Her expression softens along with her fingers before they comb up into my hair.

"So, Samuel Reyes. What are you?"

I swallow hard. "I'm a reader."

Ava lets out a pleased note in the back of her throat and my whole body tightens with wanting.

"Readers are so hot." She drags my mouth to hers, and I drown in the heady taste of her tongue tangling with mine. At some point we fall onto one of the cushy lounge seats I bought with the fantasy of Ava curling up with her favorite book in the chair.

I still want that to happen, but it's always good when furniture is multi-functional. Like how this large seat is perfect for me to sink into my librarian with steady thrusts as her ankles rest on my shoulders.

And as I suspected it would, the library immediately becomes my favorite room in my house.

Chapter Thirty

AVA

The bookshelves in Sammy's house slowly begin to fill with books. That by itself would be an enjoyable development, but something even more wonderful happens.

Sammy embraces his identity as a reader.

I've always hated the ableist notion that listening to books somehow isn't reading them. Yes, it's a different version of comprehension, but so is braille. Feeling words is different than seeing them, but it's still reading.

Sammy continues to listen to audiobooks, but now he also buys hard copies of the ones he likes. He said he wanted to support the authors, seeing as how he has money to spare. But he's also gotten into tabbing.

Once Sammy called himself a reader, the guy decided to look up what bibliophiles do, and discovered a faction of the reading population that utilizes colored tabs to notate their books.

I'll often spy a hardback on his coffee table, or in the backseat of his car, in the pocket of his briefcase that has colorful tabs sticking out from between the pages. If the Squid hears a line he likes and wants to remember, he'll find the words on the page of the physical book and mark the quote.

Also, Sammy reads across genres, including some smutty romance stories. He is extremely enthusiastic about tabbing the best spicy scenes.

For inspiration, he claims.

And because Sammy is an audio reader, sometimes he asks me to read his favorite passages aloud while he goes down on me.

Who am I to refuse?

And bless the goddess, those are often the most erotic moments of my life.

I love sleeping with a reader.

"Should I start a Bookstagram account?" Sammy asks me a few weeks after my first visit to his house.

We're in the library, and he's shifting titles around on a top shelf to fit his latest purchase. He's tall enough to reach by only stepping up on the bottom rung of the ladder.

"If you think you'd enjoy it, sure." I try to scratch Kraken while also holding my book, but she keeps attempting to bite the pages. I also try not to drool over how sexy the Squid looks while organizing his shelves.

"I might. It's just...look at this." He waves toward his collection. "This beauty is criminal to keep to myself. I think I need to share it with the world."

I smile to myself, hearing the genuine excitement in Sammy's voice rather than his common teasing bravado. "I think you'd have a beautiful Bookstagram account. Just don't let social media overwhelm your life." I've seen that happen to some of the book content creators I follow. Where they over-commit or get too focused on an esthetic they feel obligated to maintain. Then they burn themselves out, forgetting why they started their account in the first place. The simple love of books.

I want Sammy to hold onto this reader joy forever.

"Good point." He sighs. "Besides, I'd probably just end up taking a bunch of pictures of you reading. And then I wouldn't share them. I'd just look at them when I'm alone and missing you. And then I'd get all horny and sad and my pool would flood my house."

I glance at the dramatic Squid over the top of my book to find him staring at me from across the room. "Is this your weird way of asking to sit with me?"

He grins and nods.

I scoot over to give Sammy space, then deposit Kraken in his lap when he settles beside me. Sammy swipes a set of noise-canceling headphones off a nearby table, slips them on, cues up a book on his phone, then reads as he plays with the kitten and cuddles next to me.

And I try to read my book and not melt at how perfect this moment is.

I've been having a lot of perfect moments over the last few weeks, ending up at Sammy's house more often than my own. It's only, he's closer to the college and to The Jewelry Box. Most afternoons, he'll get done at the build site, swing by my place to pick up Kraken, then have dinner and a cute cat waiting for me at his home.

That's right. Sammy can cook.

Apparently, his parents always had a live-in chef and Sammy would spend hours in the kitchen with her, learning how to make different meals. And now he makes them for me, and I wonder what else I don't know about him.

Other ways I might have misjudged the Squid I deemed a playboy.

Sammy seems like such a straightforward, surface-level guy. But dig past that first playboy layer, and there's so much depth. He's the man who is cautious about letting strangers close because of a lifetime of being taken advantage of. A guy who doesn't know how to show his friends how much he loves them, so he tries to make their lives better with strategic chess moves and expensive gifts. He's the man who cares for me when my period cramps get so bad, I give in and use my magic, then crumple the next day when a migraine overwhelms me.

At first, I was sure he only wanted a hook-up.

But this is turning into so much more.

Can I have a real relationship?

If we keep on like we are, will he ask me to change my behavior? To quit The Jewelry Box and rely solely on him?

I could. Other than that period day—which wouldn't have been a problem if I hadn't already sneakily soothed Rodrigo's thumb when he jammed it in the printer door and eased Kathleen's ankle pain when I saw her limping and she described tripping on the uneven concrete outside the library entrance—Sammy keeps me fully stocked in magic.

But I don't want my physical well-being to be reliant on someone else.

And I don't want to be one more person in Sammy's life who is using him.

Chapter Thirty-One

SAMMY

I didn't think there was a way Ava as Pearl could become more beautiful on stage.

But then I settle myself in the VIP section, watch her strut out on stage, and lose my breath when she locks eyes and smiles at me.

Ava acknowledging my existence when she's wrapped in a sparkling string bikini and wearing her lace mask is next level. The club seemed crowded when I first walked in, but everyone else ceases to exist as I experience my witch's performance as if for the first time.

She is a vision. A temptress. All through her set of songs she flashes her gray eyes at me. Smiles and taunts with her hips. Makes promises to me with her body.

Her pale skin grows pink, partly from exertion, but I bet a good deal of that flush is magic filling her reserves. *How much of it is from me?*

Whatever the amount, I want to give her more. I want to be an endless supply to keep her happy and healthy.

I love you, I say through my eyes when our gazes clash. *Yes, I'm drowning in lust for you, too. But the current is only so strong because I love every part of your soul.*

I don't know if Ava interprets my silent message, but something must make a difference to her because she alters her routine. Normally, every dance she does is different, but she always—other than the times I tempted her with boxes and a kitten—ends on the pole, then strolls off the stage without a backward glance.

Today though, Ava slips to her knees and crawls. Her lithe body is cat-like as she stalks, not off stage, but toward the VIP section. I'm out of my seat and at the edge before I can consider if she wants me here. Then, in front of a crowd of clubgoers that know Pearl doesn't interact with customers, she reaches out, hooks a finger in the collar of my shirt, and drags me close until her lips brush my ear.

"Thanks for the boost, Squid. Check your phone."

Then she plants a kiss on my cheek, no doubt leaving behind an outline of her pearlescent lipstick.

I might never wash my face again.

Pearl pushes me away, as if the dancer is done with me. She's handed out a favor to a lucky bastard and is going back to her ice queen ritual.

As I resettle in my seat, I feel the stares of awe and jealousy directed my way.

They're well-deserved. I'm the lucky asshole who gets to be with her tonight. Though none of them realize that I'm *that* fortunate.

Slipping my hand into my pocket, I pull out my phone. Just as I'm wondering why Ava wanted me to look at the device, her name flashes with a new text message.

> Ava: From the way you were just drooling, I can bet you're pretty hungry. Meet me at the food truck on 8th in thirty minutes. Dinner is my treat.

I don't want to wait even that long to see her again, but if I bust into the backstage area, Yasmin will probably ban me for life and find another architect for The Underworld. Instead, I settle my tab and head to the front door to bother Aspen where he's checking IDs before people can go in.

"I thought you passed your bar exam," I say, pointedly staring at his Security shirt. "Shouldn't you be lawyering now?"

"Lawyering is not a word." The big, bearded Elemental waves a couple inside. "It's practicing law. And I've been interviewing. Just got an offer from a firm. I start in two weeks."

"That's awesome!" I clap a congratulatory slap on his shoulder.

The Petal Pusher doesn't look as enthusiastic as I'd expect.

"Yeah, I guess," he grumbles. "But Cat doesn't work at the office."

Ah, yes. No more security shifts at The Jewelry Box means no more working with his girlfriend.

"But," I point out, "now you can come here as a customer. And stare at her all night like a creep, instead of spending some of your time out here"—I wave at the line of impatient people wanting to get into the hot club—"collecting cover charge."

Aspen tilts his head, wearing the start of a smile. "True. Rafael comes here to creep a lot."

"Exactly. Now it can be a couple bonding activity. You and your boyfriend getting buzzed and gawp at your girlfriend. Sounds like a blast."

Aspen chuckles, and I clasp his shoulder again before strolling off in search of my own magical woman I unabashedly obsess over.

Ava is already at the food truck, likely having taken a back exit to avoid being seen. Cactus Crepes, owned by a Petal Pusher named Terra, tends to park in this area to feed the late-night clubgoers. Lots of places only serve drinks, and everyone gets tipsy and starts craving delicious street food. Ava waits off to the side, the light of the truck setting her to glowing.

She's taken off her mask, changed out of her skimpy outfit, and washed as much glitter off as she could manage. Black yoga shorts hug her toned ass and legs, and a cropped T-shirt shows me flashes of her stomach. Her hair, which was previously in a high ponytail, now hangs in a messy braid down her back, topped off with a Land of Ice Cream & Snow baseball hat I gave her. After dancing in those skyscraper heals, slipping her feet into some well-worn sandals must be a relief.

My witch still looks as gorgeous as she did onstage. More so because now I can stroll up to her, scoop her into my arms, and bury my face in her neck. She smells like sweat and eucalyptus. My cock twitches in my pants as I think of other ways I could get her sweaty.

"Hello, stranger." Ava chuckles, combing her fingers through my hair and teasing my scalp with her nails. "Did you have a fun night?"

"The best." With a groan of regret that I can't push her up against the side of the food truck and ravish her, I let Ava slide out of my arms. "You were amazing. Let me get you something. You must be starving."

I slip my fingers into my pocket to retrieve my wallet, but Ava covers my hand with hers.

"I already told you," she scolds, "it's my treat."

"Ava—"

"Sammy," she speaks over my protest then reaches up to tug my hair in a gentle rebuke. "I know you're always going to have more money than me." Her gray eyes hold mine. "But I make enough to treat my man to some crepes. So tell me what you want."

You. You you you.

All my life I've felt like a walking wallet to most people. Even the ones who care about me often assume I'll be willing to pay without thought.

Rarely does someone make a point to buy *me* something.

"I...uh...need to look at the menu," I tell her, voice tight with emotion I'm trying not to spill out on my overworked witch.

Ava grins triumphantly and tows me to the end of the line. There, she takes out her phone and flips through the pictures of Kraken I sent to her before heading over here.

"I can't believe you got her another cat tree. She's never going to walk on the floor again," Ava mutters.

Little does she know my plan to design Kraken a cat castle, with a fully functional moat. Of course, that will live at my house, so the two of them will have to come over even more than they already do.

We reach the window and are greeted by Terra, who has on a broad smile and the slightly disheveled look of a woman who has been serving drunk customers all night.

As threatened, Ava pays for her cheesy spinach crepe and my napoles crepe.

We lean our shoulders against a nearby lamppost and devour the late-night snack. It's one of the best meals I've ever had.

That is until the slight scent of cigarette smoke drifts our way along with a sharp voice saying, "Miss Bellarose? Is that you?"

Ava stiffens at my side, straightening from her casual lean and turning to face the asker.

It's a young white man, maybe early twenties, wearing black jeans and a slightly wrinkled button-up shirt. He's holding a smoldering cigarette and staring at Ava with a sharp, calculating gleam in his eye.

"Hello, Barry." She dips her head, voice gone to an inauthentic pleasant tone.

His eyes drag over her, and while I find I don't mind people ogling Ava when she's Pearl on stage, *this* attention makes me want to douse the man with arctic water full of piranhas.

"Didn't expect to see you here." Barry saunters closer. "What brings you downtown so late on a school night? Don't librarians still have work during the summer?" He chuckles at his own joke, but that's not the troublesome part of his comments.

He knows who Ava is. Where she works. At least where she works during normal—or slightly extended—business hours.

And we're standing half a block from the club where she strips some evenings.

I have a strong sense Ava doesn't want the two worlds to collide. But also, that there may be no stopping this man from doing exactly that.

"I'll still be in tomorrow. Just spending time with my friends before I head home." She waves toward me, and I try not to flinch at the label that I should find complimentary.

But aren't we more than that?

Because Ava has started to feel like my everything.

Barry's attention flicks to me, then away, then back to me with an intense scrutiny. I watch his eyes widen as he stares at my face. Having never met the man before in my life, I wonder what could be so interesting about my appearance.

Then, with the hand that isn't holding a cigarette, he taps his cheek. "You got something there."

I brush my fingers over the spot, expecting some sauce from my crepe. But my fingers come away pearly white.

Pearl's lipstick.

The man watches us with a new light in his eyes as he takes a drag of his smoke and lets it out in a slow stream. "You might want to be careful, Miss Bellarose."

"Excuse me?" There's a hard note to her voice now.

The man doesn't seem to notice. Or mind.

"This area has a lot of questionable businesses. Wouldn't want rumors spreading of you spending time here. Or, you know, working at one. CFF wouldn't like it." He saunters a step closer. "Would be terrible if people started gossiping."

Ava's chin goes stone hard, and I swear I can hear her grinding her teeth.

It takes me an extra second to realize exactly what is happening here.

This guy must've been in The Jewelry Box while Ava danced. He saw her kiss me. And now he sees Ava at my side and made the connection.

And he's using that information to threaten her job?

I step forward, too, letting my mouth widen into a grin full of teeth as I loom over the man. "It would also be terrible if the brake line in your car happened to snap and you only discovered the issue when you were driving across a bridge, careening toward the side, bursting through the guardrail, and plummeting toward the dry bottom of the canal."

"Sammy!" Ava gasps as the creep's face goes white.

"What?" I keep an innocent tone. "I thought we were talking about hypothetical situations that will never—ever—happen. Right, Barry?"

Instead of answering, the guy drops his cigarette on the sidewalk and scurries off. I stomp out the still glowing ember, disgust twisting my mouth.

Then I turn to Ava and find all the playful joy from earlier is replaced by worry.

"Who was that?" I ask softly, as if that'll lessen the blow of the answer.

"Abraham Fellow's TA. They're close. He's like a clone of the guy."

"And you think he'll make trouble for you?"

Ava crumbles up the empty wrapper from her crepe and tosses it in a nearby trash can, no longer meeting my gaze.

"I don't know. Maybe."

Well, I know one thing for sure. Barry is about to get a permanent ban from The Jewelry Box.

Chapter Thirty-Two

AVA

Going out with Sammy has had another benefit: I realized how much I missed simply hanging out with people. I tend toward introversion, and with the mental drain of my day job and picking up more Jewelry Box shifts, I got in the habit of not leaving my home for anything other than errands.

Realizing the rut I was falling into, I decide to keep my promise and ask Veronica to get drinks.

"Oh my god, that asshole!" My librarian buddy seethes with righteous indignation on my behalf as I finish telling her about my latest run-in with Fellows. This time, I'd gone to one of his advanced-level classes—per his request—with the intention of spending the period walking them through finding, vetting, and citing primary resources. Instead, I sat in the corner while Fellows went on a thirty-minute tangent, taking up more than half the class. Then, after I did my best to cover everything in my diminished time, he had the audacity to tell me he was expecting a more thorough review and suggested I come to his next class with a better lesson plan.

"There are other professors that do annoying shit, but I swear that guy is the bane of my existence."

"He's your nemesis." Veronica clinks her tequila sunrise against my heavy-on-the-gin gimlet. "I had one of those at my first job. The guy would assign these super research-intensive projects to freshmen, a lot of whom were first-generation so they were just trying to figure college out, and he wouldn't even invite me to come talk to them! The ones who did find their way into the library were in total panic mode. More than one literally broke down crying in my office because they were so stressed out by the guy." She shakes her head with a grimace.

"You get it." I cheers her with my drink and take a long, satisfying sip.

Bitching with someone who understands is one of the most relaxing pastimes. Once again, I feel a tug of regret that I chose to work at a place with an almost non-existent staff. I'd love to be able to just pop my head into Veronica's office to relieve a bit of the day's frustration.

As if reading my mind, my friend bumps her shoulder against mine. "I passed your resume along to the head instruction librarian, Jeanette. She was impressed and said you'd still have to come in for a short interview, but pretty much told me the job is yours if you want it. Right now, everyone else is planning on covering the opening, but I know they don't want to be spread thin if they don't have to."

Goddess, the offer is tempting. But I still can't get past the guilt that I'd be leaving the CFF library in even worse shape if I left now.

Please let them be interviewing some quality director candidates, I beg the Dark One. If I knew a director was coming in, I could explore this decision with so much less stress. If I chose to stay, I'd know my workload would be lighter. If I chose to leave, I'd know the library would have the same number of staff it's had the past year.

"I'll think about it. You said she's not due for...?"

"Two more months. And I swear I'll only bring it up once every time I see you." Veronica sips on her straw with a teasing twinkle in her eye that has me chuckling.

Wanting to forget about my job nonsense, I happily listen to Veronica regale me with the juiciest gossip from her much larger institution. Academia may be full of book-smart people, but they do some ridiculous shit that's reality TV-show worthy. At one point she gets off her stool to try reenacting a literal brawl two professors had over lab equipment. The sloppy fake swings she takes, and my inability to stop giggling alerts me that maybe I should have stopped at my second drink and eaten more than the half a plate of bacon cheese fries.

We are both officially drunk.

Which, of course, is why we both order rides, go home, take some aspirin, and go straight to bed.

Ha! Not a chance.

Arms wrapped around each other's waists, we stumble next door to a karaoke bar where we get our own room and spend the next hour serenading each other with our favorite boy band songs and drinking cheap beer. At some point, Veronica's girlfriend calls her, then shows up soon after with a smirk.

"This is my Jojo, and I love her!" Veronica declares when the black-haired, tan-skinned woman strolls into the room. The librarian launches herself at the new arrival, peppering her girlfriend's high cheekbones with sloppy kisses. Jojo hooks Veronica around the waist with one arm and raises the other to wave at me.

"Hi. You must be Ava."

"At your service," I say in my most regal voice as I dip in a low, wobbly curtsy that earns a cackling laugh from Veronica.

Jojo's smile is kind and resigned. "Looks like you need a ride home, too."

"No, no," I assure her, stumbling my way off the low stage. "I'll call my Squid."

Veronica's beautiful girlfriend gives me an odd look, but I forget about it as I dig through my purse for my phone and text Sammy to come pick me up. While we wait for him to arrive, Jojo laughingly lets Veronica drag her onto the stage, and the two of them sing a perfect rendition of "WAP."

"Did someone have a little too much fun?" The question sounds next to my ear in a teasing rasp, and I turn to grin up at the handsome Squid who has magically appeared.

"My Sammy!" I throw my arms around his neck and kiss him deeply, tasting a spike of his peanut butter lust even as I breathe in his fresh rain scent.

I love my Sammy, I think to myself, but don't say out loud because my mouth is busy kissing him.

"That's Samuel Reyes." Veronica's attempt to whisper to Jojo fails because she's still holding a microphone. I pause our making out and spy a dazed smile on the Squid's face. "He's very rich. And good in bed. But Ava doesn't care about any of that." Next to me, Sammy snorts, and I lean into his chest. "All she cares about is that he got her a cat." The librarian pouts at her girlfriend. "You never got me a cat."

"Time to go home," Jojo announces.

Veronica and I groan, but eventually let ourselves be herded out of the bar. After tearfully hugging each other goodbye, my library friend climbs into her girlfriend's waiting car.

"Did you bring the Mustang?" I ask Sammy as I wrap my arms around his waist and kiss the hollow dip at the base of his neck.

Mmm. Peanut butter.

"I-I...yes. Gods, Ava." Sammy pinches my chin and tilts my head back so I can see his deep blue eyes. "I need to drive. No sexy kisses."

I jut out my lower lip and he groans.

"No. Fucking hell dimensions." Sammy rests his forehead against mine. "You look too fucking cute when you do that."

"I'm not cute," I inform him. "I'm a sexy stripper."

"You are sexy," he agrees. "And cute." He kisses my forehead. "And drunk. So I'm going to take you back to my place and tuck you into bed."

"That is *not* sexy," I grumble as he leads me down the street to where the beautiful blue convertible is parked. The wind in my hair and the rush of the fast car distract me as we drive. I raise my hands up like I'm on a roller coaster and only bring them down when Sammy asks if I want to drink some water from my amazing blue cup.

The cup Sammy got for me.

I love my Sammy.

But I'm too busy sipping on my straw to say it out loud.

When we get to his giant house, Sammy parks the car and leads me inside, where Kraken sprints up to us, her little paws skittering on the floor as she runs. I pick her up and press her soft body against my cheek until she squirms to get down.

Though he promised to take me to bed, Sammy guides me to the kitchen first and arranges me on a stool at the island. There I watch him dice an onion, peppers, and a tomato. As he sautés the veggies in a pan,

Sammy cracks a few eggs in a bowl and whisks them. The savory smell teases my nose, my mouth fills with saliva, and I lean forward to watch him work. His forearms flex as he slips the eggs into the pan and stirs to scramble everything together. With a smooth slide, he transfers the steaming meal to a plate and sets the food in front of me.

I devour the delicious offering under his watchful eye.

Only when I'm fed, watered, and changed into one of Sammy's T-shirts does he finally fulfill his promise to tuck me in.

"I'm totally down to fuck," I murmur as my eyes close, lids heavy with happiness.

"Raincheck." Sammy's lips brush the corner of my jaw. "I'm beat."

"Okay," I sigh, my voice fading off the end of the breath. "Only because you're tired."

His chuckle is a soothing balm against my eardrums after the loud karaoke music. Everything about him soothes and comforts me. Makes me feel safe and cared for.

I love my Sammy.

But I drift to sleep before I can say it out loud.

Chapter Thirty-Three

SAMMY

Ava is groggy and grumpy after her night of drinking, glaring at me through squinted eyelids when I attempt to wake her gently.

"Leave me alone," she growls like a pissed-off honey badger.

Will she attack me? I'd probably enjoy it.

"I'd love to keep you in my bed all day," I inform her while pressing kisses to where her shoulder peeks out of the shirt I lent her. "But you've got work. And I know how involved it is for you to call in sick."

Her colorful, overstuffed schedule lives in my memory. Then a worry tugs away my teasing.

"Is this more than a hangover?" I keep my voice hushed to avoid causing her more pain. "Do you have a migraine?"

"No," she groans, rolling away from me and toward the edge of the bed. "I drank my brew before going out." She scowls at me over her shoulder, hair a tangled mess and eye makeup smudged under her eyes. "This is a normal hangover. And I know I look like death. And you're over there looking..." She gives a vague wave toward me.

I glance down at myself, taking in my lack of a shirt and loose gym shorts. Normally I'd be dressed for the day by now, but a part of me half hoped Ava would decide to call off work and stay in bed. Then I could snuggle in with her. But that domestic fantasy is not to be.

"I'm looking...?"

Her delicious mouth digs deep frown lines into her lush face. "Shut up. You know how you look."

"Do I?" I drag a hand down my torso and play with the waistband of my shorts. When I was in college, I had a six-pack, but those things are hard to maintain if you want to eat like a normal person. Still, I do swim a few—hundred—laps in the pool every other day. "Are you trying to say that I'm...bang-able?"

Honestly, Ava could say that I'm mildly attractive, and I would keel over from happiness.

She heaves herself off the bed with a groan and shuffles toward the bathroom, growling over her shoulder. "If I were in the mood to bang, then sure. But since I'm not, you're just aggravatingly hot, and I need to not look at your fuckable face."

I'm tempted to ask how I'm not currently bange-able, yet still fuckable, but decide to give the woman I love some space while she recovers from her drunken karaoke fest. Reclining on the bed, I stare at the ceiling with a goofy smile as I recall how tipsy and happy she was last night. And how I was the one she called to pick her up and take care of her even though she could just as easily have called an Uber back to her condo.

Though I do have her cat here.

Speaking of which, the little feline must be getting hungry. Wonder where Kraken has snuck off—

"Ah!" Ava's yelp shoots me off the bed and into the bathroom where I'm briefly mesmerized by her naked, wet body, fully visible through the glass door of the shower. Then I remember her sound of distress and shake away the need to insert my consciousness into the droplets that are slipping down the slopes of her breasts to catch on her pert nipples.

"What's wrong?" I rasp, proud of myself for managing a full sentence, even if it only consisted of two words.

"Cat!" she snaps, pointing to the wet tiles at her feet. Dragging my eyes downward—fuck, every inch of her is soaked—I finally reach her toes where I spy a sopping wet kitten batting at the shower spray.

Don't laugh. Don't even smile. Be a firm disciplinarian.

"Naughty Kraken." My scolding tone could use some work as I stroll forward, open the door, and scoop up the wet cat. "Let your mama shower and peace. Can't you see how naked and wet and sexy she is?"

"Sammy." Ava grinds my name out, and damn all the gods I only get *more* turned on. And hell, I can see her skin pinking with magic. She knows how much I want her right now. Still, I manage to retreat with my dripping cargo.

"I'll dry this monster off and make you breakfast." After announcing the peace offering, I stride out of the bathroom, using the retreat to tattoo the gorgeous image of a showering Ava into my brain. It is now a core memory I need for survival.

As I call on my Elemental power, the normal rocking wave sensation slow to draw up through my chest when I'm so thoroughly happy, I swear Kraken's meow is resentful when I ease the water from her fur.

The little feline is a Squid, I swear.

When Ava enters the kitchen a half hour later, she's much more put together. Only the lines of strain around her eyes indicate her head still hurts. Even though I want to kiss her and fill the air between us with bantering and teasing, I bite my tongue. That's not what she needs from me right now. After a bland breakfast of eggs and toast that she only eats half of—probably slightly nauseous too—Ava pushes off her stool.

"Do you mind driving me to work? Or dropping me off at my car? I left it parked near the bar." She rubs her temple, face scrunched. "Gods, I probably have a ticket."

"I can drive you. No problem." And I really want to, but I also have another option that might bring a happy shine to her miserable morning. "Let me grab my keys."

I jog to the front hall, scoop up my keys, plus an extra set, and slip on a hoodie I left in the hall closet. There's no need for me to visit the build site near Ava's condo today, so I'd planned to stay home and work on designs for Yasmin and her BDSM dungeon. Maybe when Ava gets home she can give me some input.

I trip over that thought.

Ava coming home. As if my place is hers.

And I realize I want it to be. Badly. Before Ava, I was anxious about letting anyone new into my space. But now I don't even think of it as mine. I want it to be ours.

Not too fast. Don't scare her.

Still, I'm jittery with excitement when I return to the kitchen in time to see Ava scratching Kraken under the chin and muttering apologies for yelling earlier.

"Ready to go?" I gesture toward the garage entrance.

Ava grabs her bag—look at that, most of her stuff is already here—and follows me. But when we step into the garage, she stumbles to a stop. I pretend nonchalance. Not letting on that I'm holding my breath.

"Do you...is that...why do you have the same car?" Ava's expression is pure confusion as her eyes flick from my royal blue Mustang to an identical one parked right beside it. The one that got delivered yesterday. The one she was too drunk to notice last night.

"Well, you see, this one," I pat the hood of the closest muscle car, "is mine. And that one," I point at the twin convertible, "is yours."

She loved driving mine so much, why not get my girl her own?

At least that's what my love-drenched mind had thought a week ago when I called the dealership about it.

But now I'm looking at her frown, staring at the downward curve of her lips, and losing confidence for every second that passes where the corners don't tilt up.

"I—I'm not joking," I swear, holding out a set of keys with an octopus keychain dangling from them. "It's yours."

Ava raises a hand, but not to accept the gift. Instead, she presses her fingers against her closed eyelids, as if her head is in even more pain. "I don't want a car, Sammy."

Dread is a mucky swamp in my gut.

"I thought you liked it." My voice is weak with worry. I messed up. I'm messing this up. "That you *would* like it."

Ava lets out a sigh that sends her shoulders drooping more than her hangover pain already had them.

"Is that why you bought it for me?" Her eyes are still closed as she asks. "Just because you thought I would like it?"

"Yes?" The word tilts up into a question because now I'm not even sure. Of course it's just because I thought she'd like it. No ulterior motive whatsoever.

Definitely not bribery to get her to fall in love with me.

"We're going to have to talk about this later," she says with another soul-crushing sigh. "When I can think. And when I'm not about to be late for work."

"Ava—"

Her hand wave cuts me off. "Please, Sammy. I just need to go to work."

"Okay." I nod. Too many times. And as I drive a quiet Ava to the job I know will stress her out even more, I try not to panic over her words.

"We're going to have to talk..."

Talk.

This isn't something I can buy or gift my way out of. Not something I can fix with money.

Ava's love isn't for sale.

And I think I just destroyed my shot at earning it.

Chapter Thirty-Four

AVA

When the provost sends me an email about meeting in the next hour, I try not to curse him at the last minute nature of the request on a day I'm sporting a hangover. I would be in a lot worse shape if Sammy hadn't fed and hydrated me, but there's still a fuzzy ache in my brain that I really want to use my healing magic to dispel.

A migraine would be worse, I remind myself.

That is, if I have one. And I'm not sure that I would with how full my internal cauldron is. Turns out Sammy thinks I'm sexy even when I'm a drunken mess. Or maybe it was that shower encounter that filled me up. He definitely wasn't turned on in the garage when I was too confused and muddled to even think of accepting his gift. A car? Gods, the guy needs to put some boundaries on his spending.

Still, I'm flush with magic, and I rarely find myself without a supply of power nowadays.

Maybe I should get in the habit of using it more often. For myself and for others.

I decide to brew myself some hangover curing tea at lunch, and I'll forgive the provost if this is to discuss the logistics of having library director candidates visit campus. I would be happy to offer a thorough tour of the facilities and host introduction sessions with the staff.

Whatever is needed as long as we finally get the position filled with a qualified candidate.

I respond back that I'll see him in an hour, then try to get as much done as I can before needing to jog across campus to reach the provost's office.

I knock on the closed door and hear a muffled, "Come in."

When I step into the impressive-sized office, I'm surprised to see that in addition to Dr. Hampton, the provost, there's another person in the room.

Abraham Fellows sits in a wing-back chair in front of Hampton's desk. The history professor eyes me with a narrow stare and a sense of smugness.

Is he on the library director hiring committee?

I feel like I'm missing something, and there's also a sourness in my gut warning me I'm not going to like where this meeting is headed.

"Ms. Bellarose. Sit down." Dr. Hampton waves me toward a rigid wooden chair, a much less comfortable choice to the seat Fellows claimed. "We have a concerning topic to discuss."

Curse of the Dark One. Are there no candidates? Are we looking at another semester without anyone taking the lead in the library?

I keep these panicked questions to myself and settle on the hard chair, wishing I'd arrived before Fellows so I could get the cushy seat.

Hampton leans back in his plush leather chair and focuses entirely on me. "It's been brought to my attention that you have a second job," he says.

The topic, so different than the one I thought we were here to discuss, takes a moment to settle in my brain. But when I grasp it, my first thought is *How did he find out about the university position?*

As I try to figure out how to explain that all I have is a tentative job offer that I wasn't truly considering because it's a temporary position, the provost must interpret my silence as confusion. Or evasion.

"Your other job...at the prostitution club," he explains with a terse sigh, conveying his utter disappointment in my apparent sexual proclivities and stained moral character.

Did he just...call The Jewelry Box a prostitution club? Yasmin will love that.

Understanding settles over me, and I firm my jaw to hold back an aggravated sigh.

And so the time has come.

A part of me always expected this to happen. Only, I thought I would be confronted while in my Pearl getup. That the condemnation would happen while I was surrounded by other dancers and Yasmin's security guards.

Not on a Thursday morning alone in an office with a man—two men —who have misinterpreted the type of sex work I perform. And why is Fellows even here?

No matter.

One thing I've perfected after working at the club is how to keep an impassive expression on my face no matter what. Unless one of these men pulls a kitten out of his jacket, they're fucked if they think I'll break.

"Did you just call me a prostitute?" I ask, voice cold as ice.

Hampton straightens in his chair and clears his throat. "I'm telling you the facts as I know them."

"What facts?" I offer an exaggerated glance around the room, as if expecting to find the evidence he's basing his conclusions on. "All I've heard is that you think I have a second job as a prostitute. Which I don't."

And that's not even a lie. Even if the provost considered stripping to be prostitution, I have never taken any money from my position at The Jewelry Box. Check Yasmin's books, and my name will never appear there. Check my tax records and the only income I have listed is from College of Freedom and Faith.

For this exact reason.

"Really?" Fellows smug voice chimes in, and I turn to face his triumphant smirk. "Then how do you explain this?" He thrusts his phone forward, a video playing on the screen.

From the tiny speakers plays the chorus of one of my favorite songs to dance to. "Black Magic Woman." *Of course*, this *would be the song.* On the screen I watch a masked Pearl perform a perfect Bird of Paradise. I'm inverted on the pole, legs in an angled split that sends one behind my back and through my looped arms, all while I spin.

Nice. Took me three months to get that right.

The video ends, and I flick my gaze up to meet Fellows' intense stare, and I fight the urge to vomit.

Not because I'm scared or anxious.

But because I taste cheap chocolate on my tongue that lets me know he's turned on.

Fellows is getting off on the fact that he's seen me close to naked, and now he gets to use that to punish me. No doubt he expects me to burst into tears and beg for forgiveness. To plead for them to keep quiet about my extracurriculars and promise to be a good girl. And these two men will go home high on their sense of self-importance and moral superiority.

But they didn't take one thing into account.

They don't have power over me.

At least not as much as they believe, and I'm not about to give them any more. Not when I have fury fueling me and the best poker face in the city of Phoenix.

"To be clear," I say, my voice sharper than they've ever heard from the kind, helpful librarian, "you went to a strip club, saw a blonde woman on stage, videotaped her without her consent, and then thought it was appropriate to show this video to me? Your coworker?" I tick the offenses off on my fingers, then face the provost in time to see the color draining from his cheeks. "Don't we have a morality clause in our contract that is supposed to protect me from this?"

Fellows splutters at my side, his bobbing mouth searching for words. "B—but it's you!"

"That woman and I are two different people." Pearl gives nothing to anyone. Meanwhile, Ava Bellarose has been bending over backwards to support this administration for far too long. "I came to this meeting expecting to discuss the ongoing issue of the empty library director position. Not to be shown pornographic images professors illegally obtained." I scoop my bag off the floor and straighten my more-than-knee-length skirt. "In the future, I will not attend a meeting with Professor Fellows unless an HR representative is present. Preferably my lawyer as well. And I suggest you prioritize properly staffing the college's library rather than alienating the few employees you do have."

"This—she—you can't—" Fellow's brain seems to be malfunctioning in the face of a confident, rather than cowed, woman. "Richard! You can't let her just—just say that!"

Richard. Hah. Of course. They're probably golf buddies. I wonder if they talked about this meeting before it even happened. Maybe had a circle jerk at the idea of setting me in my place.

They didn't expect me to come from a place of power. To be willing to piss them off. Maybe lose my job.

But that's exactly what I am willing to do. Even more so because I know others can't.

If I get fired, then I'll take Veronica's offer. Or maybe I'll start collecting the cash that gets tossed at my feet every Tuesday. I have options, and they're a set of six-inch heels allowing me to tower over these men.

Not every person who comes into this office has the same man-killer shoes as me.

But hopefully, after today, these men will think twice about underestimating and bullying a normally friendly woman.

"Abraham, be quiet." The provost hushes Fellows with a furious glare then turns a weakly apologetic smile my way. "I didn't mean to make you uncomfortable, Ms. Bellarose. This has all been a misunderstanding."

I give him the same face I offered to Sammy when he held up hundreds of dollars to attract my attention.

You are nothing to me, my expression says, and I see the withering of his last speck of confidence as it hits him.

"I have work to do." I stride purposefully toward the door. At the last moment, I throw a parting comment over my shoulder. "And an email to HR to write."

Chapter Thirty-Five

SAMMY

Ava's text to meet her at Land of Ice Cream and Snow is short and leaves me feeling like I'm about to get my heart broken.

Is she doing it here so I can drown my sorrows in frozen dairy while getting comforted by my cousin?

It's not a terrible plan, other than the fact that I'm convinced we're perfect for each other, and we should never break up even when we both perish and travel on to a death dimension.

Small things like that.

"What's with the pacing?" Harley, Quinn's older sister, watches me from her seat on a barstool as she licks a scoop of Fiery Goddess in a sugar cone. August based the spicy-sweet flavor off his love for Quinn, and it has a permanent spot on the menu.

"Nothing." I try to laugh nonchalantly but end up sounding like I belong in an asylum. "Just…had too much coffee."

And bought my girlfriend a fifty-thousand dollar car to make her love me.

"Right." Harley brushes her red curls over her shoulder to better converse with her sister, who's busy typing on her laptop. Quinn works as an accountant, remotely most days, and will often set up in an empty seat in her partner's Ice Cream Shop. "Do you know what's wrong with the twitchy Squid?"

Quinn flicks her eyes to me then back to her computer. "No. But I bet it has to do with Ava."

Even the sound of her name is beautiful.

"Oh." Harley returns her taunting eyes to me. "Did you mess up? Is this pre-break-up pacing?"

I glare at the evil Pyro and thank all the gods that the bell above the door chimes and in strolls the witch I've been waiting for.

At the sight of her in a form-fitting pencil skirt and a starched blouse buttoned to her collar, I'm ready to become a puddle at the toes of her sensible Mary Janes. Her high ponytail swishes as she scans the shop, her eyes alighting on mine.

When she smiles, I let out a breath I didn't realize I was holding.

She wouldn't smile like that if she was going to cut me out of her life, right?

Ava approaches me, but it's not fast enough, so I stride to meet her halfway and wrap my arms tight around her waist.

Let me hold you while I can.

"How's it going?" I ask, trying not to sound like I'm needy, wanting to pry into her skull and collect all her inner thoughts.

Ava presses a quick kiss to my mouth and huffs out a frustrated noise. "It's been a triple scoop day. I need some sugar, stat."

That I can do. Ava lets me keep my arm around her waist as we head to the granite counter where August waits with a welcoming smile. Ava doesn't argue with me when I pull out my card to purchase her waffle cone of Death by Minty Chocolate, but she does unearth some cash from her bag and stuffs it in the tip jar. The small gesture has me wanting to take her home, strip her down, give her five orgasms, then massage her feet.

But I guess I can wait until she finishes her ice cream.

And as much as it worries me, I want her to tell me what put the tight lines of stress around her eyes. What kind of day requires three scoops?

We settle at a booth, away from Harley's curious smirk.

"Want to tell me what happened?" I ask, proud of how calm my voice sounds.

And in between licks of her large cone, Ava relates the horrific meeting she had with that asshole professor and the provost. It's a good thing that I am sitting on the inside of the booth with Ava blocking my exit or else I might've stormed out of this ice cream shop, driven across the city to her campus, and doused the entire department with a wave of saltwater rage.

How dare they treat Ava that way? How dare they treat any woman that way?

"That is the most disgusting thing I have ever heard. What can I do?" I clench and release my fists. "I just...I can't fathom you having to go back and work with those despicable human beings."

"I haven't decided what I'm gonna do yet. All I decided was that I was taking an early day and getting an ice cream cone and meeting you." Ava presses into my side, her plush body molding to mine and spiking my arousal. "You being here, that's what I need from you. Thank you for coming."

I think about the stress that meeting must have put Ava under and how it probably fueled her natural propensity towards migraines.

Was the amount of poultice she drank last night enough? Did the pain break through, and she's on the cusp of hours of agony?

"Of course. I'll come whenever you ask. How's your head?" I let my hand settle on the base of her neck and press my fingers into tense muscles. She lets out a happy little sigh as I massage the area, but then gives me a soft smile and slowly shakes her head.

"Don't worry. I don't have a migraine. Not yet"

"And we can make sure that you don't have one." I kiss her forehead. "We'll fuel you up tonight, get you drinking a whole bunch of tea, and you'll feel fine in the morning. And we can brainstorm what you wanna do about those fuckwads." Fury rattles through my body. "One option is I buy the whole college and fire that guy. Or I can build you your own library. From the ground up. Make all your own rules. Full of books and stripper poles."

Ava's gray eyes rest on me with a furrow between her brows, her lips ticking upwards. "Sammy, do you know why I texted you the moment I got out of that meeting?"

"So, I could feed you ice cream and fund an elaborate revenge plan, obviously." Which I will do. I will pour millions of dollars into making Ava happy and comfortable at her job.

But the witch slowly shakes her head. "I didn't come to you because I wanted you to fix the problem. Definitely not with your money." Her hand finds mine, squeezing like a small hug. "I sought you out because you make me feel better."

Yes. The stress. She needs magic.

"Because I'm a horny battery for you." I try to focus on how hot she is in her librarian get-up, a trace of cream on her lips. There's a stirring in my chest and below my belt.

"No." Ava rubs her thumb over my knuckles. "Because I love you."

The ice cream shop goes entirely, eerily quiet.

Oh. I see what this is.

I'm dreaming.

Or maybe I'm hallucinating. I did buy a lot of catnip for Kraken. Maybe I inhaled some of it, and now I'm living out the most glorious fantasy that my brain can come up with. That has to be the case because if it's not then that means that Ava Bellarose just told me that she loves me.

Me.

"I...don't understand."

Now my fantasy Ava is frowning, and I regret saying that out loud.

"You don't understand what I mean when I say that I love you?"

"I...yes." But even as I say this, I draw closer to her, tentacle-ing my arms around her body, slipping my foot between hers, fisting my fingers in her clothes. Trying my best not to let this dream get away from me.

How could she love me? I haven't done enough. Haven't given her enough.

"When I say I love you," Ava speaks slowly, concern clouding her stormy eyes, "I mean I love you. I mean when something big happens in my life, good or bad, you're the first person I want to tell about it. It means when I'm angry or scared or uncomfortable, I know that you can make me feel better. It means that I don't know what's gonna happen next in my life, but I want you to be there with me when I figure it out. It means that you're my... You're my favorite person, Sammy. I love my mom, and I love my friends, but I'm *in* love with you. It's an active thing that I currently exist in and want to exist in every single day with you." Her callused hands cup my face, and she appears truly worried. "Does that make sense? I'm sorry, I didn't think I'd have to explain it. You love people. People love you. You know that, right? You know that people—me included—love you, right?"

"Of course!" In theory. I'm breathing very heavy, and I'm worried I might be hurting Ava with how tightly I'm clutching her. But if I was, she would tell me because she is brutally honest with me most times.

And the way she just mapped out her love for me, that was brutal.

That was *carve past my rib cage grip my heart in her perfect hands* brutal.

I might die.

A good death. A "happy smile on my face as I lie in my coffin" death.

It's just that I don't know if I can survive the amount of elation that is coursing through my body. My magic is fueled by sadness, and I accept that I will never be able to manipulate water again in my life because how could I ever experience any type of negative emotion again when I have Ava Bellarose's love.

But again, I am probably high on catnip.

"You can't get high on catnip, Sammy."

"Did I say that out loud?"

"Yes. And there's something that you did *not* say out loud. And it's okay if you haven't said it because you don't feel it. I don't expect you to tell me that you love me just because I told you that I loved you. I do want you to know that I don't expect it as an exchange. And if you need time—"

"I love you!" I bellow, so loud she flinches back. But I can't dial down the volume on my voice. "Oh, my Gods! I fucking love you, Ava Bellarose! What the hell?" I'm panting now, feverish to the point I might need some magical healing. "What in all the hell dimensions?! You thought *you* were going to be more obsessed with me than *I* am with *you*?" I choke on a scoff. "That's ridiculous!"

I crash my mouth into hers, because how dare she believe for a moment that she loves me more than I could love her. I don't care if I've made this woman up in my mind. I am the ridiculous over-the-top one in this relationship, and she will not take that crown from me.

My kiss is frenzied as I press her deep into the booth seat. She tastes of mint and chocolate and sweet waffle cone. She smells of eucalyptus and seduction and mine. I delve my tongue into the woman that I love. I press the tips of my fingers into her starched clothes and soft skin. I twine my hand in her silky ponytail. I give her every piece of me, filling her with the magic of love-fueled lust. And I look forward to doing this every single day forever.

"Sammy!" August bellows loud enough to pierce my horny love haze. Reluctantly I let off kissing a bewildered witch to glance at my cousin where he scowls at me from behind the front counter. "Don't even think about having sex in my shop!"

I glance around and remember I'm in public. I'm in reality.

And Ava just said she loved me.

"Yeah!" Harley points a mock glare at us. "Only August and Quinn get to do that!"

Quinn groans. "I told you that in *confidence*."

Harley smirks. "Yeah. *Confident* that I'd share it at the opportune moment."

Chapter Thirty-Six

AVA

I quit my job.

Well, I handed in my two weeks' notice.

Okay, I actually gave them a month's advance notice that I was leaving, but that was mainly because I wanted to give the administration a decent amount of time to get their collective heads out of their asses in order to start the interview process for my replacement. And hopefully the replacements for all the empty positions. And I wanted to help Rodrigo brainstorm a way for the library to move forward while it was so understaffed. I could tell the man was frustrated that he would be the only one left, but when I explained my reasoning, some of his animosity lessened.

That's the best I can hope for.

After I handed in my notice, the next day funny enough, I got offered the position of Director of the Library. It would come with a pay raise and a signing bonus. Isn't that fantastic?

I politely declined.

It's one thing to work at an underfunded, understaffed library. Honestly, that's most libraries.

But when the administration decided the best use of their time was digging into my personal life and scolding me for it, I had to admit defeat.

No. Not defeat.

I had to admit that the institution had toxicity at its core, and there was no way I was going to change it without destroying myself in the process.

My mental health is worth more than my pride.

And now I am set up to take over the instruction librarian position at Sammy's alma mater when the current worker goes on maternity leave. I know that it's not a permanent solution. I know that while I'm working one job, I'll need to be applying for others. But I still think this is the healthiest move. Plus I'll get the chance to explore a different kind of library environment, and I can decide if I want to stay with small colleges or possibly work at larger universities. And maybe I'll even get the chance to stay at the university. They could potentially have job openings, seeing as how their library has a much larger staff and they are proactive about filling empty roles.

In the meantime, I'm not gonna be particularly worried about money. And not because I'm dating a millionaire—although I bet that if I suddenly found myself without enough funds to pay my rent, Sammy would find a way to sneak money to my landlord.

But no, the reason that I won't worry about money is because I've started accepting the tips that I earn at The Jewelry Box.

When I told Yasmin that I was quitting my strict job, she informed me that she then expected me to start pocketing the money I earned while working on the stage. She made a good point about it being honestly earned, and the fact that I haven't been accepting it could be rubbing some of the other dancers the wrong way.

I never wanted any of my coworkers to think that I thought I was above stripping for a living. My reasoning was always that I didn't want to risk losing my day job, and with the lust fueling my magic I *was* getting payment, in a way. I thought taking the money was taking more than I deserved.

Yasmin disavowed me of that notion. Now I'm finding out that I have actually been earning a lot of money every week. Even just dancing on Tuesday nights and occasionally Saturday.

But I have made Sammy swear not to throw any money or jewelry or anything else on the stage for me. We are not going to be in the same situation that he is with August, stuffing his cousin's tip jar every chance he gets.

The Squid agreed, but that means he shows up and cheers the loudest and insists on buying me regular ice cream cones. Also, he spoils our cat to a ridiculous proportion.

But now I try to spoil him.

"What is it?" Sammy asks when I wake him up with a kiss and a small gift box on his chest. We are in his bed, a luxurious king-sized monstrosity that makes me never want to sleep in my condo again.

"It's called a birthday gift, old man." I prop my head on my hand to stare down at the surprised Squid.

"How did you know?"

"August." I reach out to finger-comb his hair away from his face. "Would've thought you'd be going on and on about it for weeks. Your special day. Blow jobs every hour on the hour."

His blue eyes widen. "Do I get that?"

I smirk and flick the package he hasn't touched. "How about you open this gift first." My snarky tone is a shield to cover up nerves. Maybe the present is a bad idea.

But I want to show Sammy I listen to him. And that I care.

With careful fingers, the Squid slides the lid off the box and stares at the contents. His unusual silence has me babbling to fill the void. "I thought about getting you a strand of pearls, but you probably still have that first one," I joke. "Thought this might be better. Maybe. I don't know. Just, I talked to my mom and told her about you and how I love you. And she's still got all these connections in New York, so when I asked her about instruments, she connected me with a guy who makes custom pieces." Sammy still isn't saying anything, and I'm starting to panic. "But it's nothing. I can return it."

I go to grab the gift, but it's gone, Sammy holding it away from my snatching fingers.

"Ava." My name is a rasp in his voice. "You got me a harmonica?"

Not just any harmonica. A one-of-a-kind, gold-plated harmonica with a squid design etched into the metal and the initials SR on the underside.

"I know it's not your grandfather's." I lie on my back and stare up at the ceiling, unable to meet his eyes. "But I wanted to give you something that meant something. Because I take from you all the time. And I just want you to know I'm sorry that I use you." Then I turn my head to meet his eyes. "I love you. And know that if someone hurts you, on the outside"—my fingers trail the scar on his arm—"or on the inside"—I jerk my chin toward the gift—"I want to be the one healing you."

Without warning, he rolls on top of me, pinning me to the bed with his body and kiss and eventually his hard cock. Sammy whispers his love against my magic-infused skin over and over. And when we lay in a tangle of sweaty sheets and post-orgasm bliss, he plays a Happy Birthday to himself on his new gift, a wide grin messing up some of the notes.

And a few days later, as I stroll onto The Jewelry Box main stage, wearing my mask because I still prefer the slim bit of privacy it provides me, I feel his eyes on me. I glance to the VIP section, but while it is full of people, I don't see my Squid. I scan the entire club and finally pick him out by the bar. Sammy sits with Rafael, and he chats with Cat, but he stares at me. When our eyes meet, he holds up his drink in a toast and blows me a kiss.

I stick out my tongue at him in response, which earns me a grin.

And that's all I want in payment from him.

Epilogue

AVA

A Few Months Later

Sammy holds my hand harder than necessary as we approach the front door of Damien's house. The man called us with an urgent request I couldn't say no to.

One I didn't *want* to say no to.

"You sure you want to do this?" Sammy asks, as if he can read my mind.

I squeeze his hand back and knock on the front door. "Definitely."

The entry swings wide to reveal Marisol. The teenager has on a brave face, but there's a watery quality to her eyes as if she's been crying or is about to.

"Thank the gods," she heaves out the prayer. "She's in the kitchen."

I follow behind the teenager, tugging Sammy along with me, and we come on an odd scene. A white woman with waist-length brunette hair sits on the kitchen island. Damien stands beside her, holding a blood-soaked rag against her arm.

An arm that has a long piece of metal piercing it.

"Ava is here," Marisol announces, hurrying to the woman's side. "I'm sorry, Silvia."

The woman looks at Marisol with a distracted kind of curiosity. "Why do you keep apologizing for something that's not your fault?" There's no sign of pain in her voice. In fact, her tone is relatively flat. "That's a bad habit."

"You tripped on my bag," Marisol wails before burying her face in her hands.

Silvia's eyes widen a touch. "Damien, I think your sister needs a hug. From you. I'm not good at hugs."

"I don't." Marisol sucks in a few breaths, clearly trying to calm herself. "I'm good."

Damien keeps the bloody rag in place and turns his own wild eyes on us. "Ava. Your magic. Can you do anything?"

I can feel Sammy's cloud of worry beside me, but I let go of his hand and cross the kitchen. I've never studied anatomy, so I don't know if the metal has punctured anything important, but I can instinctively tell where the woman is injured and that the bleeding will increase rapidly once the metal is removed.

"Hi." I smile up at the woman. "I'm Ava Bellarose. A witch with healing specialty." I assume Damien bringing up my magic means this woman is in on the whole mystical world thing.

"Silvia Harlow. Stoner. Though that doesn't seem to help me from injuring myself with the element."

"Maybe if you kept your space more organized, this wouldn't have happened." Damien growls the words, sounding more intense than I've ever heard the man.

Silvia gives him a blank look. "I know where everything is. That's all the organization I need."

"Yeah, you'll never lose track of your materials when they're lodged in your flesh!"

"Marisol, your brother needs a beer," Silvia says. "To calm his nerves. He's experiencing hysterics."

"I'm not hysterical!" he hollers. The kitchen sink turns on without warning, the aggressive spray complementing the Squid's seething.

My bet: Damien is anger-induced.

I bite my lip, suddenly wildly interested in getting to know Silvia better.

But first, let's make sure she doesn't bleed out.

"I can help," I say, taking control of the conversation. "Do you have a marker?"

Marisol turns the water off then yanks open a drawer and pulls out a Sharpie, brandishing it my way. I accept it with gentle fingers and sneak in between Damien and Silvia. He seems intent on staying close to her side.

"Since you're a Stoner, we shouldn't have to worry about infection. We'll just slide out the metal, and I'll set to work healing the muscles, veins, and skin. Okay?"

"Yes," Silvia says without a hint of wariness in her voice.

I lean in close to get a better look at the wound. It seems to be a smooth piece of metal, which is good.

"Are you able to tell if there are any splinters?" I ask. "Or when we take it out, would you be able to sense if there's any piece we missed?"

She nods. "I'll know. I would have taken this out myself, but I thought these two would faint at the sight." The Stoner tilts her head toward the Cortez siblings and Damien scowls in response.

"You need a healer," he insists.

She huffs out a breath and gives me a go-ahead wave.

Knowing her skin must be tender, I'm gentle as I sketch symbols around the injury. "Can you take the cloth away and wash off the blood quickly?" I ask Damien. "I just need to write a few more." There's already gore on my fingers, but I need relatively clean skin.

Jaw tight, Damien nods and removes the cloth. He twists his wrist, drawing a stream of water from the sink. Then, with gentle wave motions, the Squid cleanses the woman's skin, the hovering orb of water turning pink as her blood mixes in with the liquid.

More blood immediately starts to seep from the punctures, but I write faster, surrounding the wound in witch's language.

"Okay. Ready. Do you want to magic it out, or do you want us to slide it free?" I ask my patient.

Silvia sighs. "Damien can do it if he has the stomach for it."

The man's strong fingers pinch the end. "Tell me when."

I rub my hands, feeling the tingle of magic from what Sammy did to me in bed this morning. "Go."

The Squid slips the metal out with a sucking noise, Silvia lets out a slight gasp, and I push my magic into her wounds. The symbols guide the power, and in a matter of seconds we watch her skin knit together. But I keep pushing, knowing there's healing needed deep in her arm. Only when I feel nothing left to mend do I step back, shaking the sharp pricks from my hands that make it feel as though I sat on the limbs and they fell asleep.

"That's quality work." Silvia examines her arm.

The rigid quality of Damien's stance relaxes, and he turns grateful eyes on me. "Thank you."

"No problem—"

"We're using the master bathroom. To clean up," Sammy announces, setting his hands on my shoulders and guiding me away from the kitchen group, through the Cortez house. Down a back hall, we come upon a large bedroom with a massive bed. Sammy maneuvers me around it to a lovely bathroom equipped with a full tub.

I wonder how filling it up coincides with strict water regulations. Maybe Squids have special water reservoirs they can pull from.

Sammy runs the sink for me and even squirts the soap in my hands so I don't leave bloody fingerprints everywhere. As I scrub under my fingernails, I smile. I feel spent, but good, glad I could help our magical community in this small way. And now that I'm working a job I enjoy and regularly sleeping with a man I love, I have magic to spare.

I dry my hands, then turn to find Sammy crowding me back against the counter.

"Touch yourself," he demands.

"What?" I gape up at my normally easygoing boyfriend.

"Right now," he growls. "In front of me. Show me that pretty pussy. Finger yourself until you're soaking."

"Goddess. I just finished washing *blood* off my hands. Do you have a period kink?" I quirk an eyebrow at him. "If so, that's going to have to be a shower sex situation."

"I didn't think I had one until you said *shower sex*. We'll come back to that." Sammy reaches down to fist the hem of my sun dress and pushes it up over my thighs until he has an uninterrupted view of my turquoise cotton boy shorts. "Did you pick this color for me? For your Squid?"

"I don't know why you think calling yourself a Squid is sexy," I chide him, chills racing over my skin.

"I don't call myself *a* Squid." Sammy's thumb fiddles with my waistband. "I call myself *your* Squid. And I think you like it."

"Oh really?"

He makes an affirmative noise in the back of his throat as he sinks to his knees. "Know how I know?"

"I'm sure you'll tell me." I try to sound flippant, but my words come out breathless as he presses a hot kiss to my mound through the soft fabric and his rising lust stirs the sparks of magic under my skin.

"I know because you clench these lovely thighs together whenever I say *Squid*." Damn him, the move is involuntary and sandwiches the hand he placed between my legs. "And because I saw that toy you bought yourself. The one in the bottom drawer of your bedside table."

Fuck. I'm caught.

"It was a gag gift from Harley." Which is true.

"Maybe so. But that didn't stop you from using it. From slipping that tentacle dildo into your tight pussy." He smirks up at me from his lower vantage point. "Admit it. You've got a squid tentacle kink."

My pale skin flushes pink. But this is Sammy. I can tell him anything.

"Fine. I have a tentacle kink."

"And...?"

"And I think it's sexy when you call yourself a Squid," I mutter.

"That's a good witch." Sammy whispers the praise as he tugs down my panties. "And good witches deserve all the lust magic they can handle. I plan to fill you to the brim, Ava."

His thumbs part my folds, and at the first swipe of his tongue I grasp the sink hard to support my weak knees. Every part of my body is alive with pleasure and magic fed by Sammy's arousal, which only amps up my ecstasy, knowing how turned on he gets by tasting me.

"You're impossible," I moan as he dips his tongue in deep, teasing me with my dirty fantasies. He hums in the back of his throat and slips my underwear all the way off so he can guide one of my legs over his shoulder. With that support, I pry off one of my hands and delve it into his silky hair, fisting the strands and holding him to me. "Be a good boy and make me come," I tell him. His fingers clutch me harder. The possessive move warms me, and even as the pleasure in my body builds, I find myself softening. My hold gentles, and I stroke Sammy's head as he takes care of me. As he feeds his lust by inciting mine. Gazing down, I find him staring up at me, the skin around his mouth wet with my arousal.

I smile and tell him, "I love you."

Magic bombards me—rich peanut butter on my tongue—almost as much as I receive when Sammy orgasms while buried deep inside me. My love turns him on, and the simple joy of that has me laughing before I gasp through a delicious release.

When I come down from my high, Sammy is standing, his arms wrapped around me, holding my body close to his as the last shudders ripple through my muscles.

"You didn't want me to be without magic for even five minutes?" I ask, finally catching up with why he's been so anxious this afternoon, and why he practically jumped me in this bathroom.

Sammy was worried. And that makes me love him even more.

"Never." His chin rests on top of my head. "I know sometimes they sneak through. The migraines. That your magic doesn't always hold them back. But I'll do everything I can to make those times rare."

I have to swallow hard, choking on the amount of love I heard in that simple declaration.

"Thank you." I tilt my chin up, resting it on his sternum to gaze into his ocean eyes. "But even if you couldn't, I hope you know I'd still love you."

His dark blue stare holds mine, and his normally teasing face stays serious. "I do. I know." Sammy cradles my cheeks with his warm palms.

That's taken him some time, believing I want him without any kind of exchange. But therapy and my constant reassurances are helping.

I smirk. "I think Damien has a crush."

Sammy's grin is a slow wave washing over his face, but it doesn't recede. "I thought the same thing."

"She seems unaware," I add.

My Squid nods, more delight sparking in his eyes. "What a shame.

For him to be pining after a woman who could give a shit. Almost makes me feel bad for the guy."

"Almost?"

Sammy's evil delight softens. "Those women—the ones that don't need you—they're dangerous."

I hum in the back of my throat.

He presses a kiss to my forehead. "They could destroy a guy. But sometimes, they love you back. And then you're the luckiest fucking Squid in the world."

"I feel pretty lucky myself," I murmur.

"Good," he says, wrapping his arms tight around my body. "Because I've tentacled you. And I have no plans to let go."

No complaints here.

Thank you for reading! Did you enjoy? Please add your review because nothing helps an author more and encourages readers to take a chance on a book than a review.

And don't miss more from Lauren Connolly with her fun contemporary romance, RESCUE ME. Turn the page for a sneak peek!

You can also sign up for the City Owl Press newsletter to receive notice of all book releases!

Sneak Peek of Rescue Me

PAIGE

One of these houses is mine. I'm just not exactly sure *which* one.

A sigh pushes out, weighty and exhausted, from deep in my chest. The sun set hours ago, back when I was still on the highway. Trying to read the tiny print on each of these mailboxes isn't easy after staring out the windshield for the past two days. My eyes practically crackle, begging me to close them.

Sleep. Just go to sleep.

"That one! I...I think."

I pull up alongside the curb, letting the heavy engine rumble on as I flip through photos on my phone. Martin sent me a picture two weeks ago, a selfie of him with a large tan house behind him that looks like the one I've stopped in front of. Unfortunately, the homes on either side of it are mirror reflections.

Normally, Martin's preference for uniformity doesn't bother be. Tonight, though, I wish he had picked a weird bungalow with daisies painted on the siding and a turquoise front door. Just so I know, without a hint of a doubt, that I am parking in front of *my* house.

And I am definitely parking because I need to pick one of these clone homes before I drive myself mad puttering around this neighborhood all night.

As I shut down the engine, the whole car settles as if she's ready to sleep for the night.

"Enjoy your rest, Penelope," I mutter to the steering wheel.

I need a bed bad. A pounding started in my temples way before I even crossed the Louisiana/Mississippi border. The headache comes courtesy of long hours in the car paired with my hair being pulled up into a high, messy bun. I'd let the heavy mass down if I wasn't terrified of its condition. Two days' worth of greasiness has built up. I doubt removing my hairband would even do anything. The hair would likely continue sitting on top of my head, permanently reshaped.

My priorities have changed: before a bed, I need a shower. The vision of scrubbing a thick lather of shampoo into my scalp plays in my brain like a porno. I can imagine the transformation of the knotted mess into its normal smooth cascade.

"Butter on bread," my mom always says when she affectionately tugs on a strand.

Not sure I approve of being compared to a boring slice of white bread, but I take comfort in the fact that she's simply referring to my complexion and hair color rather than my personality.

When I push the car door open, the heavy New Orleans air embraces me. It is almost as warm and wet as an actual shower but nowhere near as refreshing. The humidity sits on my skin, weighing me down as I trudge up the front walk of a house that I hope is mine.

The easy solution would've been to just call Martin on Friday night when I decided to change my travel plans. That way my fiancé would be waiting out on the porch, ready to wave me down.

Instead, I chose the surprise method. I'd like to convince myself that this is a romantic gesture.

I just couldn't stay away from you for two more weeks!

In reality, my silence arises from shame. Whenever I let my thumb hover over his number, I couldn't even imagine how the conversation would go.

"Hey, honey! Guess what? I lost my job!" I whisper under my breath and pause with my foot on the bottom step leading up to the elevated porch.

Well, I guess I *could* say that.

Now that I'm here, potentially a few steps away from Martin, the words don't seem so inadequate. Depressing? Yeah sure. But I can clearly envision his face, how his blond brows will dip in the middle as he scowls. Not *at* me but *with* me. I can taste the glass of red wine he'll pour me as he rages over the unfair treatment.

That's when I realize why the need for surprise. I don't actually want to *talk* about how I got fired from my dream job. All I want is to see my anger reflected in the face of my partner. To feel connected to him in a way I haven't in a while.

With the moving plans, and Martin preparing to start his residency down here, and me trying to finish up all my large projects before going remote, we've barely talked. I can't even remember the last time I looked him in the eyes during a conversation. We usually just shout to each other from opposite rooms.

And sex? Well…it's been some time.

As I knock on the mystery door I hope is mine, I make a resolution. Whether I find Martin in this clone house or the one next door or the next street over, when I finally locate my fiancé, the first thing I'm going to do is stare deep into his eyes. I'll hold his gaze until our connection is firmly reestablished. Then—after a shower—I'm going to jump his bones.

Light spills into the dark night from around the edges of the curtains. At least that means whoever lives here, hopefully Martin, is still awake. After the polite taps of my knock ring out, the steady pad of footsteps sound behind the door. I brace myself, ready to stare my fiancé down.

Only, Martin doesn't open the door.

A small slim woman dressed in a robe stands before me. She is adorably petite. I could practically fit her in my pocket. Her bare feet peek out from under the floor-length robe, and her long brown hair lays in a damp mass over her shoulders.

Envy spikes hard through me. Clearly, this woman has just taken a shower. My greasy strands weep in envy.

Also, her appearance makes it clear my navigation skills have failed me. I am no closer to my own glorious shower, having no idea which one of these houses Martin bought for the two of us to live in.

"Sorry. I thought this might be my house. Do you know a blond man? About so tall?" I hold my hand a few inches above my head like the sleep drunk idiot I am.

I'm ready to continue describing my fiancé out of pure desperation when I notice the woman's face. With a stranger knocking on her door at midnight, I would expect confusion or annoyance. But if I had to guess, her slack-jawed, wide-eyed stare is closer to horror.

Apparently, my need for a shower is even direr than I knew.

"I told you I'd get it..." The familiar rusty voice drifts from behind the stranger as my fiancé trots down a set of stairs visible just over her shoulder.

The showered girl shuffles back, so I have a clear view of Martin, clad in only a pair of gym shorts, his hair just as gloriously damp from a recent cleaning as the woman in front of me.

Our eyes meet. His top half stops, but his bottom half doesn't get the memo. Instead, one of his bare feet slips on the wooden step, and he lands hard on his ass, shocked gaze never leaving mine.

So, this *is* the right house.

It's just everything else in the world that is wrong.

Whatever way I might want to interpret this situation is made impossible when I flick my eyes back to the stranger, who I now realize is wearing *my* green, cotton robe. Red splotches scorch along the tops of her cheekbones, and guilty tears pool on her lashes.

Something dark and sickening rolls in my stomach, but I flash freeze it. After one last look at the boy I've loved since my senior year of high school, I turn to the girl he chose to hurt me for.

"You can keep the robe." Reaching out, I clasp the doorknob. "And the man." I wrench the door closed on the most devastating scene of my life and sprint back to my sleeping car.

Penelope revs to life, more dependable than any man could ever be.

I shift into first gear and tear down the street, not caring who I wake up. With the roar of my sweet girl's engine, I can't hear Martin shouting.

But I can see him. In my rearview mirror, he sprints down the street after me. I skid around a corner and lose sight of him.

And he loses me.

I drive in an emotional fog, unable to dislodge the frozen ball of grief in my chest. The devastation sticks to the inside of my skull, blocking my ability to think.

It's only when I almost run a red light that I realize I shouldn't be driving.

Pulling into the next parking lot, I somehow end up in the drive-through lane of a fast-food joint. Functioning on autopilot, I roll down my window when I reach the speaker.

"What do you want?" The woman asks with the complete disinterest that can only be achieved by someone employed for the night shift at a drive-through.

The question hits me hard. Acting as a chisel, it splits the ice in my chest apart.

Grief flows free.

"What do I want?" I laugh, high-pitched and manic. "Oh, I don't know. How about a job? Or a home? Maybe my dignity?"

And now I'm crying.

"Um...we serve chicken."

I've gone insane. Martin's betrayal has turned me into a raving loon who drives around New Orleans in the middle of the night scaring fast-food workers.

This isn't me. I'm not this *type of weird.*

"Oh. Right. Of course." Swiping away the tears blurring my vision and pulling in a few choking breaths, I attempt to read the glowing menu. "I guess a family meal then."

"Eight, twelve, or sixteen pieces?"

The cracked ice in my chest has given way to a massive aching hole.

"Better make it sixteen."

"You want it with sides?"

I'm not going to be able to manage many more of these questions without the crazy laughing/crying returning.

"Yeah, whatever sides are popular. And biscuits, please. I'm gonna need a whole lot of biscuits." A sob makes the last word come out choked.

She rattles off the total, and I pull around to the window to pay. A short woman wearing a goofy chicken hat gives me a kinder smile than I was expecting after my breakdown.

"I slipped an extra biscuit in there," she whispers while passing me the armload of fried comfort.

"Thank you," I mutter, keeping my eyes to myself and hoping I never run into this lovely woman again.

For a moment, I park and consider consuming the entire order myself.

The idea is tempting.

But I still need a shower and a bed.

Penelope's engine purrs like a comforting embrace, as I pull back out on the road. The headlights point toward my childhood home.

My parents are about to get a late-night visitor, bearing fried chicken and a broken heart.

Don't stop now. Keep reading with your copy of <u>RESCUE ME</u> available now.

And visit www.laurenconnollyromance.com to keep up with the latest news where you can subscribe to the newsletter for contests, giveaways, new releases, and more.

Don't miss more of the *Casual Magic* series coming soon, and find more from Lauren Connolly at www.laurenconnollyromance.com

Until then, discover Connolly's fun contemporary romance RESCUE ME

When the universe screws you over, adopt a dog.

Paige Herbert doesn't know how she lost control of her life. Friday morning, she had her future planned. Sunday night, she's jobless and staring at her half-naked fiancé and a woman wearing her green robe.

Taking refuge in her childhood home, Paige decides this time around her life partner will have four legs instead of two. But her newly rescued pit bull is in bad need of obedience training...and the perfect guy for the job has Paige forgetting the past.

Dash Lamont doesn't want to go back to jail. Out on parole and working at an animal shelter, he's focused on living life by the rules. And number one on the list: avoid temptation.

And then, in walks Paige.

The woman parks in the middle of Dash's well-ordered life, demanding his attention with her offbeat conversation, sinful curves, and dream of a refurbished classic Chevy. Despite his decision to keep his distance, he somehow finds himself agreeing to her plea for help.

As the two spend more time together, awkward attempts at flirting, late-night dancing to jazz music, and a chance taken at a Halloween party lure the hesitant pair down a sensual road.

But when sins of the past work against the newly budding romance, Dash will need to decide whether to take his chance on love or stay in his safe lane, watching as Paige drives off without him.

Please sign up for the City Owl Press newsletter for chances to win special subscriber-only contests and giveaways as well as receiving information on upcoming releases and special excerpts.

All reviews are **welcome** and **appreciated**. Please consider leaving one on your favorite social media and book buying sites.

For books in the world of romance and speculative fiction that embody Innovation, Creativity, and Affordability, check out City Owl Press at www.cityowlpress.com.

Acknowledgments

Thank you to everyone who helped make this book happen! A special thanks to Tyler who keeps me filled in on the library tea even though I've set my name tag aside. Thank you Katie for fielding my Phoenix and cat queries. Thank you Lesley for being an amazing agent.

In every book I have to give a big shoutout to my parents, who are the reason I have this career. You listen to me talk about magical stripping librarians at the dinner table, and that makes you rockstars.

And of course, my heart is full of gratitude at the thought of how many readers have joyfully read this silly magical series. I hope you enjoyed getting tentacled by Sammy!

About the Author

LAUREN CONNOLLY is an award-winning author of contemporary and paranormal romance stories. She's lived among mountains, next to lakes, and in imaginary worlds. Lauren can never seem to stay in one place for too long, but trust that wherever she's residing there is a dog who thinks he's a troll, twin cats hiding in the couch, and bookshelves bursting with stories written by the authors she loves.

www.laurenconnollyromance.com

facebook.com/LaurenConnollyRomance

x.com/laurenaliciaCon

instagram.com/laurenconnollyromance

About the Publisher

City Owl Press is a cutting edge indie publishing company, bringing the world of romance and speculative fiction to discerning readers.

Escape Your World. Get Lost in Ours!

www.cityowlpress.com

facebook.com/CityOwlPress
x.com/cityowlpress
instagram.com/cityowlbooks
pinterest.com/cityowlpress
tiktok.com/@cityowlpress

www.ingramcontent.com/pod-product-compliance
Lightning Source LLC
Chambersburg PA
CBHW020653030726
47498CB00002B/496